b,

NOVELS
Aaron

LITTLE BOY LOST
Enlightened
Abandoned
Vanished
Discovered
Escaped
Sacrificed

NOVELLAS
Mastering the Ride
Papi

Published by DREAMSPINNER PRESS
http://www.dreamspinnerpress.com

# AARON

JP Barnaby

Dreamspinner Press

Published by
Dreamspinner Press
5032 Capital Circle SW
Ste 2, PMB# 279
Tallahassee, FL 32305-7886
USA
http://www.dreamspinnerpress.com/





ISBN: 978-1-62380-018-5

Printed in the United States of America
First Edition
October 2012

eBook edition available
eBook ISBN: 978-1-62380-019-2

For Chris, who believed in *Aaron* and in me. A light in the darkness, my safe place, and my friend. I loved you then, I love you now. I'll love you always.

"Whenever I'm weary from the battles that rage in my head, you make sense of madness when my sanity hangs by a thread."

—Richard Marx

# ONE

THE boy's heart slammed against his ribs as his sheets bound him, wrapping tendrils of cotton around his trembling arms and legs. Hot breath exploded from his lungs in sharp bursts as he fought against their hold and he tried but failed to keep the blinding fear at bay. Sweat rolled down his back in the dark, stifling space as he pulled his arms free of their nocturnal bindings. As he searched the dark corners of his room, several minutes passed before his fear burned off into white-hot rage. Two years had passed since the attack, but night after night, his dreams continued to torture him. It was a wonder he ever slept. Even with the regimen of pills his so-called doctors forced on him, he just felt like a walking corpse.

The description fit so well because everything inside him had died.

He forced back the wave of nausea that plagued him every morning when the drugs wore off, and pushed back the blankets. Peering between the heavy blue curtains, he focused on the Midwestern sky outside. Each of his days was full of repetition and habits, some far stranger than others. For example, the weird game of Russian roulette he played with himself each morning dictated that if the sky was blue and the sun was shining, he could find it within himself to brave just one more day. If, however, he saw a dark and ominous sky, he would roll to his side, face the wall, and pull the covers up over his head. Invariably, his mother would come in to check on him, wanting nothing more than to kiss his forehead or smooth his sleep-disheveled hair, but she never did. Instead, she tried not to mourn the loss of her son but to embrace the broken, disfigured boy left in his place.

The sun's harsh rays caused him to squint as he gazed through the gap in the curtains, so he forced himself to get up. The long-sleeved T-shirt clung to his body, soaked in the sweat of a late summer morning. The boy bundled clean clothes tight against his chest, thin socks sliding across the slick wooden floor as he shuffled to the bathroom to start his daily routine. Everything in his life revolved around routine. Every mood, every activity, seemingly every thought was closely monitored and controlled through the drugs. Just once, he'd like to get through a day without being nearly incapacitated by fear and pain, and be a fully functioning human being again.

At eighteen, his life was over.

The dark hardwood floor, heavily paneled curtains, cherry wood furniture, and navy-blue bedding gave his bedroom a special kind of gloom, so things brightened just a bit in the adjoining bathroom. Decorated in light blues and peaches, the room had an oceanic theme of shorelines and seashells. The décor should have calmed him, but it didn't. He probably hated that room more than any other in the house—his nakedness, his reflection, his shame were all on display there, harshly spotlighted by the energy-efficient bulbs in the fixture above the sink. The boy turned on the water in the shower, allowing it to heat to its highest tolerable level, and stepped back. The long-sleeved T-shirt and sweats, which seemed to grow larger with each passing week, fell to the floor along with underwear and socks. Staring at the faded pattern on the shower curtain rather than looking at his own body, he pulled the plastic back and stepped into the tub.

As the water cascaded over his hair and face, he could see each and every one of his scars, even with his eyes closed. They were burned into his retinas like a horrifying roadmap of his mistakes, and it seemed that even a momentary reprieve from them remained beyond his reach. He glanced up and saw his shampoo, body wash, and other necessities carefully organized in the rack that hung from the shower head. Everything in its place—everything except him—he had no place anymore. He didn't live; he didn't fit; he simply existed. The washrag scratched his skin as he washed with practiced, detached efficiency, taking great pains to stop scrubbing when his skin was only pink and not red. Even though it had been more than a year since his mother had found him on his knees in the shower, scrubbing his skin raw, he didn't want to scare her like that again. That morning, just a few months after he'd been released from the hospital, he'd had one of his most vivid and realistic nightmares. When his mother finally talked him out of the shower, she sat with him on the bathroom floor keeping a foot of space between them while he rubbed aloe into his scarred limbs. The way she strained to keep her hands at her sides made something inside of him hurt. She wanted so badly to help him, but she couldn't.

No one could.

Instead, she filled him with tranquilizers from the stash given to her by his latest shrink, and told him stories from his childhood as he stared blankly at the ceiling and tried to find meaning in the tiny patterns in the plaster. The safety and innocence he'd felt as a child had been ripped from him, almost as if they never existed. He had not mentioned that to his mother but remained quiet as she told him how he used to love playing in the bathtub. She tried so hard to reconnect him with that boy. Several shrinks tried the same tactic with him, attempting to reconnect him to his early teenage years. His mother, however, went much further back, trying anything to help her son. It never worked, and he wished that it would, even if just for her sake. Unfortunately for them both, the fantasies of deep-sea diver or mad scientist that he used to live out on the side of the tub with paper cups and bubbles were over. That boy was dead, abandoned on the floor of a garage that smelled like gas and fear and blood.

After slamming off the water in the shower, he reached out, ripped the towel from the rack, and pulled it behind the curtain. Steam hung heavy and thick in the small windowless room, and the scent of bodywash, though almost indiscernible, hung with it. The boy swiped a soft towel over his arms, legs, and torso in distracted, automated movements, but his skin was still damp when he pushed the curtain to the side and grabbed desperately for his clothes. He refused to unlock the bathroom door or even wait until the fan dissipated part of the steam. His shirt stuck to his skin as he dressed, but only when everything was covered, his scarred flesh hidden, could he take a full breath. The black comb shook in his hands as he smoothed down his short hair with a practiced touch, not bothering with gel or spray as other boys his age might be inclined to do. It simply didn't matter. People saw only one thing when they looked at him: the ugly, jagged scar that ripped his face from right ear to the middle of his throat. So, really, the way he styled his hair, or didn't, was inconsequential—no one was looking anyway. His parents had considered plastic surgery, but Aaron couldn't stand the thought of being ripped into again, torn, disfigured, touched by another set of hands, even a doctor's.

Aaron pushed that thought from his mind and started to brush his teeth as he stared at the painting hung over the sink. Calming, almost relaxing, it proved to be the best part of his morning routine. A peace and serenity lay within the complex geometric shapes that filled its black lacquer frame. At first, when he'd come home from the hospital, bandaged and nearly incapacitated, he'd ripped the bathroom mirror from the wall. His mother found him screaming, his hands nearly shredded, as if destroying the mirror would remove the image of his ruined face from his mind. It hadn't occurred to him to put anything in place of the mirror. However, his mother, the one person who knew him best, felt in some way that the painting would be better than the bare, discolored wall. She had his father hang the painting while she shopped for accessories to match it. It took Aaron nearly six months to realize that she searched for the perfect towels and bought beautiful little shell-shaped soaps because she was at a loss for how to help her broken son. He also realized that she had been right; the bare wall would have been a constant reminder of why the mirror was gone. It would have been almost as bad as the mirror itself.

*Almost.*

Leaving his towel and discarded clothes on the floor, the boy grabbed his MP3 player and a battered paperback from his cluttered bedside table and ambled down the stairs toward the kitchen. He felt almost childlike in his oversized clothes—clothes that had fit just a few months before. He stayed very close to the railing, curled in on himself, and stopped at the bottom to look around.

"Good morning, Aaron," his father said brightly, only to have his smile falter when Aaron just nodded and walked past the table where the older man sat, relaxed and deep into his morning routine. The huge polished table, where his family had dinner together every night, stood sentinel between the kitchen and the open family room. Aaron was thankful for that airy design because he'd started to feel very claustrophobic around his family—smothered by his mother's attention, his father's disappointment, and his brothers' resentment.

His younger brothers, Allen and Anthony, hadn't come downstairs yet. Aaron, Allen, and Anthony—their straight As, as his parents had joked before their first A became an F.

As on any other weekday morning, his father sat drinking his coffee and reading the paper. His pants and shirt were pressed to perfection, his tie neatly tied. The only thing missing was the jacket that hung on the back of his chair, ready to complete the perfect picture that was his father. John Downing was the epitome of stability and success, which just underscored his son's inability to cope with life. Almost too good-looking, his father's black hair was cropped into an efficient and elegant example of corporate style, with the flecks of gray, no doubt caused in large part by Aaron, giving him a distinguished air. It was his eyes that gave him away, however. His clear, vibrant blue eyes which most would describe as kind, held a deep sadness. The light that had been kindled with the birth of his first son had dimmed. Aaron didn't look at his father often anymore, maybe even less often than he looked at anyone else. Before his life was destroyed so brutally in that garage two years ago, Aaron had been the image of his father. He had the same chin, the same nose, the same black hair, and the same blue eyes. Attractive and well liked, Aaron had been just like his father, who, as a corporate attorney in downtown Chicago, was smart and successful. John Downing served as a constant reminder of the man his son would never be.

Aaron leaned against the gleaming surface of the kitchen counter and grabbed a banana. He wasn't hungry, but eating something helped to defray the constant arguments with his mother about his weight loss. Though he never said it aloud, it didn't matter if he ate, or if he wore his seatbelt, or even if he looked both ways before crossing. He was dead anyway; what difference did it make? It was only a matter of time before his body realized it, and he would finally have some peace.

Moving a little closer to the wall by sheer instinct, Aaron heard the thundering footsteps of what could only be his younger brothers, as they pounded down the stairs. They both greeted him with a quick "Hey, man" before making their way to the table. Chairs clattered and scraped against the wood floor as the boys sat down with their father. John Downing started talking to Anthony about a play from the younger boy's last soccer game, and it wasn't long before both of the boys were laughing and joking with their dad while Aaron stood seemingly forgotten in the corner of the kitchen. Only their quick, anxious glances gave away the fact that he was never forgotten.

For over two years it had been that way: polite nods, the briefest of required conversations. People treated him like a china doll: one wrong word and he would crack. For the most part, sadly, it was true. Though his younger brothers knew, at least conceptually, what had happened to him, sometimes they did say things that set him off. Allen would mention Juliette, or Anthony would tell him he was going to kill him if he didn't stop clicking the pen in his hand. They were horrified afterward by their slips. Of course any normal person would have taken such comments in stride, but Aaron was far from normal.

He had become a complete stranger to his own family.

At the time Aaron's world had changed, Allen had been fourteen and Anthony only ten. Aaron knew that, while he was still recovering in intensive care, his parents had sat his brothers down and explained as much as they could to them, given their young ages. Allen understood for the most part, but they had tried to shield Anthony from some of the horrific truths. Unfortunately, Aaron couldn't hide all his scars, so eventually Anthony was faced point-blank with the brutality that had been visited upon his hero. When Aaron first came home from the hospital, the younger Downing boys hadn't understood that their older brother, the one they had played catch with, the one who had taken them to the movies and the arcade, was a different person. He wasn't fun. He wasn't outgoing. He was frightening and screamed in his sleep every night, terrifying them to the point that they started to sleep in the rapidly finished basement. Aaron had offered, halfheartedly to move to the basement, but the cement walls and the cold concrete floor reminded him of the place where the men had taken him. He couldn't even make it down the steps. Thankfully, his parents wanted him close so they could help him.

It wasn't too long before they had started to sedate him, anyway.

His mother was already nearby at the stove, finishing up their eggs, by the time Aaron came out of his thoughts. Since he was always so quiet, neither his parents nor his brothers had noticed that he hadn't been paying attention to anything around him for the last fifteen minutes. Of course, Aaron had done it frequently: completely shut down his attention to the outside world. These periods of complete dissociation from everything scared him. He was terrified that one day he'd get trapped in his own head and never find his way back out again.

His head was a fucking scary place to be.

Michelle Downing took the plates of eggs, bacon, and toast to her husband and younger sons at the table. Aaron hadn't really even noticed that she'd been standing next to him cooking. He looked away from her stressed features and the premature gray in her hair, all caused by him. Her petite frame was where Aaron got his small stature, but that was one of the few similarities between Michelle and her eldest son. Where Aaron had inherited his father's black hair, as had Anthony, Allen and his mother had chestnut curls. Aaron was the only child to get his father's blue eyes. His brothers both had his mother's soft brown eyes.

They had once been a typical close American family, John worked while his wife stayed home to raise their boys. Now their younger sons were left pretty much on their own while their mother struggled to care for their damaged older brother. They no longer went on vacation because Aaron didn't deal well with change. They rarely went out to dinner because Aaron didn't deal well with groups of people. They took turns going to Anthony's soccer games or Allen's wrestling matches because they didn't want to leave Aaron alone.

It was as if they were all merely surviving, in the dark with no light on the horizon.

Aaron watched his family talking quietly as they ate around the table, and felt a stabbing pain of loneliness. They were the happy family, and he was just the freak that lived upstairs. Physically, everything in the house was the same, from the apple accessories in the kitchen to the big-screen television in the family room where they used to watch baseball together. *He* was different. There wasn't a place for him anymore, even though his chair sat empty at the table waiting for him. Without another word, he set the unpeeled banana back on the counter and walked past the table where his family sat glancing at him with surreptitious looks. Opening the sliding glass door directly behind his father at the head of the table, he walked out onto their huge deck and closed the door behind him. It felt better out here, less suffocating, with fewer expectations. He sat down on one of the patio chairs, looked over their small, well-maintained yard, and thought about how much he hated days like this, days where he just couldn't turn off his mind.

He squinted into the morning sun as his mother joined him on the deck. Out of the corner of his eye, he could see that she was wearing an oversized gray sweatshirt that probably belonged to his dad. She handed him an instant breakfast drink. He took it, opened the top, and sucked it down in one long drink. Mr. Handley next door stepped out onto his own deck as Aaron handed his mother the empty container. Aaron could feel the old man's eyes on him across the fence and wondered if he could hear Aaron screaming in the night. He heard his mother's quiet sigh as she reached down to smooth back a wayward piece of his hair, and he jerked away violently. He hated the fact that he couldn't even stand to be touched by his own mother. With a visible effort, she forced the hurt from her face as he looked up, but then turned and walked back into the house without another word.

Pulling his music player and the book from his pocket, he settled back on a nearby chaise, ignored his portly neighbor, and lost himself in someone else's life.

SPENCER THOMAS pulled the garbage can from beneath the sink and took inventory. Six empty Samuel Adams bottles and one Jack Daniel's bottle. He knew that the Jack Daniel's bottle had been mostly empty from the weekend binge, but it still didn't make him feel any better. He needed to have a talk with his father. Since the good doctor let his practice go, the drinking had gotten worse. The nightmares had gotten worse. Their lives had gotten worse.

With a sigh, he closed the cabinet door and left the alcohol graveyard in peace. It would be hours before his father emerged from the dark cave he called a bedroom, so Spencer ambled down the hall and into the rec room. He picked up his mother's framed picture from his desk and looked at her face for the millionth time. Miranda Thomas died about three months before she was supposed to deliver her son, whom she left premature and in the hands of his father, Henry. Spencer had heard stories of his mother from his grandparents and from his aunt Nelle, but never from his father. No one had to tell Spencer he'd gotten his shaggy brown hair and introspective hazel eyes from her. Even his freckles and pale complexion were a gift passed down to keep his mother alive in him. From his father, he'd inherited a small chin, a button nose, and an ingrained lack of self-control. They made for an interesting combination.

The phone in his pocket vibrated as he dropped into the plush leather chair in front of his desk. He pulled it out and checked the display.

*Doorbell*

The message might have seemed cryptic to anyone else, anyone that could hear and didn't get a text message from the front door. After he jumped out of the chair, he retraced his steps and jogged back up the hall. Instead of turning right to head into the kitchen, he turned left at the end of the hallway toward the living room. A silhouette stood just beyond the door's frosted glass. The rug slid under his bare feet as he skidded to a stop and turned the handle. A hot young delivery guy in shorts waited on the doorstep with a large box balanced on one arm. Spencer stared for a long moment at the man's muscular frame, perfect skin, and impish grin before the movement of sweet lips broke him from his musings.

"Spencer Thomas?" the guy asked, and Spencer found himself distracted by the sensual way his mouth curved around each letter as he spoke. A dark pink tongue flicked out to lick thin yet carnal lips—the edges of which turned up in a smile when Spencer nodded.

"Well then, Mr. Thomas, I have a package for you," he said brightly. Spencer took a long moment to deliberately look up and down the man's toned body. A shock of black hair peeked out from under his awful royal blue baseball hat, which matched the rest of his bland uniform. Spencer saw that the name patch across his left pec read "Nick." He dragged his eyes back up from the man's crotch to see the interest brewing in steel gray eyes.

Nick handed Spencer an electronic device and asked him to sign for the package. Like a bad porn flick, he licked his lips and watched as Spencer, who stood there in nothing but faded pajama pants and a smile, signed his name. Spencer handed the device back to the delivery guy, who then relinquished the package. Glancing at the return address, he saw it was from Dell—his new laptop for school. *Excellent*. Right then, however, he had a different toy in mind that he wanted to play with. The thin fabric stretched over his hardening cock. Spencer watched Nick's face as he stared at the bulge with increasing fascination, the conflict apparent.

He put the laptop down on the floor out of the doorway and stepped closer to the hot little delivery guy. Nick shifted the signature device to his left hand and used the right to scratch the back of his neck. *Nervous, how sweet.* Reaching out slowly, Spencer took the small machine from Nick and set it on top of the computer box. They were almost touching. Spencer hadn't gotten laid in months. That kid in the school bathroom after finals seemed like ages ago, and he'd been intimate with his hand for far too long.

"Is… is that my tip?" Nick asked. *Bingo.* Spencer took Nick's hand and rubbed it against his swollen dick with a slow, easy nod. Nick added softly, "You're a quiet one, aren't you?" Spencer entwined his fingers with Nick's and pulled, silently asking the other man to follow him. He knew from too much fucking experience that if he spoke, it would be over. Nick would think he was retarded and lose his hard-on. The sweet little delivery boy followed him down the hall to the spare bedroom without another word. He didn't particularly want to fuck in the flowery, overly feminine room that his aunt used on her visits, but Spencer didn't want to take the kid up to his room. He didn't want to risk Dad waking up to ruin his fun. His father wouldn't care about Spencer being sexually active, but it was hard to fuck wondering if your dad could hear. Grabbing a condom and the bottle of lube he kept hidden in the bathroom across the hall, he put them both on the lace-covered bedside table for Nick to see. That generally forestalled any awkward conversations about safe sex.

Their mouths collided as they met in the middle of the room. Nick toed out of his shoes as Spencer felt him moan into the kiss. He flipped the hat off Nick's head and ran a tender hand through the soft, messy locks suddenly freed from their prison. It felt like damp silk beneath his fingers. Spencer's mouth melded over Nick's as he unbuttoned his uniform shirt and let it slide down tanned, muscular arms to pool on the floor at their feet. He slid his fingers languidly along the back of his new lover's neck with a leisurely stop at one tender shoulder. Nick broke the contact and trailed sweet kisses along Spencer's jaw.

A moan reverberated up from Spencer's chest, scratching his throat as it escaped. Moving his hands between their overheated bodies, Spencer flicked open the button on Nick's uniform shorts before dragging down the zipper. He could feel Nick's erection pressing against the fabric, straining to be released, so he obliged. He slid his hand into the tight polyester shorts and then dug into the cotton briefs beneath as he felt Nick's hot breath on his neck and his lips vibrate on Spencer's neck.

*God, it felt good.*

The back of Spencer's knees hit the bed and he pulled Nick on top of him. The billowy pink comforter surrounded them as they kissed with a passion bordering on aggression, and Nick ground his hips against Spencer's in an ageless, graceless rhythm. Their heavy breaths mingled as he grabbed Nick's ass, and his cock strained against his sleep pants. Finally, after what felt like an eternity, his impromptu lover slid the material out of the way and palmed Spencer's dick. The old oak bed shifted as they moved, hard and hot against each other. With one particularly enthusiastic grind, the headboard smacked against the wall and jolted them. Spencer looked up above his head, always attuned to strange vibrations, but didn't see any damage.

Wrapping his arms tightly around Nick, Spencer rolled them and knelt between his lover's knees. Strong legs came up around his hips, heels pushed into his ass to draw him closer. Oh yeah, the kid was a total bottom. *Thank God.* He hated having *that* conversation. As much as Spencer wanted to go slow, to cherish every shared moment, he didn't let himself go there. He didn't open that dark place in his heart where hope lived—hope that he could find someone who would still want him even though he was different.

Another practiced moan, one with true want behind it, because grinding against Nick, eager, excited Nick, had his dick hard. The boy's throat vibrated under Spencer's lips. He pulled back and watched the heady arousal in his face.

"Please…. Suck me," Nick said. *Shit. Did he say "suck me" or "fuck me"?* He'd thrown his head back as he spoke, so Spencer couldn't tell. But yeah, did it really matter? The meaning was pretty damn clear. He grabbed Nick's uniform shorts and pulled them down over white ankle socks. Next, he jerked the briefs down those long muscled legs and slid a hand along Nick's flank as he did so. The guy pulled his feet loose from the confining fabric and spread himself for Spencer's approval.

Spencer certainly approved.

The uniform hid a fantastic body—sculpted arms, strong and thick from moving boxes for a living, a six-pack that made Spencer feel almost flabby in comparison, and a thick cock pointing his way home. He hooked his thumbs into the waistband of the faded green pajama pants and pulled them down over his ass as he leaned forward to suck Nick's cock. The feel of it, the decadent weight on his tongue made Spencer throb. Carefully, he lifted first one knee and then the other to get the pants down to his feet before he kicked them off. Pushing Nick's legs farther apart, he decided all that mattered in the moment was the hot guy spread out before him.

He traced the ridges of the cock head with his tongue, as he stared at the tight abs in front of his eyes. Spencer never closed his eyes during sex, not once. He couldn't afford that kind of vulnerability, especially with someone he didn't know. A tender hand stroked the side of his face, and he leaned into it. The unexpected affection was so foreign to him, his chest tightened with the feeling. Then he imagined the look on his new friend's face if they tried to have a conversation, and the tightness went away. It was a rough and tumble fuck—nothing more.

Watching Nick's face as best he could from between the boy's legs, Spencer held up that pretty cock and licked lower. He sucked one of the well-groomed balls into his mouth and traced the sensitive, bumpy skin with his tongue. Nick drove his head back into the pillow, and while Spencer couldn't see his mouth, he assumed nothing intelligible was being said anyway. The smell of sweat and musk and some kind of scented soap filled his nostrils as he buried his face deeper between Nick's legs and licked the crevasse between hip and thigh. The hand on his head became more insistent, so Spencer dragged his pointed tongue from base to tip before swallowing the impressive dick. He tried not to gag as the head slid to the back of his throat with a jerk of Nick's hips.

He pulled back and used a hand to stroke the inches not between his lips, almost kissing his hand with each bob of his head. A slick twist of his hand over the head had Nick writhing. *God, it was hot.* Looking up again, he still didn't see any discernible speech, so he relinquished the dick from his mouth and grabbed the condom and lube. Holding them up, he waited for something, a "yes," a nod, something to tell him to continue.

Thankfully, he got both.

“God yeah, man. Fuck me,” Nick said with an almost violent nod. Apparently, he was too far gone into a blissful haze to notice that Spencer still hadn’t spoken.

While he knelt up and opened the condom, Nick tried to roll over onto his stomach, but Spencer stopped him with a hand on his chest. He had to be able to see the guy’s face in case he wanted to stop. Spencer had only facial expressions and mouthed words to guide him. His partner didn’t fight it, but merely pulled his knees up to his chest so that Spencer could lube up his ass. *No muss, no fuss.*

As he pressed the blunt tip of his cock against the tiny opening, he watched Nick’s face for some indication that he’d changed his mind. When none came, Spencer pushed forward and felt the muscle give as he buried himself in Nick’s body. The groan seemed to start at his feet and drive its way up and out between his gritted teeth. Hot and tight, Nick felt so fucking good around his cock. Slowly, he moved forward until his thighs met the boy’s skin. The kid trembled beneath him with need and want, and Spencer didn’t have to hear him to know what he needed.

Nick slammed his eyes shut as his back arched and forced Spencer’s cock to keep contact with his prostate as he thrust deep. Spencer reached up and grabbed one of the pillows. Shoving it under Nick’s head so that it raised a few inches, he leaned down and kissed the boy hard. When Nick dropped his legs around Spencer’s waist, the encounter took on a level of intimacy that Spencer wasn’t used to, but he clung to it nonetheless.

He rocked his hips and made sure to keep the angle of his thrusts consistent to nail Nick’s sweet spot as his lover reached down to stroke himself. A fine sheen of sweat broke out over Nick’s body, and the sweet smell of it filled Spencer’s senses. He loved watching the lines of the boy’s throat when he threw his head back in pleasured abandon. The hand on his bicep squeezed, and the body beneath him trembled as they raced toward that glorious orgasm that crested just ahead of them both.

“Clothes…,” Nick said, and it took Spencer a minute in his lust-filled haze to realize that he’d said “close.” He drove his hands under Nick’s shoulders, grabbed them tightly, and thrust harder into the pliant, willing boy. Spencer gave up on watching for more words and buried his face into Nick’s sweaty neck.

A rumbling cry vibrated against his shoulder just as Nick shuddered beneath him and a warm slickness pumped onto his stomach. *That's it, baby.* He thrust once, twice, and again as he tried to wring the pleasure from his partner, a boy he would probably never see again after their brief encounter. A tingling, electric feeling pulsed in his balls, and he drove harder into Nick, so close… *so fucking close.* His growling moan took him by surprise as his cock erupted into the condom, deep inside the boy. *Deep. Hot. Tight. Fuck.*

Everything in his brain focused on that single, all-encompassing feeling of bliss. Harsh, ragged breaths escaped his lungs in bursts, and without thought, he kissed the boy's neck and shoulders and tried to show him what their interlude had meant to him. Such a pretty guy, sweet and smiling, he wished he could take him out for dinner or even coffee and just talk. Unfortunately, he knew that people generally looked at the deaf in one of two ways: as a novelty, or retarded. When he spoke, and his voice didn't hold that same generic cadence that everyone on earth seemed to achieve as easily as breathing, people assumed he was slow or mentally handicapped. They talked louder, slower, which of course didn't help him a bit unless he could read their lips. So they didn't bother talking to him at all. They talked around him. They treated him like some kind of animal, incapable of rational conversation.

So he didn't give them the chance.

"Oh my God, that was fucking amazing," Nick said as he came out of his sexual stupor and kissed Spencer lightly. With their foreheads pressed together, he could feel Nick's breath on his face, so he closed his eyes for just a moment to savor the feeling before he was alone again.

With a sigh against his cheek, Nick's chest rumbled with speech that Spencer didn't catch. He pulled back to look at Nick, but the boy had fallen silent. Spencer started to feel a little self-conscious, naked above a total stranger who just lay there staring up at him. After another long minute of silence, Nick pushed on his shoulders and tried to roll out from under him.

"What the hell, man? I said I had to go back to work. My boss is going to be pissed," he said before turning his back to Spencer and grabbing his uniform from where it lay crumpled on the floor. As Nick faced away, Spencer couldn't tell if he talked while he dressed, but his face seemed to be moving in a manner consistent with speech. Instead of trying to understand, Spencer simply sat on the side of the bed and waited.

"So, would you?" he asked as he turned around and looked expectantly at Spencer. *God, would you fucking leave already?* Spencer tilted his head to the side as he tried to figure out what the kid had asked him. He must have taken too long, because Nick said something about him being stupid before he grabbed his shoes off the floor and started for the door. Spencer leaned over and snagged his pants from the floor. With vicious jerks, he pulled them on and then pushed on Nick's shoulder to make him look up.

"I. Am. Not. Stupid.. I. Am. Deaf., Asshole.," Spencer told him in slow, measured speech as he had been taught from early childhood. Just for good measure, he pointed to his ear and shook his head. A look of dawning comprehension passed over Nick's face, which was replaced quickly by regret and shame. *Good.*

"I'm sorry," Nick started and put his hands on his chest to illustrate his sincerity. *Wow, really?* "I'm going to go." His exaggerated speech made it difficult to read his lips, but worse, he used two fingers to mime walking and then pointed to the door like Spencer was too slow to understand that he was leaving. *For fuck's sake.*

Spencer opened the door to the small bedroom and held out a hand to indicate that Nick should go first. The guy couldn't pick up his little signature machine and get out of the house fast enough. He didn't even say good-bye to Spencer in his haste to get away from the freak.

Spencer leaned against the door and wondered what it would be like to have a guy look past the deafness and actually see *him*.

# TWO

AARON sat quietly, picking at his grilled cheese sandwich, when his mother came into the kitchen with an envelope. He saw that it was addressed to him, but when he shrugged at her, she opened it instead. Taking another bit of soup so that she could see, he waited, remarkably uninterested, for the results of his final homeschool exams. Part of him hoped he had failed every subject so he could bow out of any further discussions of college, but the smile that spread across his mother's face told him otherwise. Looking into his mother's overbright, misty eyes, he understood what she was feeling. By all rights, he should have died that night in the garage with Juliette, so the fact that he even had results to mail was a miracle.

"I am so incredibly proud of you, Aaron. When we chose to homeschool you those last two years, I didn't know if you'd ever be… if you'd… but you did," she stammered and then handed him the sheet of paper. Underneath the pretentious state logo was a list of his achievements. He had managed to pass every subject. In a few, like English, he was sure that his results were born more of pity than the actual quality of his work.

He didn't care.

"Let's… I mean…. Can we take you out to dinner to celebrate?" The hopeful longing in her face made the polite refusal he was about to give die in his throat. Shame burned on the back of his neck like the summer sun. She had done so much for him, and asked for so little in return. Couldn't he just give her this one thing? From her expression, it looked like her whole life depended on his answer to the question.

Slowly, he nodded.

His mother did manage to restrain herself from hugging him, but just barely, and unfortunately he had reached the upper limit of his accommodations for the day. He was grateful that she didn't hug him, because one of his meltdowns in the kitchen would have just punctuated the afternoon nicely. Things were starting to get bad for him again, he could feel it. Some days were better, but lately, his depression was taking him on another downward spiral. He tried so hard to keep things from spinning out of control, but trying to hide the depth of his depression from his mother had become exhausting. Aaron tried so hard to keep the worst of his symptoms from her, because she had so many other things to worry about. Sometimes, when the demons came calling inside his head, he saw just how much caring for him was taking a toll on her. In those moments, he wished that he'd just have the balls to end her pain, and his, but he didn't. It was just one more thing in his life he wasn't man enough to do.

"Okay, well, Allen has his first date tonight, so maybe tomorrow night," she said, her beaming smile bringing him back from those dark thoughts. It was a bit of a comfort to him that Allen had a date. His brothers had to deal with so much, and finally they were able to start living somewhat normal lives, despite their psychotic brother. Aaron left more than half of his sandwich on the plate, but finished his soup, tipping up the bowl and drinking it. He hoped that would appease her almost constant need to feed him.

"Mom, I'm going to go lie down for a while," Aaron told her as she took his dishes to the counter near the sink. The combination of all the pills and omnipresent suffocating depression made Aaron feel tired, lethargic. Some days, this tiredness allowed him to finally escape for a few hours in the dreamless sleep of a midafternoon nap. On other days he would just stare restlessly at the ceiling or the TV, even the very idea of sleep eluding him.

*It started off as most of his dreams did, with that last debate practice. Juliette was the captain, but Aaron was the best on the team. They were trying to get other students involved, since it was the beginning of the term, trying to get them engaged to see which ones would make the team that year. Aaron always helped out with recruiting because the debate team was important to Juliette, and Juliette was important to Aaron. That night, the topic that they pulled from the list was euthanasia. Juliette was on pro and Aaron was left with con. It didn't matter how they personally felt about the topic, they still needed to put together a concise, effective strategy for debating the issue. Juliette explained to the assembled students that voluntary, active euthanasia was about people deciding how they wanted to live and die. The government should not be able to legislate a person's free will if they weren't injuring another party. Denying a person the choice of ending his own pain and suffering was unfair and cruel. These were valid points, and Aaron knew that arguing them would not win him any favor. His explanation of the cons of euthanasia was on a different level. By actively taking the life of a person, especially one who is in inexorable pain, one could not know if the consent given was voluntary. A person with substantial wealth could be murdered with no legal recourse. Even assuming the absence of foul play, a mistaken diagnosis could end someone's life needlessly.*

*By the end of the debate, Aaron and Juliette had been furiously hurling facts and arguments at each other with such voracity that other students discussed the possibility of intervening. That's just how Aaron and Juliette were, passionate and competitive. Friends since grade school, they knew exactly how to push each other's buttons and what their next line of defense would be; they made a hell of a debate pair.*

*The dream skipped around—the walk, the van, the screaming, the pain, the blood.*

Aaron shot bolt upright in bed, the scream caught in his throat. His bedroom was dark, which confused him further, and then he heard the doorbell ring. *The men were there. They'd never been caught, and they were there.* The men that had hurt him, had killed Juliette, they were there to finish the job. The men would kill his family like they had killed Juliette. Without thinking, without stopping to consider that his attackers would hardly ring the bell, he vaulted out of bed and practically fell down the stairs. The sight at the front door stopped him in his tracks. Intellectually, on some level, he realized that it was just Allen and his date, but Allen wore his letterman's jacket, just like Aaron had been wearing that night. His date wore a sweater and jeans, her auburn hair falling straight down around her delicate face, reminding him of Juliette.

The flashback hit without any warning.

*Juliette screaming.*

*Juliette begging for her mother.*

*Juliette begging Aaron to make them stop.*

*Juliette covered in blood.*

*The man's breath on the back of his neck.*

*The knife slicing his face.*

*The blade cutting across his throat.*

"Mom!" Anthony screamed as Aaron fell to his knees on the living room carpet. Their mother, terrified and completely bewildered, knelt next to her eldest son.

"Mom, don't let me go! Please, they'll hurt me, Mom! Please…." Aaron pleaded, trying to force the images, the memories from his mind.

Allen's date, who had no idea what was happening, began to get scared, backing slowly toward the door. Allen looked over at her, and then at his brother on the floor. If Aaron had been seeing his brother at all as he knelt on the floor trying to keep from sobbing, he would have seen that Allen's face, now ruddy and flushed, was livid. Their lives had been so fucked up for so long, and Aaron was ruining the first real sense of normalcy, the first real date Allen had ever had. Aaron knew that both Allen and Anthony must catch shit at school for their freak brother, and Allen had finally found a girl to look past that.

"Shut up, Aaron!" Allen roared, obviously humiliated by his brother's psychotic meltdown in the middle of the living room.

His hands were gripped into tight fists at his sides, and despite all the love and respect he surely felt for Aaron, Allen had seemed to finally reach his breaking point. Two years of their parents' misery, two years of night terrors, and two years of wanting more than anything to have his brother back had finally taken its toll on Allen. Shaking, he turned to his date and held out his hand wordlessly.

"Maybe we should do this another time," the girl said, with one hand on the doorknob. She looked like a frightened fawn ready to bolt.

"No, Carrie, just give me a minute, please…." he pleaded with her, and she nodded as she continued to wait with her hand on the door. Allen turned on his brother, his eyes ablaze, fueled by his date's fear.

"I am not you! I am not stupid enough to be lured into a goddamned van, tearing my whole family apart!" Allen yelled, and all the blood left Aaron's face as the flashback began to recede and he realized what he had done. Everything Allen had to deal with just living in the same house with him, and he had just terrified the poor girl before they could even get out the door. He felt like Quasimodo in the bell tower, the freak that should be hidden away for everyone's peace of mind, maybe even for his own good.

"My brother is a lunatic," Allen told his date, almost drowning out his mother's shocked gasp. Before anyone could call him back, he grabbed the girl's hand and pulled her out the front door, leaving his trembling brother kneeling helplessly on the living room carpet. It was the first time anyone had said it aloud, but Aaron felt with perfect clarity that it was true. He would never be normal. He would never be anything but a burden, a source of shame and discomfort for his parents and his brothers. Not for the first time, Aaron wished he had died with Juliette and not been left to linger in this damaged shell.

Hours later, after Aaron had been properly medicated and put to bed, Allen came in to check on him. Aaron was propped up on pillows, staring blankly at the wall near the foot of his bed. It was always like this when he was drugged, like he was in some kind of suspended animation. Unable to move because his limbs were just too heavy, unable to think because his mind was full of fog, he simply existed. If they stood him in the corner, he could have been a potted plant, except he no longer had any aesthetic value. Aaron had heard Allen enter the room, but it took him a moment in his medicated state to respond. The guilt that consumed his brother was plain on Allen's pale face.

"Aaron," he said tentatively, like a boy drowning in waves of his own self-hatred. He still smelled faintly of the aftershave he'd worn to impress his date. Before the attack, when he was still able to smile, Aaron might have teased him about it. It all seemed so frivolous. Allen pulled Aaron's desk chair up next to the bed and sat down. With almost painful slowness, Aaron's blank stare moved from the bare wall to his younger brother. Tears welled in Allen's eyes as he looked at his big brother, nearly incapacitated by the drugs the doctors prescribed. Allen waited until Aaron's eyes finally focused on him before he spoke.

"I am so sorry, Aaron," Allen said, the tears beginning to fall. "What I said to you was unforgivable. I didn't mean it, I was just…."

"Embarrassed," his brother finished for him, his eyes glazed over.

"Yes," Allen replied shamefully, looking down at the navy blue comforter that covered his brother's bed.

"Now, let me tell you something," Aaron said, as he fought the hold of the drugs and depression. Allen looked up to meet his brother's level, glassy stare. "I never climbed into that fucking van. I was dragged into it, screaming and fighting." The anger in his face, in his voice, was unmistakable, and Allen just nodded, wide-eyed and pale.

"I didn't…. They never really told us what…," Allen stammered.

Aaron could see that Allen's own behavior, his words, sickened him, and he didn't need to do anything else to drive the point home. None of this was Allen's fault; it was Aaron's. He had brought this horror down on his family, merely by surviving.

"As for the lunatic part, well, you're probably right about that. Between the drugs and the flashbacks, I feel like a madman most of the time."

Allen took several short, very shallow breaths and looked like he was suffocating, crushed by the weight of his older brother's disapproval. Before the attack, Aaron knew that Allen had idolized him. He was everything that Allen wanted to be—smart, funny, good-looking. "Aaron, I…."

"If you came in here looking for forgiveness, you needn't have bothered," Aaron said, his gaze still unfocused. "You had it before you ever left the house."

Allen dropped his head, the tears falling in earnest, mumbling something about Aaron being a much better man than he was.

"It scares me," Aaron went on, not commenting on his brother's emotional outpouring, a dreamy quality to his voice, maybe because he rarely used it anymore. "What could happen to you, or to Anthony. I'm scared all the time, even with the drugs. When I saw you standing there, you and that girl who looked so much like Juliette, I thought that maybe if I stopped you from going that I could have stopped it all from happening.

It triggered a flashback, and all I could see was Juliette and me. I had to stop you from going, to stop Juliette from dying. I had just woken from a really bad nightmare, and it was all… jumbled in my head. I'm sorry that I embarrassed you." This was the first time in two years Allen had ever sat and talked alone with Aaron. His parents had told him the basics about what had happened to his brother, but maybe he never really appreciated the extent of the damage until today, when he heard it straight from Aaron.

They both looked up at the sound of yelling—not screaming, as Aaron had become accustomed to in his dreams, but more like an argument. He couldn't make out the words through the walls and closed door, so he couldn't understand what was happening. His parents never fought, nor did they raise their voices to him or his brothers. Especially since Aaron's attack, his family forced themselves to be exceedingly polite to each other.

Making his decision, Aaron glanced at Allen, threw back the blankets, and crept to his bedroom door. He placed a hand on the wood and used it to steady himself as he turned the knob. The small click sounded loud in the confines of his room, but not so loud that it would have been heard over the shouting. Once he swung the door slowly open, the voices became discernible.

"We are not having this discussion, John. I won't do it." A soft thump, like the slamming of a drawer, punctuated his mother's disagreement. Slipping quietly from his room, Aaron crept down the hall with Allen right behind, each step bringing them closer to their parents' bedroom. Their door was pulled to, but not completely closed. He leaned heavily against the wall. The tranquilizer caused him to feel slow and stupid as he pressed his palm against his forehead to stop the hallway from spinning.

"You saw what happened tonight. It was Allen's first real shot at something normal. We can't keep sacrificing them to try to save him. It's been two years, Michelle, and he's not getting any better." His father's voice sounded heavy with tears that Aaron knew he would never shed, not over him, anyway.

"He has a name, John." The sharp edge in his mother's voice did nothing to cut the tension as it leaked from the bedroom into the hallway.

Aaron stood listening in stunned disbelief. He looked back to see Allen's horrified face staring back at him.

"Maybe we should let the professionals care for Aaron, because I don't think we're doing what's best for him," John said, and Aaron's heart ached at the resignation in his voice. His own father had given up on him, written him off to the insanity. The throbbing in his head returned, and Aaron worked hard to keep himself from sliding down the wall.

"I am not sending him to some kind of institution." Michelle's voice trembled, and Aaron couldn't listen anymore. Part of him wanted to stay and see what their decision would be, but his tenuous hold on himself made that impossible. He refused to listen to his parents' plan to get rid of him like he was an old pair of running shoes—battered, scuffed, and torn. Instead, he ignored his brother and walked silently back to his room. Crawling back to the bed that had cooled in his absence, he slammed his headphones onto his head and turned the music just loud enough so that he couldn't hear the voices from the hall.

He spent the rest of the night trying to figure out how to make his parents love him again.

# THREE

MICHELLE turned and handed Allen a plate stacked with fluffy pancakes before nudging him in the direction of the table where Anthony and Aaron sat eating. The inescapable smell of syrup surrounded Aaron as he took another buttery bite. He watched her back as she made more pancakes and an expert flip almost made him smile. She frowned as she sat down at the table with them, a much shorter stack of pancakes on her plate. A quiet sigh escaped, of sadness or exhaustion, he couldn't tell. Then, in a desperate attempt to pull her family back together, she told them that they were going out to dinner to celebrate Aaron's graduation. Allen made a crack about celebrating Aaron barely passing English when he himself would have been grounded for a D in English. The joke came completely out of nowhere, but Michelle shot her middle son a stern look showing that she was not amused, just as the house phone rang. She answered it as Allen lowered his gaze, chastised after the hour-long lecture he'd been given earlier that morning. Aaron had heard most of it as he sat at the top of the stairs, trying to avoid the pitiful looks and imagined judgments he got from his family when they could see him. The expression Allen wore told him that his brother was still disgusted with himself for what he'd said to Aaron, even after all had been forgiven.

"Mom, no, we won't be home tonight, I'm sorry. Can I stop by tomorrow evening?" Aaron heard his mother say. Anthony had already left the table, as Allen sat next to Aaron, looking deep in thought. "Yes, well, we're going out to dinner… yes, Aaron too. We're celebrating his graduation from high school. No, Mom, I won't wear the red shirt." Allen stifled a laugh as his mother rolled her eyes. "Sure, Mom, we'll meet you at Clancy's at seven. Okay, Mom. Love you too." She hung up the phone and sighed. Dealing with his grandparents always stressed Aaron out, which in turn stressed out his mother. Aaron had heard his grandmother berating his mother once for coddling Aaron. If they just treated him like a normal kid, he would be normal. They really had no clue. So his mother got it from all sides, all because he couldn't function on his own. No wonder they wanted to ship him off.

"MOM, I'm so glad that you and Dad could make it on such short notice," Aaron's mother told his grandparents as they followed the host to their table at the restaurant. He was surprised when Allen grabbed Anthony by the back of the shirt and all but threw him into the seat next to his grandmother before taking the one next to Aaron. His parents sat opposite his brothers, leaving him at the opposite side of the table from his grandparents. Aaron could have kissed his brothers; they had put a human barrier between him and his grandparents. Whenever he saw them, his grandmother tried to hug him or his grandfather would pat him on the back. Neither of them were around Aaron enough to really understand why they could no longer touch their grandson.

After they'd been seated for a few minutes, Aaron quietly studying his menu, Michelle began to make small talk with her parents while John and Anthony talked about school. They were trying to keep the focus off Aaron, which he appreciated almost desperately. While they murmured in polite conversation, their server approached the table between Aaron and Allen, startling the older boy.

"Hi, my name is Juliette, and I'll be your server this evening," she said in a falsely bright tone.

Allen and his father, who were seated on either side of Aaron, noticed how his breathing seemed to accelerate at the mention of the server's name; they both leaned forward in their chairs, looking anxious. Aaron scooted his chair toward his father in an effort to get away from her.

"What can I get you folks to drink?" the server asked, popping her gum as she spoke, her pen poised to document their beverage preferences. Probably in her late twenties, the girl wasn't bad to look at with her frizzy red hair and freckles, but her high nasal voice was grating on the nerves.

"I'll have a Coke," John said. Each member of the family listed off a litany of liquid refreshments in turn, from Michelle's iced tea to the grandparents' wine. The two younger brothers both ordered 7Up, and then Allen ordered a Coke for his older brother, who flashed him a grateful look. Aaron hated to talk, especially to strangers who would just stare at him, causing him to stutter and repeat himself until he sounded like the freak he was. *Jesus, it was a fucking Thursday. Why was the restaurant so crowded?*

"I've heard their lasagna here is excellent," John piped up to keep the conversation going, once the server had gone to fill the drink order. Sweat trickled down the side of Aaron's face as he sat in the claustrophobic restaurant surrounded by strangers. He could feel them on all sides, pressing against his space. It was hard to breathe.

"Yes, that does sound good," their grandfather said as he looked over the menu one final time before closing it and setting it next to his plate. He sat stiffly in his chair, all but swallowed by the gray cardigan that helped to warm him in the air-conditioned restaurant. Thin and nearly bald, he pushed his thick oval glasses back up on the bridge of his nose as he addressed his eldest grandson. "So, Aaron, have you decided on your major at college?"

"Aaron isn't going to college yet," Allen said, his voice full of trepidation for his brother. Aaron sat staring absently at his silverware on the table, his breathing fast and labored. Aaron was in the beginning stages of a panic attack, and he worried what that would mean for him in the middle of a crowded restaurant. His mother's face swam before his eyes as he looked up at her helplessly.

"Thank you, son, but I was asking your brother," his grandfather said pointedly, and looked to Aaron to provide a more detailed answer.

Anyone that knew Aaron knew that Grandpa was going to be disappointed on that score. Without raising his eyes, Aaron simply mumbled, "Thinking about it," to his water glass.

"Grandpa, guess what!" Anthony said, successfully grabbing his grandfather's attention as he launched into a play-by-play of his last soccer game. The goal he scored, the perfect pass he set up for the next goal, and the head pass that helped to win the game. His eyes danced, and

Aaron vaguely remembered that same excitement talking about some of his more challenging debates, but that seemed like a lifetime ago. He envied Anthony's glow as he watched from the corner of his eye, but silently thanked his brother as the conversation kept both of Aaron's grandparents busy and their attention away from him.

The server came back and distributed the drinks. When she set Aaron's Coke in front of him, he grabbed it, discarded the straw, and drank every bit of it without breathing before returning the glass to the table. The sugar and caffeine felt like drugs in his system as the carbonation calmed his stomach. He closed his eyes as the server stared at him. After a moment, John started the process of ordering their entrees, much as he had with the drinks, deflecting the attention from Aaron, whose hands had started to shake under the table.

"I'll have the linguini Alfredo," John said with a forced smile for the server. The strain of keeping up the happy family front started to show in the lines around his eyes. Michelle ordered ravioli, as did her mother. Aaron's grandfather decided to go with the lasagna, as he had talked about before things began to get tense. Anthony, always a lover of spaghetti, chose to have it with meatballs. Things were going well as Allen ordered manicotti, and then it was Aaron's turn. In a very quiet voice, he asked his plate for chicken nuggets and french fries.

"I'm sorry, sir, only children twelve and under can order from the kids' menu," she said in a mildly sardonic tone, and likely expected Aaron to pick something else. As the table went completely silent, like the calm before the storm, Aaron balled his hands into tight fists and rested his forehead on them. His breathing became even more labored, and before anyone, including the shocked server could speak, Anthony jumped in.

"Ma'am, I'm twelve. Please bring me chicken nuggets." Aaron raised his head at his brother's voice to see that the server was staring at him. Then, almost as an afterthought, Anthony added, "Could you bring my brother the spaghetti and meatballs?" That brought the server back to herself, and she looked away from the horror of Aaron's ruined face.

"I… I can do that," she said, still a little shaken by Aaron's behavior. Falling back into her learned routine, she started to collect the menus. Everyone passed theirs to Allen, and he handed them to the server. One menu slipped from her grasp and hit Aaron's shoulder before she could grab it. The apology died in her throat as Aaron jerked away from her so violently that he knocked over his water glass. He stood up with heart-clenching haste and backed away from the table.

"Aaron," Allen said quickly, getting his brother's attention. "Let's go outside for a few minutes." Aaron looked around wildly for a moment and saw his mother's sorrow. *Please don't send me away. Please. I can't.* He faced his grandparents' shock before he locked eyes with Allen. Nodding furiously, he let Allen lead him from the table and carefully around the inanely curious inhabitants of the other tables until they reached the lobby area. Not bothering to return the good-bye from the host, they practically ran for the door.

The door slammed open as Aaron rushed through it, nearly sprinting toward the edge of the parking lot. As he reached it, he stopped, putting his hands on his knees. Aaron's face had a light sheen of sweat as he gulped down air. Allen could do nothing but stand next to him, looking helpless and being very careful not to touch his brother.

"Aaron, look at me, man…. Breathe…." Allen began to take slow deep breaths. "It's okay, Aaron, just breathe." His deep breathing was exaggerated, trying to get his brother to match his pace.

An older couple came out of the restaurant, watching them warily as they shuffled past the boys on the way to their car. The man, who must have been in his seventies, used his cane heavily as his wife held his other arm. Glancing back at Aaron again as she helped her husband into their seafoam-colored sedan, the woman turned her heavily lined face to Allen and furrowed her brow. When Allen didn't say anything, she walked slowly around the car and got behind the wheel. As she pulled out of the space, she narrowly missed the minivan parked in the row behind her. The two boys watched as they rolled slowly, merging into traffic as they left the lot.

Finally, Allen looked back at Aaron, who was breathing deeply and slowly with his eyes on his brother. It helped him to have something to focus on, something to keep him anchored in the present when his mind wanted to travel back to that dark place and keep him there until he screamed.

"Thank you," Aaron whispered, and closed his eyes against the dying afternoon light as the darkness in his mind started to recede and his lungs slowly started to work again. Each breath came easier than the last, though his face and neck still felt hot and tight. The long-sleeved polo clung to his back in the heat and tension of the near breakdown. Aaron continued to take slow, deep breaths for a few more minutes until he felt calmer. When he opened his eyes, he was looking at Allen and saw his own sadness reflected in his brother's face.

"Aaron, you're my brother and I love you. There isn't anything I wouldn't do for you, man." Allen moved to put a hand on his brother's shoulder, but then remembered himself.

"Love you too, kid, even though it's me who is supposed to be looking out for you," Aaron said with real remorse. It *was* his job to look out for his brothers, not the other way around. It killed him that they had to treat him like some kind of invalid because he couldn't function. One menu hitting his shoulder and he lost control of everything. He couldn't live like that. He just… he couldn't. Something had to change. He just didn't know what he could do to make it happen.

"You always watched out for me and Anthony," Allen said, looking his brother in the eye. "We can do the watching for a while."

Aaron closed his eyes again briefly. Then after a moment, he nodded.

"Are you okay to go back inside? I'm sure Mom is wondering where we are." Allen asked and then glanced around, probably to see if their mother had followed them outside.

Aaron let his brother lead him back to the table like a naughty child. When Aaron sat down in his place, he found that the mess from his spill was gone, and he had a fresh Coke. The food had been brought out while they were outside, so he grabbed his napkin and rested it in his lap as Allen sat down beside him. If he could just get through eating without any more problems, he might be able to salvage the rest of the evening for his mother. By the look on his father's face, that cause was lost.

"Thanks, Anthony," Aaron said quietly as he picked up his first piece of chicken. Miraculously, he found that he had an appetite. The last thing he wanted right then was to cause his mother more worry, so he ate as Anthony smiled back at him through a mouth full of spaghetti.

The rest of the meal crawled along, subdued but uneventful. Aaron noticed that when the server returned to the table, she made sure to do so near their grandparents, as far as she could from him. The tightness in his chest dissolved after nearly strangling him all night, and he watched the conversation with a small measure of interest. His mother smiled at him when she noticed that Aaron had cleaned his plate for the first time in six months.

"AARON, your father and I have been talking," Michelle said quietly as she and Aaron sat alone at the kitchen table a few days later. Aaron's head jerked up and he stared at her, his heart thundering in his chest. They'd finally come to it. His mother was sick of taking care of him, and they were going to send him away. He couldn't take that. He couldn't. He'd die there. His mother must have seen something in his face, because she reached for one of his hands, which he jerked under the table, banging his fingers on the edge in his haste to get away from her. The kitchen closed in around him as he rocked almost imperceptibly in his chair.

"Please, honey, it's okay. We just think maybe you should start thinking about college." She pulled her hand back slowly, the sting of rejection still in her eyes as she watched him.

*College?* The antianxiety meds were making him feel a little slow. *Wait, if they wanted him to start thinking about college, maybe they were giving him another chance.* Aaron studied his mother and saw no real signs of deception. She didn't avoid his eyes, she wasn't wringing her hands, she had none of the outward indicators that he'd practiced watching for during debate.

"Okay," he replied, without even a moment's hesitation. If his parents were giving him another chance to stay in their lives, he'd grab onto it with both hands. If college would make them happy, he'd at least give it a shot rather than ending up in a completely different kind of institution.

"Okay? Just like that?" she asked, and her tone turned a bit wary, like she was waiting for the catch, the punch line of his joke. Her face softened when he nodded.

"I could try something like that University of Phoenix and just take online classes."

"I'm not sure that's something you want to do. Degrees like that are pointless because employers discount them. Maybe you could look into that extension of ITM over in Donner," she countered, and Aaron could hear the determination in her voice.

"Any degree is going to be pointless, Mom." The fight had gone out of his voice, but so had any hope. Aaron wanted to argue, wanted to remind her about the panic attacks he got just by leaving the house. He wanted to question her about how he was supposed to function in a classroom full of people, or hold down any kind of job. He wanted to explain to her how useless he was as a person, but the words died in his throat. None of his well-reasoned arguments would be anything new to her. She knew them all, and she could use every one of them against him as a reason to send him away. So instead, he said nothing. He'd figure out how to survive in a classroom with a hundred other people, staring at him, judging him, making him feel worthless.

With one sharp nod, he accepted his fate, rose and trudged up the familiar path to his room. Nothing would be gained by putting off the inevitable. Rather than simply lying on the bed listening to music like he did most days, Aaron grabbed his rarely used laptop from the desk and balanced it on his lap as he sat back against the headboard. The website for ITM, Institute for Technology and Manufacturing, had a wealth of information in a clean, well-managed, and organized page. It was the only type of school in the area that would be considered a trade school or junior college. Two years ago, before his life ended, Aaron was looking at schools like Stanford or UCLA, but those dreams were gone.

Clicking on *Programs*, he looked through the offerings to see what his options were. Information Technology had the largest list, with degrees in networking, programming, security, forensics, and a host of other geeky proclivities. Also listed were degrees in business, electronics technology, drafting and design, criminal justice, and apparently to round things out, health services. Out of habit, Aaron read through the criminal justice list with a pang of regret. In high school, he'd wanted to be a lawyer, like his father. Working toward that career, he'd gotten involved in political campaigns, joined debate, and sometimes helped his father do research for a case. But that wasn't his life anymore. No way would he be able to stand in front of a courtroom and be confident or articulate like his father. At this point, he needed to work with what he had left.

Starting with Information Technology, he scanned the different opportunities, searching for one that would allow him the comfort of isolation. Networking, mobile communications, project management, they all sounded like group type settings. Instead, he moved down to the Associate Degree programs. Maybe he should start smaller. More than one shrink had used the phrase "baby steps" with him. He fucking hated that term. They had no concept of what it meant to increment your life by inches.

He clicked on the software development associate degree and read the description. Yes, he liked to solve puzzles, or at least he used to. Yes, he liked computers, as well as anyone else. He felt comfortable with them, more comfortable than he did with people, anyway. Computers didn't stare at your scars or give you looks of pity and disgust. They couldn't burn you or destroy your soul. He read through the rest of the description and decided that it sounded just as good to him as anything else would. With grim determination, he clicked the *Apply Now* button and filled in the form.

When he received the response, he read through it briefly, feeling the sweat bead on the back of his neck. They would be sending him a brochure for the college, and wanted to schedule a campus tour. They'd be calling to talk to him. They wanted to meet with him. Forwarding the e-mail to his mother, he slammed the computer closed and all but threw it onto his desk. He couldn't do it. He couldn't. His breathing came in sharp, pained gasps as he rolled to his side and pulled his knees up. Curled like a baby, he stared at the wall and tried not to think about what would come next.

Just because he applied, that didn't mean he had to go.

Until it did.

Just as she took care of everything else in his life, Aaron's mother handled everything with ITM. She met with the dean to explain about Aaron's issues. She met with his instructor to give him an idea of what having him in class would mean. She didn't accept the dean's recommendation that maybe Aaron should wait before attending college. His class was scheduled, paperwork was completed, tuition was paid, and throughout the process, Aaron sat idly by and watched his life being lived without him.

As Aaron sat ordering his textbooks for the new semester, the one thing his mother let him do alone, he wondered why in the hell he couldn't just take classes online. He could register online, buy his books online, even turn in homework online—it was a fucking computer degree, and yet he couldn't take classes online. He'd signed up for only one of the recommended four courses. *Baby steps.* After talking it over with his mother, they decided to wait on taking English and public speaking. English frustrated the hell out of Aaron, and his mother planned to talk to the dean about public speaking. They were sure when they explained the magnitude of Aaron's discomfort, the school would let him take a different elective. It would take him much longer than two years to graduate at that rate, but degree or no degree, he doubted that he would ever be high functioning enough to hold down a job. Most of the time, he was barely able to make it to dinner.

Entering the credit card number that his mother had given him for the books, Aaron set the pick-up date for the Friday before classes started. His mom could take him over to the college. Even in his diminished capacity, he should still be able to walk into the bookstore and pick up a bag. Vaguely, as he clicked the order button on the badly designed bookstore site, he wondered if he would be the only student on campus whose mother chauffeured him to and from school. After a moment of deliberation, he printed the receipt and decided that he probably would.

SPENCER stood watching his father sleep, sprawled out in the recliner with a leather-bound edition of Tolkien's trilogy cracked open on his chest, the binding stretched beyond reasonable limits. He didn't take the book from his father's hands, but simply watched as it rose and fell with each rumbling snore. Henry Thomas wasn't a violent drunk, or even an angry one, but it broke Spencer's heart to see him in pain. It had been just the two of them for so long, relying on each other, and he felt like they just weren't the same anymore. He didn't know how to get their closeness back. He didn't know how to help.

Shivering lightly in the late night breeze, he closed and locked the sliding glass door and grabbed one of the throws from the back of the couch. Carefully, he laid it across his father's legs and brought it up over the man's chest. His father merely grunted and slept on. With a heavy sigh, Spencer went up to his room and pulled out his new laptop. Memories from his encounter with the delivery guy flooded his mind and made his cock begin to fill. They were marred only marginally by the delivery boy's post-sex behavior, but he could look past that and remember what being inside the boy had felt like.

Bringing up his favorite Twitter app, he watched his timeline for a few minutes to see who else was up who could distract him from worrying about his father. He talked to people all over the world in a dozen different time zones. Having friends on Twitter was easier than having them in real life. He didn't have to tell them he was deaf. He didn't have to see the fucking pity in their eyes. He could simply be Spencer, and that was okay. Talking to guys and flirting with them online was safe—it wasn't like he'd ever see them. Fucking guys over Twitter had turned into his escape.

---

**Mark John-Thomas @Mark4873**

ikr? WTF? I'm sick of hearing str8 guys going on and on about pussy. #Unfollow

View conversation ⮌ Reply ⇅ Retweet ★Favorite

---

**Todd Marshall @BottomBoi574**

I'm so bored

View conversation ⮌ Reply ⇅ Retweet ★Favorite

---

**Brandon Masters @BrandonMastersXXX**

Doing an insanely hot three way with this mega fucking stud and his boyfriend

View conversation ⮌ Reply ⇅ Retweet ★Favorite

---

---

**Spencer Thomas @Spence9876**

@BottomBoi574 I got somethin you can play with if you're bored.

View conversation ⮌ Reply ⇅ Retweet ★Favorite

---

**Todd Marshall @BottomBoi574**

@Spence9876 WTF I sent you a DM like 3 days ago?

View conversation ⮌ Reply ⇅ Retweet ★Favorite

---

**Mark John-Thomas @Mark4873**

Hey @Spence9876 Where the fuck have you been?

View conversation ⮌ Reply ⇅ Retweet ★Favorite

---

**Kyle Stacey @KyleStaceyXXX**

I love SF pic.twitter.com/387g83H8

View conversation ⮌ Reply ⇅ Retweet ★Favorite

---

**Spencer Thomas @Spence9876**

@Mark4873 Sorry I've been busy getting shit done… Checking DMs now

View conversation ⮌ Reply ⇅ Retweet ★Favorite

---

Spencer clicked the link to switch the page to his private messages, and sure enough, there was one from @BottomBoi asking him to Skype, and it pissed him off. He'd already explained about a dozen times that he didn't want to talk to him over Skype. The kid thought he would be getting great video chat sex. All he'd get was fucking silence and maybe a video to jack off to.

---

**Spencer Thomas @Spence9876**

DM @BottomBoi574 My mic doesn't work on the laptop. Can't Skype. Sorry

View conversation ⮌ Reply ⇅ Retweet ★Favorite

---

It was an excuse he'd used over and over again, but one that seemed to work. Well, except with @BottomBoi, who offered to ship him a brand new computer headset so they could talk. God, if the guy only knew what he was asking, he'd shut the fuck up. One day soon, he'd just give up and unfollow Spencer, who couldn't wait for that day.

---

**Mark John-Thomas @Mark4873**

@Spence9876 No prob man. Wanna chat?

View conversation ↩ Reply ⇅ Retweet ★Favorite

---

Mark, whoever he was, understood that Spencer didn't Skype. He'd asked once, and when Spencer refused, he hadn't asked again. Instead, they'd gone onto chat and talked there privately. It was faster and more reliable than the private messaging system in Twitter.

---

**Spencer Thomas @Spence9876**

@Mark4873 Yeah, logging on now.

View conversation ↩ Reply ⇅ Retweet ★Favorite

---

He brought up the chat window and minimized Twitter, no longer in the mood to deal with BottomBoi and his neediness. Besides, Mark was always fun inspiration for a late-night hand fuck. Just to be safe, he got up and locked his bedroom door as Mark's first message popped up on his screen.

[MARK]: been hard 4 u for days  fucking loved those pics you sent

Spencer leaned back in his desk chair and popped the button on his jeans. He might not be able to talk a guy to orgasm, but he could certainly share some hot come shots. A few videos might reside on his phone, too, but he felt reasonably sure his password would save him from curious eyes. He hadn't been brave enough to send one of those out. A still shot he could argue he'd gotten from the Internet and shared. A video taken on his phone was another story.

[SPENCER]: Think my cock is enough to satisfy you?

[MARK]: yeah it's a work of fucking art is it hard for me now?

[SPENCER]: Yeah, I'm typing one-handed if that's what you're asking.

[MARK]: it is

[MARK]: so am i

[MARK]: wish u had me over the desk right now pounding into me

[SPENCER]: You like it hard and fast?

[MARK]: fuck yeah

[SPENCER]: You want me to pin you to the desk? Drill you into it with my cock?

[MARK]: omg yeah

Spencer pulled his jeans and briefs down to his calves and spread his legs wide. The cool leather of the office chair chilled the backs of his thighs. He liked being naked and spread like that, still half-dressed, stroking his cock as he imagined the faceless guy on the other side of the chat window doing the same. He wondered if their rhythms matched and what Mark thought of as he jerked off. The blood rushed to his cock, filling it, lengthening it as he wondered if Mark was using his pictures to jack off.

[MARK]: want to ride you

[SPENCER]: I could do that, lay back on the bed and watch you fuck yourself on me.

[MARK]: tell me something about you

[SPENCER]: Tell you what?

[MARK]: don't care, anything about you

[SPENCER]: I'm starting college in a couple weeks.

He didn't know what made him reveal that about himself. Usually, he didn't share any kind of personal information with anonymous guys online. The need for a connection and the lack of blood in his brain made him stupid.

[MARK]: Jesus ur a twink?

[MARK]: fuck im so hard please let me watch?

[SPENCER]: No. And if you ask again, the conversation is over.

[MARK]: sorry tell me what you're doing

[SPENCER]: I'm getting up and moving to the bed.

His hard-on started to falter as he stood up. Spencer was rapidly getting out of the mood to play tonight, but jerked his jeans all the way off anyway. Pulling his shirt off over his head, he pulled one of the pillows up and propped it against the headboard. The screen moved up as another message came through. He ignored it for the moment and settled the laptop on the bed next to him. God, he just wanted to fucking jack off and go to sleep. He didn't think that was too much to ask. Glancing up, he saw the message Mark sent, and his dick got harder. It was a picture of the thirtysomething brown-haired guy straddled over a dildo. Naked from the waist down, his nondescript blue T-shirt had been hiked up above his nipples, which were pebbled out on his chest. The base of the dildo barely peeked out from beneath his balls, prominent because of the way his back arched and his cock jutted up toward his stomach.

It was fucking beautiful.

He grabbed his phone and reached far down between his legs. Angling the phone to miss his face, he took a picture of his hand wrapped around the base of his cock and e-mailed it to Mark.

[SPENCER]: Check your e-mail. I have something for you to ride.

A minute passed, and then two.

[MARK]: FUCK I wanna choke on that

Spencer imagined a pair of sweet, soft lips around his cock and groaned. He rolled a bit to his left, reached into his bedside table, and pulled out a bottle of lube. He popped the lid and then poured a bit directly on the head of his cock and used his right hand to spread it across his hot skin. He used his left hand, which was devoid of lube, to type. The result wasn't the polished typing he usually used because text speak drove his father insane.

[SPENCER]: take it deep

[SPENCER]: I want to fuck ur throat

He'd never done that before, but the thought just make his fucking balls ache. Having the guy trapped beneath him taking everything Spencer gave. *Fucking take it. Take my cock.* Beyond any sense of reason, he concentrated on the head of his dick, twisting his grip over it. It throbbed in his hand. Jerking his hips up, he thrust into his warm, slick fist and wished it were Mark's pliable body. He could almost feel the tight heat, and he gripped tighter.

[MARK]: rubbing stretching god so good

[MARK]: please fuck me harder

With the slow response time as a guide, he figured Mark was doing only the barest essentials of typing because his hands were otherwise occupied. One hand drove a dildo into his ass, and the other hand wrapped around his dick. God, he could almost see him as he knelt on a bed somewhere and wished he could be on top of Spencer… or under him.

[SPENCER]: want to spread you wide open across my bed and make you scream

The thought just randomly popped into his head of a guy spread-eagled and face down on his bed. He wasn't bound, although Spencer wouldn't be opposed to the idea. He simply lay there until Spencer knelt between his knees and lined his cock up along the sweet valley of ass laid out like a buffet.

[MARK]: make me scream with your mouth or your cock?

In his mind, he spread the guy's cheeks with his palms and buried his face in Mark's ass. Precome leaked from the tip of his dick as he wondered what that sweet ass would taste like, or how Mark would fuck the sheets, grinding his hips into the bed as he rode Spencer's tongue.

[SPENCER]: tell me what you want

[MARK]: god please fuck me

[SPENCER]: use that dildo

[SPENCER]: pretend it's me

[SPENCER]: get on your hands and knees with your legs spread wide fuck that sweet little ass for me

[SPENCER]: do it hard I like it hard

[MARK]: uggggggggggh yeah so hard

A smile spread across Spencer's face. The guy was certainly thinking about him and all the things his cock could do. Too bad it could never be real. He tried to push that thought from his mind and concentrate on the feeling in his balls instead, because that didn't make him feel inadequate. Suddenly, he just wanted it over.

[SPENCER]: close going to come

Speeding the motion of his hand, he focused on the spots where he was most sensitive. Years of practice told him exactly how to get himself off with minimum fuss. It would be empty and hollow, just as it always was, but at least he'd be able to fucking sleep.

[MARK]: me too keep hitting that sweet spot just like you would

Spencer rolled his eyes. Another night that would have been hot, but right then, it grated on his nerves and he snapped the laptop lid closed. Let the guy think he lost his Internet connection. He'd be back. They were all desperate, lonely guys looking to get off. They'd all be back, just as he would.

His orgasm, empty and unfulfilling, finally fucking landed on his stomach in warm, sticky blotches. The pressure behind his eyes and the burning in his throat took him by surprise. An emotional release came right along with the physical, and he turned his head into the pillow trying to stop the lonely ache in his chest.

# FOUR

AS HE expected, Aaron's mother offered to accompany him into the bookstore just to keep him company. Of course, he knew that she was afraid for him. With the groups of people on campus, would this be the day that he had a panic attack in the bookstore or became unresponsive in the bathroom? The college had been briefed about his various neuroses by his mother and the current stop in his revolving door of shrinks, but at the end of the day, it was his mother who had to pick up the pieces if he fell apart. It took a long time to convince her to wait in the car outside the quad. If he was going to sit in a room full of other people for class, he had to start doing things for himself.

As luck would have it, the bookstore was relatively quiet when he arrived. Most of the students probably already had their books.

"May I help you?" the young woman from behind the desk asked as Aaron approached. The smile faded quickly from her pointed little face as Aaron looked up, his scars illuminated harshly in the fluorescent lighting. He could tell that she was trying not to stare as she twirled her blond hair around one finger, obviously nervous and uncomfortable. Aaron handed her his receipt without a word, and she looked it over before going to the shelves a few feet behind her to get his bag of books. Looking around at the different products on display as he waited, he was glad that his mother had already taken care of getting everything else that he needed. Aaron thought that maybe his mother took a special kind of comfort in doing something as mundane as picking out his school supplies, because he was still around to buy them for. Picking up notebooks and pens was his mother's way of celebrating the fact that he needed them.

The hairs on the back of his neck stood up as he felt someone standing in line behind him. He didn't want to be here any longer than was absolutcly necessary. God, he didn't know if he could sit in a classroom surrounded by people if he couldn't even stand in line to get books. The girl stepped back to the counter and double-checked the bag's contents to make sure they matched his receipt. It seemed to Aaron that she was almost deliberately taking her time checking his stuff. It made him uncomfortable. She pushed the bag to him, but didn't let go of the bottom when he grabbed the handles at the top.

"I don't know if you remember, but… uhm… we went to high school together," she said finally. Warning bells started to sound in his head, and his heart raced. His breathing became shallow, and he tried to pull the bag away from her and leave, but she held on. "I'm so sorry about—" That was as far as she'd gotten before Aaron ripped the bag from her grasp and bolted for the door. He had no idea if she was going to express her sorrow about what happened to him, or Juliette, but whatever it was, he didn't want to hear it. He fucking hated the word *sorry*. They couldn't possibly understand what the word meant. The girl, well, all of them who tried and failed to console him, they couldn't possibly be as *sorry* as he was. He didn't want their hollow platitudes, no matter how sincere they seemed. Aaron didn't know the girl behind the counter, didn't remember her. She certainly didn't know him, at least the boy he had become. There was absolutely nothing she could say that he wanted to hear.

His hands were still wrapped into tight fists, one around the handles of the bookstore bag, the other awkwardly hanging at his side as he walked out into the quad with its perfectly landscaped lawns and modest, well-kept buildings. The campus also happened to have the best IT program within a hundred-mile radius. His parents had insisted that he go to college, even if he didn't feel like he had any kind of future. The shrinks had told his mother that Aaron should live as close to a normal life as possible, to assimilate him back into society. It was a joke. Aaron would attend this school not for its academics, but because it was ten minutes from his home. His mother stayed home to care for him and his brothers, so she would never be more than ten minutes away from him at any given time. It had been like that all his life, but now, more than ever, that proximity was crucial.

Exhausted and lost in thought, Aaron sat on one of the benches, trying to stop his heart from racing before he went back to the parking lot where his mother waited. The smell of freshly mown grass hung heavy in the air as the cool late summer morning turned into a warm late summer afternoon. He could hear a mower off in the distance, but mostly, the quiet chatter of students on the sidewalk near him was the only sound. With his bag held tightly in his arms, as if it were an anchor tethering him to reality, he stared unseeing after a long and sleepless night. The bench near where he sat was one of three in a semicircle around an abstract statue of metal concentric circles standing atop a square base. Small bushes sprinkled the open area, with little purple and blue flowers still in bloom. He should go back to the car before his mom started to worry, but he didn't want to go yet. It was peaceful here, almost serene. Aaron never really went anywhere, and this beautiful oasis of freedom was much less oppressive than the bedroom he rarely left. A girl he did not know half waved at him, until he looked up fully and the sun brought his scars into relief. Her expression changed to the shock and horror he knew so well, almost like a welcoming friend, signaling a lucky escape from a would-be conversationalist.

The hand that touched his shoulder was so unexpected and scared him so badly, he shot off the end of the bench, stumbled on shock-numbed legs, and fell onto the ground. His bag landed near his feet and his books scattered from it along the sidewalk. A searing pain ripped through his side as he landed on the corner of the statue's base and avoided screaming only by the sheer grace of God. Aaron curled in on himself, to the only protective position he could think of. Pulling his knees to his chest and covering his head with his hands, he didn't even have the presence of mind to grab his cell phone from his pocket. At that point, the only goal was to keep himself safe.

*The sound of the van door slamming was loud in his ears as he struggled against the guy who held him. His nostrils were assaulted by the stench of stale beer and sweat, as the arms remained clamped around him like a vise. Looking over, he saw Juliette struggling as hard as he was.*

*"Shhhhhh.... Calm down, kid, we're just going for a little ride."*

Flashes of that night came back, strong and unbidden, as he cowered beside the concrete base of the statue. Its solid, unyielding presence was mildly reassuring, and Aaron pulled harder against it, trying to shield himself from the attack that he knew was coming. The burns, it would be the burns first.

"Don't hurt me…. Please… d… don't touch me," he chanted over and over again to his knees, which were now almost directly in front of his face as he rocked on the ground. With his arms locked over his head, he was only vaguely aware that the figure standing over him was still looming. Then, a car door slammed in the distance, and he heard footsteps. Still, he didn't dare move.

"Aaron… Aaron, I'm not going to touch you. Baby, can you hear me?" His mother's voice filtered through the fog of fear and panic. *Thank God.* No one could hurt him with his mother protecting him. She'd even saved him that night. That horrible night she'd come through and she'd saved him.

"Mama?" Aaron's voice was shaky and quiet as he allowed his arms to fall from his head and wrap around his knees. "Mama, I want to go home." Her breathing hitched, and she sounded almost like she might cry. He couldn't even remember the last time he'd called her "mama"—probably not since he was a small boy.

"Okay, baby, we're going home," his mother replied in a soft, reassuring voice. Her voice changed then as he heard her addressing his unknown assailant.

"Did you need something?" Aaron's mother asked coldly. She was obviously upset by Aaron's incapacitation. The response that she got was strange, and sounded almost foreign, even though it was in perfect English.

"I. Am. Very. Sorry.." The guy's voice was shaky, and he spoke slowly, enunciating every syllable very clearly, like he was not used to speaking or like he thought Aaron was slow. Frankly, Aaron didn't care; he wanted to get the hell out of there. There was something about the stranger's slow, measured pronunciation that just sounded off, and Aaron found that he didn't want to look up to see the guy's face. He didn't want to see horror or pity. He wanted to go home.

"I. Was. Asking. Him. For. Directions.," the guy continued, still in that slow, measured speech. "I. Cannot. See. What. He. Is. Saying.. What. Is. He. Saying.?"

"He said 'please don't touch me'. What building are you looking for?" The exhaustion in his mother's voice filled him with shame. He knew that she just wanted to get him home, but the fact that he couldn't even deal with a guy just asking for directions caused his chest to tighten. It infuriated him that he couldn't act like a normal human being, that he had to sit cowered in the shadow of this boy who was no real threat.

"Patterson.."

"It's the building over there across the lot," his mother explained.

"Thank. You.," the guy replied, and sensing an escape, Aaron scrambled to his feet and bolted for the car, not looking up at the lost student. It was a minute or so before his mother joined him, and together they got into the car and headed home. The silence in the car was almost deafening.

His mother brought him a tranquilizer and a bottle of grape juice as he sat on his bed staring at the door. The soft whirring of his fan was the only sound in the room as he took the pill without a word. It had been a couple of weeks since he'd needed one, but today he certainly needed it. Images from the flashback he'd experienced in the quad were burned into his mind, and he knew that only the tranquilizer would make them fade. Nothing made them leave completely, but for a while, they wouldn't torture him. Still fully dressed with the exception of his shoes, he rolled on his bed to face the wall, pulled his knees up to his chest and waited for the drugs to do their job.

This day hadn't really started out so bad. How did it go so wrong?

He felt his mother's weight leave the bed as she stood up.

"Mama, I'm sorry," he said, his voice almost pleading. One day she would grow tired of his childish behavior and let his father send him away. That thought drained him of what little strength he had left. His mother sat back down on the bed, and with the powerful tranquilizer to keep him calm, briefly touched his hair. He wanted so badly to be able to cry.

"It's not your fault, Aaron. None of this is your fault, baby. Now, just take a nap, and when you wake up, I'll bring you some dinner." She stood again and left the room quietly, turning off his light and closing his door behind her. He was asleep before she made it to the stairs.

SPENCER skipped the search for his last class and ran for the safety of his car. He'd find the last class sometime before he had to be there on Thursday, but right then, he couldn't get the image of that boy's terrified face out of his head—so small, and just… helpless. He'd seen enough television shows to know that something horrible had happened to that kid. Normal people didn't just drop to the ground with a tap on the shoulder. But then, what would Spencer know about normal?

The light at the intersection that led to the main road turned red just as he approached. Spencer drummed his fingers on the steering wheel and waited, hoping that the car pulling up next to him at the light wasn't the boy and his mother. *Please God.* It wasn't. Malibu Barbie pulled up next to him in a Jetta and smiled over at him. Normally, he'd have the patience to flirt back. Even if he wasn't interested, he liked being wanted. Right then, he couldn't be bothered. He just wanted to get home and talk to his father about what happened in the quad.

The next light turned yellow, and the car in front of him stopped, forcing him to stop as well. Jesus, it was a conspiracy. The boy's face swam in front of his eyes again, terrified and lost. Spencer didn't think he could pull himself into a ball as tight as the guy did. His knees had been practically behind his head in some sort of defensive position that someone who did yoga couldn't have gotten into. Did he really think Spencer was going to hurt him?

The light on his console flashed, indicating a loud sound, and he looked up to see that the light had turned green and the car in front of him had moved. He looked around, ever cautious, and then stepped on the gas. His pulse pounded in his head, and he couldn't stop the adrenaline coursing through his body. It was almost like he was the one who'd been scared.

Finally, he caught a green light and sped up. He drove a little faster than he normally did in an effort to outrun the images in his head, to leave them at the college.

Spencer gave a silent prayer of thanks to see his father's BMW in the garage when he pulled in. After grabbing the bag from the bookstore out of his back seat, he ran to the back door. It slammed behind him, getting the attention of his father, who stood in the kitchen with one hand on his head and the other around a tall glass of something. Damn it, he'd started already.

With one look at his father's bloodshot eyes and hunched shoulders, Spencer walked right past and up to his room. He wondered, not for the first time, what it would be like to lose himself in the fog of alcohol like his father. Would it help get the boy's ruined face out of his head?

# FIVE

TWO more days of freedom left to him before he started classes on Monday, and Aaron had an idea for how he wanted to spend one of them. He just hoped his mother agreed. It was important for him to do this, no matter what the cost to his own psyche.

"Mom," Aaron said, and his mother stopped in the doorway, turning to look at her son curiously. He rarely, if ever, initiated a conversation with her, so she looked fairly surprised. "Would you mind taking me to visit… Juliette tomorrow?" It took her a minute to respond. Aaron had never visited Juliette's grave, not once in almost two years. He had still been in the hospital when her parents held her funeral. Michelle stood in the doorway while she appeared to consider it. The silence between them hung heavy in the air while she no doubt thought about the damage that visit could do to her son, or maybe the way it might help his recovery. After several long and tense moments, she spoke.

"Sure, honey. We can stop by the florist on the way."

The next morning, after making pancakes and sausage for all her boys, Michelle tapped into that strength that seemed to remain somewhere inside of her, and asked Aaron if he still wanted to visit Juliette. He said that he did, and went upstairs to change.

Neither of them spoke as they made their way to the commercial area of town. When they arrived at the small brick building with the displays of flowers exploding with late summer color, Aaron stayed in the car. His mother would pick out the flowers that she thought were best. What the hell did he know about buying gravesite flowers? It was all he could do to focus on something other than why the flowers were necessary in the first place.

"I decided to go with a mixed bouquet of pink roses, lilies, and daisies," his mother said when she returned to the car with a subtly colored mix of flowers, which she handed to Aaron. Holding them on his lap, his expression was hard and cold as he wrapped his arms around himself, almost as if he were trying to hold himself together, or as if he wanted to curl up into a ball so tight and so small that he would just disappear into it. Aaron saw his mother glance periodically at him as they headed for East Park Cemetery.

She pulled off the side of the road near where Juliette's grave must be. Aaron knew that his mother had been here a few times since Juliette's funeral. Each time he stayed home and his father tried in vain to distract him. After turning off the ignition, Michelle sat waiting for Aaron to speak or move. He did neither.

"Aaron, honey, do you want me to go with you?" his mother prompted, but he shook his head. Aaron needed to do this alone, especially since he was unsure how he would respond to actually seeing Juliette's grave, knowing she was buried there. However he reacted, his mother didn't need to see it. She saw enough. After taking one last long moment to look over the small rolling hills of green, he opened the car door. The smell of freshly mown grass flooded over him, and he climbed out of the car. It didn't take him long to find the small monument signaling the entrance to Juliette's part of the cemetery. His mother had described the statue as a marble angel with a lamb at her feet. His friend's parents had chosen to bury her in the children's section. Maybe they wanted to maintain her innocence, or it could have just been that the plots were smaller and less expensive in this section. Whatever the reason, she was here, somewhere to the right of this statue.

The cemetery was silent, almost eerily so considering it was a nice summer Saturday afternoon. The only sound to be heard was that of a mower in the distance. Grass seemed to stretch on for miles around him, but for all its airy solitude, the place made him feel claustrophobic—almost as if there should be a grave here for him, like his grave was calling for him. He should be buried here, right alongside Juliette under the granite eyes of God's chosen messenger. Sometimes it felt like he *had* joined her, suffocating, trapped inside his own head.

Balling his hands into fists, he forced himself to take slow, measured steps toward the grave, his breaths coming in quick, sharp pants. Goddamn it, he couldn't go to pieces. He wanted to do it, needed to do it, needed to see what he could get out of this physical reminder of his own fleeting mortality—maybe it would make him want to live again. Being careful not to step on the graves of other poor dead children, he followed the dates of death marked on the headstones, year by year, until he saw her name.

JULIETTE ANNE MARTIN
AUGUST 14, 1991—OCTOBER 9, 2008
BELOVED DAUGHTER

There were no bears or blocks or even angels, as he had seen on the other headstones while he had looked for hers. It was dark gray, marble, and very elegant. All at once, the realization that his friend, his Juliette, lay dead at his feet, caused his legs to buckle, and he landed hard on the soft earth next to her. The forgotten flowers fell to the ground, and dry heaves wracked his body. He wouldn't cry; he knew that. He'd been unable to cry since that night. Just as he couldn't stand to be touched, he was also not allowed the small measure of relief that crying would have afforded him.

It took a long time for him to finally get himself together. Remembering the flowers, he moved them to the grass just below the marble marker he could no longer bring himself to look at. Aaron considered just standing up and going back to the car, having done what he came here to do unassisted. Glancing over his shoulder, Aaron noticed that he couldn't see his mother's car from here, and he wondered if she was starting to worry.

"J… Juliette, it's… it's Aaron," he whispered, feeling fairly stupid for addressing the flowers and a patch of freshly mown grass. Running his fingers gently along the prickly surface of the short green lawn, he felt a mild breeze pick up and caress his face. He wondered in that moment if maybe she could hear him, but shook the thought off as a silly superstition. Nevertheless, he continued to whisper to his friend.

"It's been so hard, Juliette. The way everyone treats me, like I'm a bomb just waiting to go off," Aaron said, his voice trembling as he knelt on the cool, damp grass. "The memories, the flashbacks, I don't know how much longer I can keep doing this. The doctors don't help. The pills don't help. As selfish as it sounds, I wish you were here, Juliette. God, I feel so alone, so fucking scared all the time. I don't know if you would have wanted to live, just like I don't know if I do, but it would be so much easier to have someone that understood." His chest ached as he continued to caress the grass with his outstretched hand, talking to the idea of his lost friend. He had no idea if she could hear him, if anyone could hear him. Talking about this shit just made it all worse. The self-hatred that he felt, the feelings that he tried to keep contained, burned like acid on his tongue as he spoke about them.

Summoning all the strength he had left, he forced down the self-loathing and the thoughts of suicide, back into the place where he kept them locked away. These were things he couldn't let his mother see; she had so much else to worry about. So, after baring as much of his soul as he could stand to this empty patch of grass, he was finally ready to leave. Standing slowly, he brushed the grass off his knees, feeling suddenly guilty for the new stains it had left on his jeans. Aaron looked around slowly, noticing that the sounds of the mower were now gone, and bent to straighten the flowers on Juliette's grave.

"Happy birthday, Juliette," he said quietly, and then turned to go.

AS SPENCER flipped through the first couple chapters of his new programming book, he sighed. He'd learned most of the stuff in high school and had figured the rest out on his own. More than anything, he needed a challenge, something to keep his mind off the other shit going on in his life. While he was excited about starting college, his father's drinking worried him. Dad was the only person in his life he could really count on. At eighteen, he couldn't carry the weight of college and his father's worsening alcoholism. It had gotten better for a while, until one of his partners became involved in a lawsuit that wrecked their entire psychiatric practice. Rather than putting up a new shingle, he'd retired at forty-five to explore his other options. The only other option he'd found was in a bottle.

His phone buzzed, so he pulled it out of his pocket. Spencer didn't have many friends, so more often than not the texts came from his father.

DAD: I don't feel like cooking tonight. You want pizza or Chinese?

Spencer had expected the text. His father hadn't gotten out of bed until about two in the afternoon, and even then he looked like hell. He thought about offering to cook, but didn't feel much like it either. That kid at the college had scared the fuck out of him. One minute, he was tapping the guy on the shoulder, the next he was watching in horror as the boy freaked out on the ground. Spencer hadn't meant to scare him like that. He just wanted to find all his classes before Monday. Dealing with the interpreter that the school forced on him was enough; he didn't want to get lost and have to ask for directions.

SPENCER: Chinese

DAD: Orange chicken or fried rice?

Texting each other from the same damned house seemed ridiculous to Spencer, so he marked his page in the textbook, got up off the couch, and went in search of his father. The kitchen, spartan in its décor, was empty except for a lonely pitcher of ice tea Spencer had made earlier, which sat on the breakfast bar. The fifty-inch flat-panel on the wall of the living room was dark, and the room appeared equally empty. It took him several minutes and a few more rooms, but finally he saw his father in his office. A quiet room lined with books, it was rich with dark wood and supple leather. His father sat on the leather couch that dominated the back wall. The desk, a perfectly crafted walnut office desk with fancy bronze drawer handles and a black leather blotter, sat unused along the western wall. For all the effort his father put into managing his life the last few months, the desk could have had an inch of dust on it.

"Menu.?" Spencer asked, and his father looked up from the book in his hands. He didn't mind talking in front of his dad, because he'd been doing it all his life. His father, along with Aunt Nelle, had taught him to speak. It took forever, especially since neither of them had any experience dealing with deaf children. But somehow, between the three of them, they managed. That was years ago, however, while he still held his father's complete focus. As he got older and became more self-sufficient, his father sank deeper into a depression that imploded with his forced retirement.

*I think there is a menu on the desk,* his father signed after setting his book on the couch next to him. It showed just how far their relationship had deteriorated in the last few years that they were both sitting in the house reading, in different rooms, with absolutely no communication between them. He walked over to the desk and rummaged through the drawers until he found a file of menus. It reminded him of how organized his father used to be. From the top drawer, he pulled out a pad of paper and pen.

After scanning the menu, he wrote his order on the pad and handed it to his father. Just one more thing his father had to do for him. One day soon, restaurants would start taking advantage of online ordering, and he couldn't wait. They already used online ordering for their groceries because neither of them wanted the bother of going to the grocery store. After a cursory look through the menu, his father picked up his cell phone from the couch arm and called in their order. While Spencer couldn't hear what he said, he could read his father's lips and discern the weary sound of his voice from the way his body sagged on the couch.

*They said about twenty minutes,* he signed after tossing the phone back onto the couch. His father looked older than Spencer had ever seen him. Bags hung low beneath his eyes, which had once been bright and full of life. Growing up, his father had always been there for him, looking out for him, teaching him how to negotiate the hearing world, but lately, he watched as his greatest ally slipped farther and farther away.

*Did you get everything you need for school? I saw the charge come through for the laptop.*

His heart slowed just a bit with the concern in his father's expression. Maybe he wasn't as far away as Spencer had imagined.

*Yes. I got my books yesterday. I even started reading them,* Spencer answered with a tentative smile. For the first time in his life, he felt unbalanced in their relationship. They'd always been a team before—just the two of them against the world, but all that had changed recently, and

Spencer didn't know how to get it back. His father picked up the discarded book and opened it back to his page.

The silence weighed on him, heavy and awkward as he stood watching his father read.

"My. College. Career. Started. With. A. Bang. The. Other. Day.," he told his father in a desperate attempt to keep his attention. He'd wanted to talk to him about it when he got home, but his dad had been in no shape for a conversation. They hadn't really talked in weeks, and Spencer missed their easy way with each other. His friends in high school fought constantly with their parents, but he and his father rarely argued. Lately, his dad had been locked away in his office or his bedroom while the empties piled up in the garbage.

*What do you mean?* His father's signing was clipped and halfhearted, almost like he couldn't stand another complication right then.

*I tapped a boy on the shoulder to ask him for directions, and he freaked out.* Even just the memory of it bothered Spencer.

*Freaked out how? He did not hurt you?* His father's eyes took a quick inventory of Spencer, who smiled ruefully and dropped into the big leather office chair. Whenever he sat here, in his father's chair, he felt like a little kid at the adult table.

*No, he did not hurt me. He fell down with his hands over his head and begged me not to touch him. It scared me at first, but then I felt sad for him.* The boy's scarred face haunted him. He couldn't imagine what had happened to force such a reaction from a simple touch, but he knew what it was like to be afraid and in pain. He knew what it was to be alone.

*Sounds like he had a flashback or a reaction to some kind of trauma. What happened to him?* His father sat up straighter on the couch, his interest obviously engaged. As a clinical psychologist, someone having an episode in the middle of the quad would be of interest.

*A woman, I think it was his mom, came and helped him. I would not have left him alone. It was really awful. I had no idea what to do. Guess that is why I did not go into psychology,* Spencer reasoned with a shrug. His insides felt like ice as he thought about how scared the boy had looked.

*Seeing someone in pain is not something you ever get used to. At least, I never did.*

Spencer's phone vibrated in his pocket. Looking away from his father, he checked the display and saw that someone had rung the doorbell. It didn't seem like twenty minutes, but Spencer had no idea what time his father had called. He took the money that his father held out and went downstairs to pay the delivery man.

They sat in silence at the dining room table and ate mediocre Chinese food, his father's attention lost amid soy sauce and fortune cookies.

Later, as he stared at the ceiling and tried to find sleep within its textured surface, his nerves were out of control. In high school, he had spent most of his time dodging bullies who loved to slam him into lockers, trip him in the cafeteria, or spit disgusting projectiles at him. His heart thudded in his chest as he wondered if college could be the same, or his career after college. Would he always have to fight so hard just to be like everyone else?

The kid's face came unbidden once again to his mind, and sleep eluded him.

THE sun hurt Spencer's eyes when they opened through the crust which glued them closed, just a few hours after he'd finally fallen asleep. A dull pain in the base of his neck warned of a pending headache, and he rolled onto his side with a groan. Searching under his pillow for his phone, placed where the vibrations would eventually wake him, he hit the button to see the time. Monday, ten minutes before the alarm was set to go off. He tossed the phone onto the nightstand, rolled onto his stomach, and buried his face in the pillow. The stretch in his back and arms helped to relieve the tension mounting into a headache, but he knew he'd have to take something once he got out of bed.

His father would still be in bed when he left. It was his first day of college, and his father would miss it to nurse his hangover. The pain crept slowly toward his temples, threatening to block out the sun with its intensity. His stomach lurched with the pain, and he kicked back the blanket. The floor was cold under his feet as he moved quietly into the bathroom. The migraine meds sat in the medicine cabinet as they always did, but he resented having to take them right then. They made him feel slow and sluggish, not the best choice for his first day. Without them, however, the stabbing pain behind his eyes would only get worse.

His throat closed up around the pill even as the water from the tap washed it down. Shutting his eyes against the throbbing in his head, he wet a washrag and pressed the cool cloth to his forehead. The last thing he needed right then was to be incapacitated by a headache. Crawling back into bed, he decided to wait fifteen minutes, until the meds kicked in, before attempting to shower. Spencer reset his alarm and closed his eyes behind the cool press of fabric. *Please, just let it go away.*

The screaming pain had dulled into an incessant throb by the time the alarm went off under his pillow. Tight muscles in his shoulders cramped as he rolled to his side and checked the time on his phone. Spencer needed to be in the shower right then in order to make it to school in time to meet his interpreter. It took all his strength to make it into the bathroom and even more to turn on the shower. Rubbing shampoo into his scalp felt far better than the needle jabbed behind his eye.

By the time he was dressed, Spencer had just enough time for a quick bowl of cereal in the kitchen before he had to leave. The smell of pancakes and sausage made his mouth water as he came down the stairs. He stared, open-mouthed, as his father stood in the kitchen making breakfast for them both. His father turned, plate in hand, and smiled when he saw Spencer in the doorway. He set the plate on the table.

*I could not send you off to your first day in college without a good breakfast*, he signed and turned to walk back to the stove. Spencer stood frozen in the doorway another moment longer. His father had been so considerate. Pulling the milk from the refrigerator, Spencer poured two glasses without being asked and sat down at the table with a warm glow in his stomach.

He didn't give a fuck about being late anymore.

*I am taking Psychology this semester*, Spencer signed after they were both sitting at the table with piles of pancakes and heaps of sausage stacked on their plates. It was one of the breakfasts he'd always loved growing up. Anything in the world could be cured with either pancakes or ice cream—even college jitters.

*At least I will be good for something*, his father replied with a shrug and dumped syrup over his fluffy, buttered pancakes. Spencer hated the depression and sadness he saw in his father's eyes.

"You. Are. Good. For. Lots. Of. Other. Things. Too.. You. Could. Still. Practice. If. You. Wanted. To.," Spencer reasoned, but his dad just nodded once without comment. They lost the moment to awkward silence.

Spencer drove to school a while later, feeling lonelier than he had in a very long time.

# SIX

AARON didn't want to open his eyes the next morning when his mother called through the door that it was time to get up. It had been years since he'd used an alarm clock; the evil jarring noise made his heart leap into his throat. Even when it was set to music, it startled him so badly that it put him on edge for the rest of the day. So his mom woke him up, and her voice soothed rather than scared him. It was just one more thing that she did for him to help him cope with the fact that he barely functioned. Sometimes, as he lay staring up at the blank ceiling above his head, he wondered if maybe his mother did too much for him. She was enabling him by not pushing or challenging him so that the status quo could be maintained. Even after two years, he still felt like an infant or some kind of invalid because he hadn't made any progress. He was still that weak, scared little boy they'd found nearly dead on the oil-stained floor.

He didn't have time to lie there and dissect the issue of his abnormal psychosis right then, however. At that moment, he needed to open his eyes and get into the shower in order to start his day—his first day of college. Taking a deep breath, he opened his eyes to see a perfectly blue, cloudless sky. Maybe it would be a good day.

He rushed through his shower and the rest of his morning routine, and then grabbed his laptop bag and headed downstairs. He felt bad about making his mother worry after visiting Juliette on Saturday. He had been very quiet, introspective, when they'd gotten home. Seeing her name carved into the tombstone like that really brought it home for him. It wasn't just some horrifying nightmare. She wasn't on vacation with her family. Juliette had been raped and murdered less than ten feet from him. Before the men had stabbed him, before they had cut his face and his arms and tried to kill him, they had made him watch as they cut her throat. They had made him watch, knowing that it was going to happen to him too just as soon as they were done with her. He could still feel the cold concrete pressed under his mostly naked body, smell the putrid odor of sweat and gasoline as the boot dug into his cheek as the man held him still. The blood had poured from her as the knife slid with little resistance across her soft skin, soaking her torn sweater and finally pooling on the filthy floor.

Aaron hadn't wanted to talk about any of this, least of all with his mother. She did so much for him already, there was no way he would plant those images in her head. Those images, and other images that to him were just as horrifying, would stay locked inside him. At no time that he could imagine would he burden someone else with his nightmares.

As he walked into the kitchen, Aaron promised himself that he would eat whatever his mother put in front of him. It was the least he could do for her, not causing her any more worry than was absolutely necessary. He had already done enough. Allen passed him on his way out to school as Aaron settled into a kitchen chair. Since Allen was old enough to drive both himself and Anthony to school in the beat-up Ford Mustang that his parents had bought for them, he could afford to leave a little bit later. The two miles to the combination junior/senior high school took much less time in their day-glo orange beater.

"I hope you have a great first day, man," Allen said, and then he shoved a cereal bar whole into his mouth and grabbed his bag.

"Thanks," Aaron replied as his mother placed a plate of blueberry pancakes in front of him. Allen said something unintelligible with the cereal bar taking up most of the space in his mouth, and ran for the front door.

"If you rolled out of bed more than five minutes before you had to leave, I'd make them for you too," his mother called after Allen with a laugh. Aaron looked up at her, the guilt eating at his stomach as he noticed the dark circles under her eyes. It was obvious that she hadn't slept well last night either. He must have really scared her yesterday.

"Mom, are you busy?" Aaron asked, the words out of his mouth before he really decided to speak.

"I'm never too busy for my boys," his mother said with a smile and sat down in the empty seat across from him. Strangely pleased that she had brought pancakes for herself as well, he thought it would be really nice to just sit here at the table and eat alone with his mom.

"I'm sorry I was so… quiet. I know that it worried you. I just…. I can't…." Aaron started, but had really no idea how to finish.

*I can't tell you about all the horrible things I see in my head.*

*I can't clearly articulate what it's like to die inside.*

*I can't describe what it's like to want to scream every minute of every day.*

He had no idea what the hell he was supposed to tell her. Even during the hundreds of wasted hours of useless therapy, he'd never talked about it. The humiliation, the shame were only the tip of the psychiatric iceberg. So the shrinks pumped him full of pills and moved on to someone they *could* help.

"You don't need to apologize, Aaron. I knew it would be hard for you. To tell you the truth, I would have been more worried if you hadn't been upset by it, and I'm really proud of you for going. You walked alone across the grass, and you made it through. The Aaron we brought home two years ago wouldn't have been able to do that. I hope you can see how far you've come. Things are getting better, honey, slowly." It was such a lovely sentiment Aaron didn't have the heart to contradict her, so he remained silent. Soon after they finished their breakfast, she drove him to school.

As he stood against the wall outside the computer lab where his first class was to be held, he took several deep breaths, trying to calm the panicky, out-of-control feeling in his chest. A bead of sweat rolled down the side of his face, and he focused on a single tile on the floor. When he could breathe again, he turned and opened the door. Just as he had hoped, there were no other students in the lab yet. Walking to the very last row of computers, he took the one on the end. Dropping into the ugly fabric chair, he rolled up to the desk and turned on the machine, bringing up a free gaming site once it had booted.

One by one, students began to file into the large auditorium-style rows of tables and computers. Aaron started to get nervous when people sat in the row right in front of him. The class was going to be near capacity. He had been almost comfortable with the empty rows serving as a barrier between him and the rest of the people in the room. Just a few more students, and someone might sit right next to him. Could he deal with that? Would he have to change sections? Would he have to drop? Aaron didn't see the fucking point of going to college anyway. It's not like he'd ever be able to hold down a job. He knew he would be a burden on his parents, and then his brothers for the rest of his life, which he hoped wasn't drawn out.

He noticed the empty seat next to his was marked "RESERVED." He wondered if his instructor, Dr. Mayer, had done that to give him the chance to sit alone. The panicky feeling in his chest started to loosen when his instructor came into the room and dropped a worn leather backpack on the table at the front. He was a younger guy, maybe in his late twenties, with shaggy brown hair and glasses. He looked fairly at ease in his khaki pants and solid blue polo. It was casual classroom attire. He dallied at the front of the room for several minutes, pulling things out of the backpack. It seemed he was waiting for the students to settle so class could begin. Dr. Mayer had just put up the syllabus on the computer projector when the lab door opened and a teenage boy entered with an older woman. His long brown curls were windswept as he climbed the stairs, walking right toward Aaron, who prayed silently they would take the seats across the aisle from him.

The boy, who Aaron now noticed had a strong build and probably a day's worth of stubble on his face, sat down right next to him, pulling the reserved sign off the monitor. He looked over at Aaron with hauntingly deep hazel eyes, smiled shyly, and then turned to watch the woman sitting next to him. Aaron wondered why he was paying more attention to the woman than to the instructor until she started moving her hands. The boy took the vibrant blue messenger bag off his shoulder, his eyes never leaving the woman as she kept using sign language to communicate to him.

He was deaf.

His black T-shirt stretched tight over his shoulders as he crossed his arms, still watching the woman as she relayed the content of the lecture. With each successive line of the syllabus or announcement Dr. Mayer made, the woman repeated it in controlled, practiced gestures. It became apparent to Aaron why they made him sit in the back. The boy may have been able to read lips from the front row, but his companion's signing would have been distracting to the rest of the students in the hall. By putting him in the back, the distraction was at least minimized.

The first class was all about the syllabus, expectations, et cetera, and Aaron sat quietly, mostly listening. He found himself increasingly distracted by the boy on his left as he listened to the lecture through the hands of the woman. A sense of familiarity or similarity gave Aaron pause, because he understood all too well what it was like to have to rely on others in order to survive. Unable to imagine what it would be like to be deaf, to have the hardships the guy had to suffer through, he felt a surge of empathy as he turned back to the lecture.

Just as he caught up to what Dr. Mayer was reading from the syllabus, his breath froze in his lungs. A quarter of his grade would depend on a partner project. He couldn't do a partner project. Just the thought of being that close to someone, of the time it would take to complete while they stared at him with horror and revulsion, made him shut down completely inside. He could feel the blood pounding in his temples as the panic took over, and the room started to get smaller.

It was all he could do keep it at bay until his mother arrived.

"Mom, you need to talk to the instructor. I can't do a project with someone," Aaron pleaded with his mother as soon as he had shut the car door. She had arrived right on time, and was waiting for him when he exited the building at a run.

"Take a deep breath and calm down, Aaron. Whatever it is, we will work it out. Now, tell me what happened." Her calm was unnerving him. How could she be so calm when he was falling apart? He hadn't wanted to go to college in the first fucking place, but now that he was there it gave him something to do. It allowed him to think about something else, focus on something other than the miserable reality of his life. His college career was about to end before it ever really got started.

There was no way he would be able to graduate without this class, no matter who his mother talked to. It was the prerequisite for the next course in the series. He'd be stopped in his tracks if he couldn't take it. The problem was, there was no way he would be able to work so closely with someone else. *What the fuck was he going to do?* His hands automatically tightened into fists, as they always did when the panic attack started. Whoever he was paired with, they would pity him, stare at him, maybe even request another partner because they were repulsed by him. *Oh God.*

"Aaron, you need to calm down. I will talk to your instructor. What is the worst that could happen, honey? Think about it. You drop the class, or you split up the work with someone and never see them again. Maybe I can get him to let you do the project on your own. It will be okay."

Aaron looked into his mother's worried face and nodded, taking a deep breath. She was right. The worst thing that could happen is that he was done with college. He had already lived through so much worse. Sitting back in the passenger seat, he closed his eyes, trying to work through the fear, work through the panic. His mother would take care of it; she always took care of it. *He would be okay.* He didn't have to go to college. It wasn't a matter of life and death. *He was okay.*

After ten minutes of deep breathing and talking himself down, he finally opened his eyes to see his mother smiling at him.

"Why are you smiling?" Aaron asked, genuinely curious. The moment didn't seem particularly happy or amusing to him.

"Even as recently as six months ago, you wouldn't have been able to calm yourself down when you started to panic. You would have to have taken an Ativan."

He thought about that for a minute. She was right, but he pushed the idea away immediately because he didn't want to hope. If he started to hope things were getting better when they weren't, that would devastate him further when his parents finally sent him away. No, he wasn't getting better. He would continue to have to rely on his mother, to not have friends, to merely exist. While he was medicated, he could dream about having a normal life, but when the drugs started to wear off he'd remember it could never be possible for him. So, when his mother insinuated that he was getting better, he filed the comment away to study when he could once again dare to hope. His mother seemed to understand.

As soon as they arrived home, his mother called Dr. Mayer's office to talk to him about the project, even going so far as to suggest that Aaron work on it alone. However, since the point of the project was collaboration, he wouldn't budge. Programmers, he reasoned, often had to work in teams to accomplish their objectives. Dr. Mayer wanted them to start working on their team-building and professional social skills. By the time the conversation was over and she hung up the phone, Aaron wanted to vomit.

Okay, twenty-five percent of his grade. If he aced the rest of the course, he could pass without doing the project at all. That raised his spirits. With a renewed sense of hope, he headed upstairs to start reading his first assignment.

The next day in class, Dr. Mayer started to lecture about program structure. Aaron watched him over the top of his flat-panel monitor, making sure to pay closer attention than he had ever done in any class. High school, from what he could remember, had been easy. He would listen to a lecture, do his homework, maybe study for a test or two—mostly in history—and then be done. Finishing high school through homeschooling was altogether different. Even though there were no other students and Aaron was sitting at his own kitchen table, he felt restless and anxious. Focus, memory, everything seemed to be a problem for him like they had never been in the past. His mother had a rough battle just to get him to the point where he could meet the state's requirements for graduation. At the time, Aaron didn't see the point in continuing his high school education, much like he didn't see the point in going to college. The two positive things that had come out of both finishing high school and going to college were that the gestures seemed to give his mother a purpose, like she was making a real difference. It also kept his mind off the horrible images that continued to torture him.

Aaron checked his watch as the instructor paused, to see there were still nearly twenty minutes of class left. He waited, but it seemed the lecture was over for the day. The woman two seats over sat quietly, and the boy next to him looked around curiously. Since they didn't have lab work, maybe that meant they were getting out early. Aaron was fairly excited by the prospect.

"Okay, guys, I'm going to end there to give you time to get to know your new project partner and maybe start work on your plan," Dr. Mayer said, bringing up a class list on the overhead. Aaron felt the sweat begin to bead on his forehead, and the room was suddenly much hotter to him, his shirt collar suffocating him. The instructor was going to assign their partners. He couldn't do it. He just couldn't stand the look on some poor girl's face when she saw he was her partner. Taking a deep breath, he tried to force himself to calm down.

"As I call your name, stand up so that your partner can find you." Okay, fuck calming down. When his name was called and everyone turned to look at him, they would all just stare. Everyone fucking stared. He was a sideshow freak. Grabbing his laptop bag from the floor, he bumped the boy next to him by accident as he threw his notebook, textbook, pen, and recorder haphazardly into one of the pockets and nearly turned over the chair in his haste to get out of the room.

"Mr. Downing!" The instructor called after him as he reached the door and took off at a dead run toward the parking lot, not even stopping to call his mother to tell her he would be early. When she arrived, nearly fifteen minutes later, she found him sitting huddled into a small ball at the top of the stairs to the lab building with his arms wrapped around his bag, staring at his shoes.

"Aaron, honey, let's go home," his mother prompted a third time when her first two responses were met with a terrifying silence. Finally, Aaron looked up, blinking in surprise to see his mother standing there. Slowly, he stood and followed her to the car on deadened legs. He sat in the passenger seat, still as stone, until they reached the driveway in front of their house. His mother pulled her keys from the ignition, removed her seat belt, and turned to him. Before she had a chance to ask, he answered her question.

"Dr. Mayer assigned our project partners today," Aaron said in a lifeless voice.

"You don't like your partner?" his mother asked.

"I never found out who it was." Aaron spent the next ten minutes explaining to his mother why he had felt so trapped and why he needed to get out. She nodded, like she understood, but she didn't. She couldn't.

"I'm just going to have to drop the class. I can't let another student fail because of me," Aaron sighed as he got out of the car and walked up to the house. Each step felt like he was dragging himself up the walk. He couldn't wait to get upstairs so he could lie down. It seemed as if, lately, he had been the poster child for lethargy. In the afternoons he would get a soda from the fridge, use it to wash down a few pills, and chase unconsciousness.

When Aaron got inside, he headed upstairs first to change into a long-sleeved T-shirt and sweats. He knew from experience that the more comfortable he was, the easier sleep would come. Well, except they were hot as hell. All his clothes, every piece was designed to cover his skin—from the long-sleeved shirts to the full-length pants. He never wore anything, not even in midsummer, that showed the scars on his arms and legs. They sickened him. It was enough that he couldn't hide the ones on his face and neck. They were all a constant physical reminder of his nightmare, haunting him through every waking moment.

When he came back down for his soda, he heard his mother talking. Since they were the only ones home, he had to assume she was on the phone. Feeling faintly guilty about listening to her conversation, he turned to go back upstairs, but stopped when he heard his name.

"No, Aaron is all right. He was just… uncomfortable with the method you chose for pairing your students. He didn't want a room full of people staring at him as he stood up to find his partner," his mother said, and it sounded like she was starting to lose her patience. "No…. No… you couldn't have known." God knows his instructor could not have predicted that Aaron would run out of class. Most of the time, Aaron really had no idea what would set him off, and he'd been living with his neuroses for over two years.

"Yes… I will talk to him about it. Thank you for calling."

*She would talk to Aaron? Not that she would talk to Dr. Mayer for Aaron? Talk to him about what?* Mildly irritated, he walked into the kitchen as she set the cordless phone on the counter. Continuing on to the refrigerator, he grabbed a soda from the bottom shelf. Should he just stay and talk to her now, or go up to his room? Sleep sounded really good right now. Unfortunately, his mother had made the decision for him.

"Aaron, could we talk for a minute?" she asked in a voice that left little question she wanted to have a serious discussion with him. Her posture was almost rigid and her expression determined. He opened his soda, considering, and finally resigned himself to the inevitable. Taking a seat across from her at the table, he braced himself.

"I'm going to drop the class," Aaron told her, trying to beat her to the punch. He had no idea if she knew he'd heard her conversation, but he hoped she would take that decision and leave it at that.

"I agree that is one option," his mother said, surprising him. He didn't think she would take that as a viable option. When she did, he relaxed, just a little. "There are other alternatives too."

"Such as?" Aaron asked without any real interest.

"First, I want you to think about something. Dr. Mayer doesn't generally assign partners in his classes. This is the first time he has ever done so. Usually, he lets students pick their own partners, but he did it to save you the anxiety of finding one on your own." This did surprise Aaron. He knew that Dr. Mayer would probably be a lot easier on him than he needed to be, but to go out of his way like that just to make one of his students feel more comfortable.... It wasn't just the mark of a good teacher, it was kind.

"Why do you feel like you can't do a project with another student?" his mother pressed, bringing one hand up to cup her chin as she prepared to consider his answer. He just wasn't sure he could give her one. She wanted him to reason out his fears, to justify his panic when there was no logic to it. If he could act rationally and logically control his emotional responses in the first place, none of this would be an issue. So, rather than trying to explain the fear, he tried to describe it.

"When I think about having to spend the amount of time needed to complete this project with a stranger, to see them stare at me, to feel their judgment and their pity, I feel panicky," he said, trying to articulate the feelings as well as he could.

"Okay, I can accept that. I cannot say that I understand, because I don't, and I won't patronize you by saying that I do." It was one of the first times in his life that his mother had spoken to him like an adult. He found he appreciated it, more than he could say. It was mildly disconcerting, though, because he was so used to her trying to placate him. "So, what if you and your partner did a majority of your work through instant messaging or texting or e-mail?"

In his head, Aaron started to protest, but since he couldn't find a logical reason, he closed his mouth. What if all the work could be done over the computer? He could e-mail his instructor when he had a question, and that was okay. The better question was, why hadn't he thought of it? He had been so preoccupied with the thought of having to interact with someone that it never once occurred to him that it wouldn't have to be in person.

"I… I guess I could do that," Aaron admitted, but his mother's expression did not change. It didn't brighten as he expected it to.

"Are you sure that's all you're worried about, Aaron?"

"What do you mean?" Aaron asked, mildly confused. What else would it be?

"Now, you can certainly tell me I'm wrong, and maybe I am. I'm wondering if there's another reason you don't want to work with someone, why you avoid people in general. Your best friend was murdered, and I'm wondering that you think maybe if you let yourself get too close, too invested…."

Aaron stood up abruptly and left the room. He was afraid of what he might say if he opened his mouth. He was afraid of what he might feel, what he might relive if he allowed his mind to go there.

Making sure his mother hadn't followed, he stopped briefly at his parents' medicine cabinet to grab one of his anxiety pills. After a moment of thought, he changed his mind and took one of the tranquilizers instead before going into his bedroom. His mother would not let him keep the medication in his room for fear he would kill himself with it. Downing the pill with the soda, he set the can on his desk and then threw himself onto his bed. Aaron lay on his stomach, his face buried in his pillow as he tried not to think about Juliette. Even now, he couldn't remember the good times with her without hearing her scream.

What he couldn't admit, not even to his mother or to any of the dozen shrinks, was that when he thought about Juliette, when he heard her screaming in his head, it also brought back everything they had done to him as well. It made him feel selfish to focus on his own trauma when he had survived and she hadn't. He should be cherishing his second chance at life and not squandering it, locked away and not really living.

These were the last thoughts he had before finally, mercifully, the tranquilizer put him to sleep.

# SEVEN

SPENCER felt a hand on his arm and looked up to see Dr. Mayer. After pulling the messenger bag off his shoulder, he dropped it on the floor and signed to Karen, his new interpreter, that she could go. He could talk to his instructor without her. She nodded and left with a wave. His face flushed a little as he turned around to face Dr. Mayer. It was only the first week. He had no idea what he could have done already. Images of sitting in the principal's office with his father year after year flashed in his head.

"I wanted to talk to you about your project partner," Dr. Mayer said slowly, enunciating his words very clearly, which Spencer appreciated. Sometimes people talked too fast for him to catch, or worse, talked with their mouths full of food so that he had no idea what they said. "His name is Aaron Downing, and he was sitting next to you during the lecture."

*Of course he was. Fucking Karma.*

He'd recognized the guy as soon as he sat down. How could he not? It wasn't just the scars he remembered, but the haunted, dead look in the… in Aaron's eyes. Besides, a panic attack in the middle of the quad wasn't something he would forget any time soon. At least Spencer would be able to find a way to apologize for scaring the fuck out of him before term started. He didn't know if Dr. Mayer had any more idea what had happened to the guy than he did, so he didn't ask, but his instructor answered the question anyway.

"Without violating his privacy, I can tell you that Aaron…. Well, he needs a little compassion. I matched you together because, from talking to his parents, I think it may be easier for him to work with a partner without actually speaking—like through text, chat, or e-mail. My brother is deaf, so I had a feeling you might feel more comfortable working that way as well. Terry can talk, but he feels more comfortable with written communication. Is it the same for you?" Dr. Mayer looked a little self-conscious about his revelation but kept meeting Spencer's eyes.

"Yes.," Spencer said, choosing not to elaborate.

"He is also very shy, so if you could introduce yourself to him, that might make things go a little more smoothly." *Yes, I'm sure that will go very well. Hi, my name is Spencer, sorry for scaring the holy fucking shit out of you in the quad the other day. Can I get your cell phone number so we can text like normal antisocial human beings, since we are both too fucked up to have a conversation?*

"Okay. I. Will. Talk. To. Him.." Spencer adjusted his bag with nervous energy pulsing through him. He wanted to just get to his next class and not think about it anymore. He didn't want to know if the kid remembered him. Of course, Dr. Mayer could not have known about the incident in the quad, but it seemed like an awful lot of responsibility to put on his shoulders in the first week of class. He raised his hand in a half wave to let Dr. Mayer know he was leaving and then escaped the room with a speed that bordered on flight.

His hands continued to shake until he reached the small study area at the end of the hall. Fishing into his pocket, Spencer pulled out a couple of dollar bills and forced them into the vending machine to get a soda, because he'd learned long ago that sugar made everything better. Pancake syrup, ice cream, cookies, soda—it seemed his mood had always been influenced heavily by his blood sugar. He opened the bottle and found salvation in its perfectly carbonated depths. *Thank you, Jesus, and hallelujah.*

According to the time on his phone, he had about half an hour before his next class, so Spencer dropped into one of the chairs and tossed his bag onto the table in front of him. He wondered where Aaron Downing was right then. Maybe they'd have another class together and he could talk to him before their next class. He took out a piece of paper and wrote down all his electronic information—chat, cell phone, e-mail. Adding a note at the bottom to make his intentions clear, he slid the paper into the front of his programming book and put it back in his bag.

Spencer had four classes that term: Freshman Programming Design, psychology, Calculus I, and Freshman Composition. Programming and Calculus would be his favorites, by far. He'd always been an analytical person to whom math and science came easily. The English class, unfortunately, was a requirement, and he prayed to whatever God would listen that he wouldn't have to ever read his work aloud. He'd picked psychology to fill one of the humanities electives that he dreaded. He'd much rather fill the time with science electives, but the school wanted them to have a well-rounded education—whatever the fuck that meant. Physics would have been more his style, but at least he had a built-in psychology tutor if he needed it. Maybe it would give him and his dad something to talk about.

The class starting in… twenty minutes… was Calculus. He'd already talked to the instructor, and together they decided he could forego an interpreter. Sitting in the front of the class, he should be able to get the gist of the lecture, and Dr. Lanman said she did a majority of the lecture on the whiteboard. The tension left his shoulders as he thought about a whole ninety minute math class without people staring at him like they did in the programming class. Even that kid Aaron had stared. When he did, Spencer got a good look at the scars on his face and neck. God, he couldn't even imagine what had happened to cause that kind of physical and psychological damage.

His phone vibrated in his pocket. Pulling it out, he checked the display and saw a text from his father.

DAD: What's up, doc?

Spencer laughed. It had been a joke of theirs for as long as he could remember. One day when he'd been watching cartoons, he heard the phrase and asked his dad if it referred to him. He was a doctor, after all. After that, every time his father wanted to see how he was, that's the phrase he used. His father had asked it after his first day at school when the hearing kids made fun of him. He'd asked it after the principal called him for Spencer's behavioral problems. He'd asked it to get Spencer to finally tell him he was gay.

SPENCER: Not much. Got through my first class of the day without getting in trouble. Sitting here waiting for my second.

DAD: Up for Mexican for dinner?

SPENCER: La Caretta?

DAD: Yep. Get through the day without punching anyone, and we'll go out to dinner.

SPENCER: I think I can do that. No one has said anything to me at all except my programming teacher.

DAD: Was there a problem?

SPENCER: No. Remember me telling you about that kid from the quad, the one that freaked out?

DAD: Yes.

SPENCER: He ended up in my programming class, and Dr. Mayer made us project partners. The kid's name is Aaron, and Dr. Mayer asked me to introduce myself because he's really shy. He said that Aaron needed compassion.

SPENCER: I saw him up close today. He's got horrible scars on his face. I feel so bad for him.

DAD: Just take things slow, Spence. He will come around. But, if he shows any violent tendencies, tell me immediately and we'll talk to your instructor. Okay?

SPENCER: Dr. Mayer said that Aaron would want to work over the computer, mostly, like I would. That is why he paired us up.

DAD: That was very considerate of him.

SPENCER: That is what I thought too. Class now. See you at four.

DAD: See you then.

Spencer clicked off the phone and put it back in his pocket. It never occurred to him Aaron might have violent tendencies. He just assumed by what had happened in the quad that the kid had been hurt badly by someone. No, he couldn't believe that Aaron had been the aggressor in whatever happened to him. First, the kid was only like five and a half feet tall and didn't weigh anything. He would have to be insane to start a fight with anyone. Someone had hurt him, and badly.

After picking up his bag, he headed off to his Calculus class as his mind raced about his new partner.

The next morning, Spencer got to school early so he could wait for Aaron in the class and talk to him before it started filling up. He didn't want his interpreter there, because his new partner seemed kind of skittish of people. The room was empty when he entered and climbed up to the very last row of seats. Taking the seat Dr. Mayer had designated for him, he took his programming book out of his bag and set it on the desk next to the keyboard. The piece of paper with his contact information stuck out of the top, but he left it there while he waited.

The nervous energy made his limbs vibrate, and he tapped his fingers against the desk in some tuneless rhythm. He'd never heard music, but he could feel it vibrating under his feet when Dad played it at the house. The habit was born more of anxiety than music, anyway. With a sigh, he turned on the computer. He could play solitaire until class started.

A shadow fell over his face a few minutes later, and he looked up to see Aaron passing him to sit in the same seat next to Spencer. He had dark circles under dull blue eyes, and his complexion was almost a light gray. The way he'd run out of class the day before made Spencer think maybe the partner thing was a source of stress for Aaron, so he decided to just bite the bullet and do it.

# EIGHT

WHEN Aaron entered the lab, he was surprised and a little disappointed to find he wasn't alone. As he climbed up, past row after row of empty seats, his attention was focused on the boy that was sitting in the seat next to the one Aaron sat in. For a moment, he considered moving to the other side of the aisle, but then decided that someone else would just sit next to him anyway, and sat down his stuff at his regular seat. Briefly, he wondered where the boy's interpreter was. Aaron turned on his workstation, watching the screen as he waited for it to boot. He was startled completely out of his thoughts when the boy next to him said his name.

"Aaron," he said in a slow, measured timbre, his pronunciation slightly different than Aaron was used to. He looked over at the boy and noticed for the first time that he was relatively short-statured, just like Aaron. His shaggy brown hair was in naturally curled disarray because of the slight humidity, and his nose and cheeks were dusted sparingly with freckles. Aaron did something he would normally never do: he met the boy's gaze. He wasn't sure what had made him do it, but he found the other boy's hazel eyes were full of kindness and wonder rather than judgment.

Aaron merely nodded in response.

"My. Name. Is. Spencer.," the boy said in a very slow, punctuated speech. The words sounded only slightly off from what someone would expect as a standard cadence, but in his panic, Aaron hardly noticed. "I. Am. Your. Project. Partner.." Spencer handed Aaron a piece of paper with his e-mail, cell phone number, and instant messenger contact information. Printed in neat block writing below that was a note that read, "It is easier for me to work like this if that is okay with you?"

In response, Aaron quickly turned around with panic fluttering in his chest and created an account on the site Spencer used for instant messaging. He sent him a chat invitation and waited while Spencer responded. It only took a minute for the first chat window to pop up.

SPENCER: Thanks, this makes things easier for me.

AARON: Me too.

Aaron typed in his e-mail address and cell phone number, breathing a sigh of deep relief that he'd drawn this boy as a partner, and that Spencer had sought him out. Had Aaron believed in fate, he might have chalked this pairing up to that, but he didn't. Believing in fate would mean that what happened to him, what happened to Juliette, was supposed to happen, and he didn't think God was that cruel.

AARON: How did you know who I was?

SPENCER: Dr. Mayer told me, plus you were the only one whose name he didn't call besides mine. It would have been a process of elimination, anyway.

AARON: What did he tell you about me?

SPENCER: Nothing really, just that you keep to yourself, but that he thinks we will work well together. And I don't have to use my interpreter.

Aaron didn't have any reply to that, because he knew exactly what it was like to rely so completely on others to be able to function. Other students were starting to file in now, taking their places among the graduated rows of computers on their Formica tables. He checked his screen as another message came up.

SPENCER: You want to chat later and talk about the project? We should start deciding what we want to do, and maybe put a plan together.

AARON: That's a good idea. Around 7:00?

SPENCER: Cool.

It occurred to Aaron as he saw Spencer's translator making her way up through the throng of other students, that he had just done what he had set out to do. Well, actually, Spencer had really done most of it, but regardless, it was done. He had met and actually talked to his partner, gotten contact information, and set up a time for them to work later. A warm glow of accomplishment, one that he hadn't felt in a very long time, blazed in his chest. He thought it might be pride.

The lecture continued along similar lines as the day before, program structures and object-oriented structures. He found the subject matter rather fascinating and started to subconsciously apply some of the concepts to a program he'd been constructing in his head since the project had been assigned. Aaron got completely into the material and found he didn't want the lecture to end, but too soon Dr. Mayer dismissed them. Aaron hung back as he usually did, waiting for the other students to file out so he didn't risk any accidental contact. Spencer turned to him after he'd packed up and waved before pointing to his watch. Aaron nodded at the reminder to be on at seven.

He started to say he remembered, but then after rolling his eyes at himself, just nodded.

"Aaron, do you have a moment?" Dr. Mayer asked as Aaron headed down the steps and toward the door. Aaron changed direction, and after letting a group of girls pass, moved to stand in front of the table that instructors used to hold their stuff during lectures. There wasn't enough of the blond wood for it to really be called a desk—it was little more than a glorified side table, but it put an effective buffer between them. Dr. Mayer was currently using it to put away his laptop and notes. As Aaron waited, the professor looked up.

"Thanks for staying. I just wondered if Mr. Thomas talked to you today?" Dr. Mayer asked as he zipped up his bag.

"Mr. Thomas?" Aaron asked, running his hand over his short hair. Was he one of the administrators or something? He started to feel a little uncomfortable. Had he done something wrong?

"Spencer Thomas is your project partner. I asked him to introduce himself so that maybe you would feel a little more comfortable with the idea of a partner," Dr. Mayer said with a slight frown. He appeared to be disappointed because he thought Spencer hadn't done as he'd asked.

"Yes, I'm sorry. I don't think he ever said his last name," Aaron told the desk, not looking at the instructor. "We chatted on IM for a few minutes before class." Then he decided he might as well do the thing properly. "We are meeting up online later tonight in order to get started."

Aaron scuffed the toe of his shoe along the floor, embarrassed by the gap that existed between himself and a normally functioning person. He wanted to thank Dr. Mayer for helping him to find such a good partner, but he couldn't find the words.

"That is fantastic, Aaron!" the older man exclaimed, and then in a lower voice, almost conspiratorially, he added, "You have an incredible amount of potential as a programmer. Your code on that first assignment was some of the cleanest and most concise I've seen. That shows not only talent, but creativity. I didn't want to see you stumble on a solvable problem." Of course, this man had no idea what did or did not constitute a solvable problem for Aaron, but Aaron did appreciate what Dr. Mayer had gone through in order to help him. He also appreciated the kind words the professor had said about his potential. It had been a long time since he felt like he had any potential, any purpose, or any future.

Maybe, in time, he would find he did.

"HOW was class?" his mother asked when he'd gotten in the car. As he told her about the unexpected conversations, both with the new boy, Spencer, and his professor, her face grew more and more excited. Not only had he moved forward with his project and stayed in the class, but his instructor felt he had a knack for something—something other than failure and panic. His mother said she had always known computers were the place for him, because all mothers know what's best for their children. She also promised to have dinner out of the way early so he'd have plenty of time to get ready for his chat session with Spencer.

With an extreme effort, he managed not to roll his eyes. Jesus, she made it sound like some kind of date. If dating were even a remote possibility for him, he could see her getting excited, but he hadn't even dated before the attack. It wasn't that he didn't want to, he was just scared. Juliette may have guessed at it, but he was pretty sure his mother wouldn't be excited to know he was gay. But, true to her word, his mother made a quick dinner of grilled cheese and tomato soup so Aaron was in his room by a quarter of six. Opening up the file on his laptop for the project specs, he began to read.

*PING*

The sound of his chat notification startled him out of his thoughts, and his heart jumped into his throat. Looking down, he noticed that, without conscious thought, he'd taken a page full of notes about the project and his ideas for what they could work on. He had drawn out several crude interfaces and a few logic flowcharts for subroutines and objects to support his ideas. The more he read in the specs, the more excited he'd gotten about working on it. It had been so long since he'd been excited about anything, he almost didn't recognize the feeling.

Aaron looked up at the screen to see Spencer's waiting message.

SPENCER: Hey.

Aaron grabbed his laptop and pulled it to him, putting his hastily scribbled notes aside.

AARON: Hi.

SPENCER: Have you read over the specs?

AARON: Yeah, I just finished. I have a few ideas about what we can do.

SPENCER: Me too, but they're going to be a challenge. One of them involves using social networking APIs.

AARON: That's cool. I'm up for a challenge

A challenging project would take his mind off less pleasant things he would otherwise be thinking. If he kept his mind busy enough, maybe he could get through this semester without a complete breakdown.

SPENCER: Okay, the specs essentially say we can do pretty much whatever we want so long as the program is a desktop app with a menu and your basic standard interface. The program just needs to serve some useful function, but I want to go beyond that. I was thinking about a client app that will monitor your social networking sites and respond to certain messages. Like a bot, but smarter.

AARON: Like what?

SPENCER: Maybe monitoring your account and responding to tweets like #FollowFriday. When someone tells their friends to follow you, it could automatically generate a thank you tweet. Or it could go through all the tweets directed at you and randomly generate #FollowFriday tweets.

AARON: All with the documented Twitter API? I heard it's pretty programmer friendly.

SPENCER: Yep.

AARON: I've never used Twitter, but it could send out a tweet with the song you're listening to, or what movie you're watching based on the metadata. We could even connect it to YouTube and tweet videos the user is watching or rating.

SPENCER: We could combine them into one big Twitter app.

AARON: It would be more work.

SPENCER: True, but when we're finished, we could load it up onto a Freeware site and start getting our names out there—maybe add some stuff to our resumes.

AARON: That's a great idea.

They continued to talk late into the night about the design for their new software. Downloading a screen share program, they drew up specs and mapped out ideas to submit for their proposal. Before Aaron even realized it, it was after midnight. They had been chatting for over five hours. He couldn't help but be a little shocked, because he didn't even talk to his own family for five hours in a month, much less one night. Spencer was surprisingly easy to talk to, especially about programming, because he seemed to be very passionate about it, just like Aaron was.

SPENCER: This was great, man, but I have an 8 a.m. class. Damn interpreter. =)

AARON: I can't believe it's midnight already. I'll see you in class.

SPENCER: K, night.

AARON: Good night.

Aaron turned off his laptop in kind of a daze, the machine hot against his legs. Setting the computer on the bed next to him, he realized he was sitting against his headboard. He didn't really even remember moving to the bed, but he must have at some point because that was where he ended up. One word, almost foreign to him now, resonated through his head as he set the computer on the desk and started getting ready for bed.

*Fun.*

Talking to Spencer, planning their project, had been fun.

# NINE

FOR the first time since he'd started college, Aaron found he was actually looking forward to going to class. The previous night had been a great start to their project, and Aaron was excited about showing Spencer the code he'd written that morning. It was elegant, and some of it was truly inspired. People generally didn't look at software development as something creative or artistic, but merely as a means to an end.

"You're ready early today. I'm surprised. I heard you typing away last night when I went to bed," his mother said, pulling her long brown hair into a loose ponytail as she went to the stove.

"Yeah, Spencer and I got a little carried away last night talking code," Aaron told her as he distractedly doodled a few more logic structures in his notebook at the kitchen table. When his mother took a peek over his shoulder as she set the syrup next to her son, she saw complex diagrams with squares, diamonds, lines, and arrows. He wondered if she understood any of it.

"That looks complicated," she said, turning back toward the counter to start mixing the waffles. Before she could measure out the mix, Aaron turned to face her.

"Mom, do we have any bacon? I'd love some bacon and eggs." Aaron noticed his mother held on to the measuring cup in her hand, but just barely. In the last two years, he'd never asked for anything. Whatever she made, he ate, with no enthusiasm. If they went out to dinner, he had no preference on the restaurant. He didn't even care what kind of soda they had in the house; he drank whatever his brothers drank. It was a huge shift in his behavior, but he needed to give her some kind of hope. He didn't want to be sent away. Since she'd mentioned earlier she had gotten bacon at the store the day before, he thought that might be a way to fake normalcy for her. Her expression showed she would have slaughtered a pig in the back yard at that point to give him what he'd asked for.

"Sure, honey, I'll make bacon and eggs," she said almost casually. He knew it was a monumental thing to her, but she looked over at him like she expected him to have changed. He sat, continuing to draw his complex shapes on the pad in front of him, not acknowledging the magnitude of the moment. His heart lightened.

With hands that trembled slightly, she made her son his bacon and eggs.

As they ate, Aaron explained the symbols and flows to his mother. It was possibly the longest conversation they'd ever had, and he could tell by her glassy gaze she hadn't understood a word of it. By the time Aaron went to throw on his shoes so she could take him to campus, he could see a glimpse of tears in her eyes.

"You look so much like your father. During those fleeting minutes when you're not angry, I can sometimes see the boy I knew. You talk with such enthusiasm about this project, and about programming in general. It just… it gives me hope my son might one day emerge from that shell where you've been living," she told him with a light in her eyes that hadn't been there in a while. Embarrassed, Aaron turned away. He couldn't bring himself to take away her hope.

Once he was in the computer lab at school, Aaron continued to work out some of the design of their new program as he waited for Spencer. He'd just finished detailing the tweet object parameters when he saw his partner walking up the stairs toward him. Spencer half waved at Aaron and dropped into his seat, punching the power button on his lab PC. Aaron smirked, knowing exactly how tired Spencer was feeling because he was feeling it himself. Spencer avoided the braided security cable that connected the monitor to the table as he set his bag down next to him. Aaron watched Spencer log into chat, and Aaron quickly followed suit.

SPENCER: I'm fucking wiped.

AARON: Yeah, me too, but I have a few more ideas. Oh! And look at this.

Aaron loaded the code he'd written from his thumb drive and turned the flat-panel monitor as far as the security cable would allow so Spencer could see it.

SPENCER: I love the generalized parameters for the module. That will make it a hell of a lot easier to reuse. Brilliant, man!

Aaron chuckled at Spencer's enthusiasm, pleased he'd made him happy. Then he stopped short. He hadn't so much as cracked a smile in more than two years. He didn't deserve to laugh. He didn't deserve to be happy. Juliette couldn't laugh, and it was all his fault. She couldn't enjoy the joke. She was gone. He had led her to that van like a lamb to slaughter.

SPENCER: Aaron, are you okay? You look kind of sick?

"Aaron.?"

Aaron looked up and saw that Spencer had one hand up to reach for him, most likely to put a hand on his shoulder. Aaron wrenched back so violently he nearly fell off the rolling chair. Spencer jerked back as well and stared at Aaron, remorse and pity written clearly all over his pale face.

Aaron felt anxious, like his skin was crawling, but he also felt embarrassed by his display in front of Spencer. Quickly, he typed out a message in the chat window.

AARON: I'm sorry. So, should we pitch this idea to Dr. Mayer?

Aaron was trying to change the subject before Spencer could ask about his bizarre behavior. Spencer looked at him for a long moment, and Aaron could feel his gaze even though his eyes were fixed determinately on the keyboard in front of him. Finally, his chat client displayed a new message.

SPENCER: Sure, we can show him our idea after class if you want. There's no point going forward if he doesn't approve.

Even after Dr. Mayer had started class, Aaron was distracted and upset by his reaction in front of Spencer. It had never really mattered to him what people thought of him, because he never stuck around long enough for it to matter. It used to, he could remember that clearly, but now he was in and out of the restaurant, or in and out of the doctor's office, or in and out of the classroom before anyone could speak to him. He didn't make friends, didn't form relationships. So, if some guy stared a little too long in the hall or some girl tried to talk to him in the library, he could just brush them off. This time, however, he couldn't just walk away. He needed to work with Spencer in order to get this project done, not only for his own grade, but for his partner's. It was more than that, though. Aaron found he didn't want to brush off Spencer or walk away. For the first time in so long, he'd found someone he could talk to, at least superficially connect with over code, if nothing else.

Without ever intending to, over the five hours they'd spent chatting about code, Aaron had found a friend. That thought scared the hell out of him.

Aaron was drawn out of these thoughts when the lights in the lab came up, signaling the end of the lecture. He still felt shaken and off balance. Spencer didn't make any move to touch him again, but rapidly typed out a chat message.

SPENCER: We could just put together something and e-mail it to Dr. Mayer?

Great, Spencer thought he was a freak, just like everyone else. He doesn't even want to stick around to talk about their project with the instructor—the project Aaron was so excited about. To Aaron, it looked like Spencer couldn't wait to get away from him, and Aaron couldn't blame him. He wished sometimes that he could get away from himself.

Quickly, he typed a message to Spencer indicating that was fine with him. He didn't even wait for his computer to log off completely before he was out of his seat and down the stairs two at a time. In his haste, he nearly knocked over a boy just getting out of his aisle seat in the second row. He didn't stop until he was outside. As soon as his mother stopped in front of him, he was in the car and they were gone.

"AARON, are you finished eating?" his mother asked gently as she reached to take his dinner plate.

He nodded, noticing the rest of the family had already left the table. The smell of the meatloaf his mother had made had dissipated. The sound of the news filtered quietly from the living room, but otherwise, the house was fairly quiet. Aaron started to get up from the table when his mother spoke again.

"Honey, you've been preoccupied since I picked you up from school. Did something happen in class?"

On the surface, her voice was pleasantly curious, but there was an underlying tension there. She was worried about him. Looking to his left and away from his mother, Aaron stared out the glass door leading to the weathered deck. A little boy and girl played in the back yard of the lot adjacent to theirs. They couldn't have been more than five or six years old. The girl's hair was in pigtails, and she wore a set of denim overall shorts while the boy was in a Superman T-shirt and red shorts. As Aaron watched, the boy slid about halfway down the slide and then jumped off, his arms out in front of him as if he were flying. He grabbed the girl's hand as he hit the ground, and together they took off for the other side of the yard, laughing as they ran. It took a second, but then Aaron realized that he'd just witnessed Superman saving the girl. He wondered when the little boy would learn there was no Superman, and the girl was never safe.

Turning his eyes back to his mother, Aaron hoped the pain radiating through his chest wasn't as apparent to her as it was to him. He couldn't tell her that he'd laughed in class. It would give her hope, a hope he certainly did not feel and would not expect. He couldn't tell her that he'd freaked out when Spencer tried to touch him, or how any of that made him feel, because he couldn't take away her hope either. Without hope, they'd send him away. Right now, he just wanted to go upstairs and try like hell to do something about his homework. That would help him forget everything, at least for a while, and he wouldn't dwell on what it meant.

"No, Mom, everything is fine. I'm going to go up and work on my homework." His mother nodded, the worry lines deepening in her face. He could tell she was trying not to let on she was hurt he wouldn't confide in her.

Of course he saw it; he always saw it.

It certainly wasn't personal. If he was going to open up to anyone and talk about what was bothering him, it would definitely be his mother. He heard her soft sigh as he left the room. A few minutes later, Aaron walked into his room and flipped on the light. The grief started to overwhelm him as he stood quietly in the doorway. Any little trigger seemed to set him off lately: the laughter in class, the boy playing a superhero. Sometimes it was just a bleeding paper cut. How was he supposed to get through life like this?

Aaron decided to forego his homework tonight. The depression had left him drained, and he didn't feel like taking any pills to make it better. The sun hadn't quite set as he changed quickly into a long-sleeved T-shirt and sleep pants and then crawled into bed with what little energy he still had.

He was asleep within minutes.

*THE sound of his heart thudded in his ears as he lay with his bare stomach on the cold, smooth concrete, the knee between his shoulder blades a constant reminder of his helplessness. The smell of grease, gasoline, and sweat hung heavy in the air, almost like a fog, penetrating and inescapable. Scalding, blinding pain all over his body tugged at his consciousness. Each place where they had hit him, cut him, or burned him pushed him closer to that sweet oblivion, that darkness in which he knew it would all stop.*

*He could hear Juliette crying beside him—soft, agonizing sobs that were at least marginally less painful to listen to than her screams. Her piercing screams of pain, anguish, and fear as she begged for them to stop, as she begged for her mother, had torn at his soul. He knew by the raw tenderness of his throat that he had made the same piteous cries, but he refused to allow his mind to remember why. He couldn't stand the memory of the man's breath on the back of his neck or his pleasured grunts in his ear.*

*Summoning all his last reserves of strength, he turned his head to the left, laying his right cheek against the cold dirty floor as his eyes found Juliette's. The haunted, pleading look in her eyes suddenly made him feel ashamed. He closed his eyes briefly, trying to make it stop. They flew open again at the sound of Juliette's horrifically interrupted scream. Her head was pulled back hard by her hair until her face was pointed toward the ceiling. The flash of metal, the spray of hot sticky blood was so quick*

*Juliette's panic-stricken voice was cut off mid-scream. He watched in horrified disbelief as the life drained from her warm brown eyes.*

*A sharp pain in his scalp caused him to fight. He knew he was next, and he thrashed and kicked, punched and screamed, trying anything he could to stop the coming horror.*

*He saw the knife coming, angled toward his throat.*

His mother's face swam across Aaron's vision as he fought against the hands that held him down. The harder they held him, the harder he fought. He screamed and thrashed, and finally, they let go. His conscious mind started to take control of him, pulling him from the dream, and he saw his mother's frightened face more clearly. Aaron tried to calm himself as her voice registered in his mind.

"Aaron, baby, please.... Please wake up."

Aaron opened his eyes again and looked around, seeing that it was his father and brothers who had been holding him. As he stopped struggling, they pulled away, and he crawled up against the headboard of his bed, pulling himself into a tight ball.

"D.... Don't.... T.... Touch...." He took a deep breath, trying to will his pulse to slow, to stop pounding in his head. "Please, don't touch me," Aaron finally pleaded quietly, and they all backed away to give him some room. He continued to rock slightly, his back against the headboard, his face on his knees. Their voices reached him as they spoke softly to each other, but he didn't even try to understand what they were saying. After a few minutes, someone sat on the edge of the bed. Looking up, Aaron saw his mother holding out a small bathroom cup and a full glass of water. Everyone else must have gone back to bed, because now they were alone in the room.

Without comment, Aaron took the cup and dropped the pills into his palm. Two pills this time. He must have really scared her. After popping the pills into his mouth, he washed them down with the water and lay back down in his bed. Her hand shook as his mother covered him up with the blankets, being exceedingly careful not to touch her son. She murmured soft platitudes to him: "It's all right now" or "Try to rest," maybe even an "It's all over." He didn't much care what they were. The sound of her voice was soothing, and he suspected they were as much for her comfort as they were for his. As he watched, she turned off his bedroom light, her soft sniffle barely audible even in the stillness of the room. Then she left, closing the door behind her.

He tried to muster up some measure of guilt for scaring her so badly, but the room became fuzzy and blurred as the tranquilizers began to take hold of him.

# TEN

DR. MAYER started class, and Spencer glanced at the empty seat next to him before settling his attention on his interpreter. The way Aaron had jerked away from him the day before had hurt. Did he really think Spencer would hurt him? Spencer thought they'd gotten along really well as they talked about the project. Maybe it was reflex, something he couldn't control. But then, why did he look so fucking sad when they started talking? He had no idea what he'd done to screw things up already, but he was determined to make it up. Logging into his chat client, he saw that Aaron's status was offline. So instead, he pulled out his cell phone.

SPENCER: Hey, you want me to take notes for you today?

Nothing.

With a sigh, he dropped the phone back into his pocket and took very good notes so he could copy them for Aaron. Maybe when he reached out to touch Aaron it reminded him of the quad. He never did apologize for that. Damn it. He didn't want to do it over text message.

SPENCER: Are you around?

SPENCER: Want to talk later about the project? I had some ideas.

By the time class ended, he'd sent half a dozen texts to Aaron with no response. He fucking wished he could call Aaron, even if neither of them liked to talk, but of course he wouldn't be able to hear. Instead, he was forced to just pack up his stuff and hope Aaron came back to class.

He found it wasn't just the project he worried about.

"What did he do before he jerked away? Had he said anything?" Henry Thomas asked his son as they sat across from each other at

D'Margio's. They'd decided neither of them really wanted to cook. Spencer was still upset about Aaron's outburst the day before, and Henry seemed more than happy to talk about it. It was an opportunity to talk to his dad, and he refused to pass it up.

"No., We. Were. Just. Talking. About. The. Project.. Then. He. Got. Quiet.. He. Looked. Sick.. I. Asked. Him. If. He. Was. Okay., And. He. Jerked. Back.. Wait.... I. Reached. Out. To. Touch.. He. Just.... He. Looked. Like. He. Needed. A. Friend." Spencer took a drink of his water to quench his suddenly dry throat.

Henry picked up his glass of wine and took a small sip as he watched his son. "Maybe it had to do with being touched. A lot of victims of violent crime do not like to be touched, especially rape victims," he added as an afterthought.

"Oh. God.. You. Do. Not. Think...," Spencer started and set his glass down. Revulsion rolled through him as he thought about someone hurting Aaron like that. It had to be something else. Maybe he'd been hit by a car or his high school exploded. Grasping at straws, he tried to think of anything else that might cause the kind of fear he saw in Aaron's eyes.

"I don't think anything. I haven't even met the guy."

"Maybe. You. Should.."

"What?" Spencer's father asked, his voice heavy with skepticism, but Spencer was already sitting up straighter in his seat.

*Dad, this guy needs help. You are one of the best trauma psychologists in the country. Whatever has happened to him, maybe you can help.* Spencer signed quickly, excitement making his movements more pronounced. It seemed so easy, so natural for his father to treat Aaron. Maybe it would help his father too.

*Spencer, I am no longer a practicing psychologist. If his trauma is as severe as you describe, he is probably already in therapy,* Henry reasoned as their food arrived at the table.

"Would you like Parmesan cheese, sir?" It was lucky Spencer caught the question to his father, because when the server turned to him, he was standing at Spencer's shoulder in the crowded restaurant, and Spencer couldn't get a good look at his face. The server asked his father if they needed anything else and then wandered away to help another table that had flagged him down.

*No, but you still have your license. Can I just bring him over to do homework so you can meet him?* Spencer knew his father. He wouldn't turn Aaron away once he'd seen the pain in Aaron's eyes. The alcoholism hadn't affected his deep-seated need to help people.

*What is his name?*

"Aaron. Downing.," Spencer said rather than spelling out the name. His father's brow furrowed, but he didn't comment for a long moment. He wondered if maybe his dad knew Aaron's parents or something.

*You can bring him over because I want to meet your friends*, his father insisted, but Spencer could see the light in his eyes. *A challenge.*

HARSH, bright rays of light filtered through his half-open curtains and caused the incessant throbbing of his head to escalate into a full-blown pounding as Aaron finally started to wake. He moaned and rolled onto his back, a wave of nausea washing over him. Taking a few deep breaths, trying not to vomit, he brought one hand to his face, noticing as he did so it felt like lifting lead. Shielding his eyes against the bright light, he looked over at his bedside clock and was shocked to find it was nearly five in the evening.

As he shifted to his side and let his legs fall over the edge of the bed, it felt like someone had turned the gravity in his room way up. Everything was dull and heavy. He sat up slowly, feeling a rush of light-headedness as he stayed perched precariously on the side of the bed. Putting his head in his hands, he tried to fight the vertigo and nausea as he continued breathing deeply, staying as still as possible. He thought back, trying to remember what the hell happened. *Had he drank last night?* Aaron did drink sometimes, stealing whiskey or tequila from his parents' liquor cabinet when things got too hard. They still kept his pills in their medicine cabinet, afraid Aaron would do something drastic, but they never said anything about the missing liquor.

A remnant of the dream he'd had the night before came back to him, as did the panic attack which had caused the need for the tranquilizers. Aaron stumbled and tripped as he nearly ran for the bathroom, getting the toilet lid up just as he vomited what little there was in his stomach. The screaming and the blood spattered across his memory caused him to continue to dry heave long after his stomach was empty.

His mother found him a few minutes later on the bathroom floor and stood by helplessly as he stumbled back into his bedroom, finally making it to his desk. Aaron practically fell into the well-padded chair and rested his forehead on the cool polished surface of the desk. His mother went downstairs, returning quickly with a small plate of dry toast and a can of 7Up.

"Thanks, Mom," Aaron said quietly as she placed the food on the desk. Usually, his mother didn't like the boys to eat in their rooms. She was afraid she would find fuzzy dishes in a month or two, but she was obviously making an unspoken exception. As he took a bite of the toast, she went into the bathroom, and he heard the water running. He popped the top on the 7Up and took a long drink, trying to wash the acrid taste from his mouth. Aaron's mother returned a moment later with a cold wet rag which he took gratefully, wiping his face and the back of his neck. The nausea had finally started to subside.

Aaron finished two of the slices of toast and promised his mother to come down in a little while for some fruit. As he took another drink of the soda, he leaned down to pick up his laptop case. Pulling out the laptop, he carried it and the soda back to his bed. Thankfully, the room had stopped spinning, allowing him to feel steadier on his feet. Propping his pillow against the headboard, he sat back and opened the laptop. Carefully setting his soda on the bedside table, he turned on the laptop and waited for it to boot. The process seemed arduous, his body and mind still sluggish from the aftereffects of the large dose of tranquilizer the night before. Turning his attention back to his laptop, he entered his password and let it finish loading.

Just as Aaron clicked to open his e-mail client, an IM window popped up. Since there was only one person on his chat list, there was little doubt who it was from.

SPENCER: Where the hell have you been?!?!

Aaron was taken aback. He missed one class; it didn't really warrant that strong a response, did it?

AARON: I wasn't feeling well. I kind of slept through class.

SPENCER: I've been texting you all night. You were so freaked out after class. I just wanted to make sure you were okay. Are you okay, Aaron?

He sighed. Was he okay? No, he wasn't okay, not by a long shot, but what should he tell Spencer? If they were going to work together on the project for the rest of the term, Aaron knew he had to tell Spencer something. He would probably have to do a lot of explaining for his behavior before the course was over.

AARON: I don't know what you want to hear.

SPENCER: Look, man, we all have issues, some worse than others. I like you. I think we could be good friends. It sounds like maybe you could use one. I know I could. If you want to talk about it, just tell me what you're comfortable with for now. I'll do the same. Deal?

There was a long pause during which neither of them typed anything. It seemed they both knew they were on the verge of crossing a line, one Aaron hadn't been anywhere near since the attack. Though had he sat and analyzed it, without fear and doubt clouding his judgment, he would have seen he already considered Spencer a friend. No matter how hard he tried not to.

Nothing good ever came from calling Aaron Downing a friend, but with a heavy feeling in his chest, he typed his agreement.

SPENCER: Being deaf, I don't make friends easily. Most people either think I'm mentally challenged or don't want to put in the effort.

And there it was—Spencer was asking Aaron to let him in, to be his friend. Could he? Could he trust that Spencer wouldn't just take what he shared and use it to gossip about the scarred freak? Instinctively, he knew he could trust Spencer. But really, what had his instincts ever gotten him? If he'd had good instincts, as soon as that van had pulled over by them, he'd have grabbed Juliette and run. The problem was, Aaron was so fucking tired of being alone. He decided to give Spencer the polite public version of what had happened to him, and hope it didn't scare off his potential new friend.

AARON: During my sophomore year of high school, when I was 16, my best friend Juliette and I were walking home from debate practice.

Aaron took a deep breath. God he remembered that day so clearly. He and Juliette had been talking about going to their school's spring dance together. There wasn't anyone Juliette particularly wanted to go with, and besides, no one had asked her. Aaron didn't want to come out to the whole school by showing up with a guy. So he'd decided to ask her if she wanted to go with him, as friends. He'd never talked to Juliette about being gay until that night. Deep down, he didn't think she'd have a problem with it; he was just scared to admit it. On their way home, she'd just come right out and asked him, infusing the question with her usual sense of humor. The fact she knew him so well was just one of the things he loved most about her. She was his best friend, and she never judged him, she just listened.

God, he missed her so much.

AARON: It was just after 9. Practice had run late because Juliette and I were trying to get some of the other students involved. The school year had just started, and Juliette was working on getting the team together. She was the captain. As we were walking past an elementary school playground, a dirty white van pulled up to the curb. I thought it was some kind of delivery van and the driver was lost. Juliette and I slowed down when we got to the sidewalk. The side door opened, and two guys jumped out. One grabbed Juliette, and the other grabbed me. They took us to some kind of abandoned mechanic's garage and tortured us. I have scars on my arms, my legs, my back, and my chest, in addition to the ones you see on my face and neck. When they were done, they killed Juliette. They tried to kill me, but they screwed up the job.

SPENCER: OMG Were they caught?

Aaron thought "Oh my God" just about covered it. He'd never told anyone but the police and his mother anything about that night. Even then, he didn't get into details, and there were parts he refused to talk about. They understood, or at least they appeared to. It didn't matter. The physical evidence they found at the scene and at the hospital told them what they wanted to know, what Aaron could not talk about. It didn't stop the shrinks, though. He just told them all to go to hell.

AARON: No, they were never caught.

SPENCER: How did you get away?

AARON: They didn't tie us up; they just took turns holding us down. Either they didn't bring anything, or they just liked to watch us struggle. My cell phone was in my pocket. After they left and before I lost consciousness, I turned it on and dialed. My mom had been going out of her mind because no one could find us, and I hadn't answered my phone, which was off while we were in practice. She got the cops and the cell phone company to trace our location through the GPS in my phone, and they found us. They said 15 minutes later and I would have lost too much blood....

The chat window stayed quiet for a long time, and Aaron wondered if he'd gone too far, told Spencer too much. The poor guy probably had his e-mail up in another window, e-mailing Dr. Mayer to beg for a new partner, and Aaron couldn't blame him. He spent most of his life drugged into oblivion so he didn't have to deal with himself. Why would someone not forced to deal with Aaron do it willingly? It took another two minutes for the next message to come through, and when it did, it wasn't what Aaron had expected at all.

SPENCER: I once destroyed a high school band room.

AARON: What?? Why?

SPENCER: When I was in high school, my aunt Nelle and my father were having a conversation about the cause of my condition, and they didn't realize I was reading their lips. Hearing people forget sometimes that I can understand what they're saying even though I can't hear them. I had a really hard time for a while after that. I wanted to play guitar, and when the band director said they weren't "equipped to accommodate my special needs," I lost it. My dad was understanding, considering the fact I'd caused about $5000 worth of damage he had to pay for....

AARON: Something caused you to be deaf?

It took a few minutes, which meant that Spencer too was trying to decide how much of his story to tell. Aaron couldn't blame him; that's exactly what Aaron had done when editing his own gruesome tale.

SPENCER: My mom was mugged and then died while giving birth to me about 3 months too early.

AARON: I'm sorry.

SPENCER: Me too. Not so much about the deafness, because I don't really know what I'm missing since I was born deaf, but because I never got to meet my mom. I have pictures, and Aunt Nelle tells me stories about her, but I really wish I'd known her.

The chat window was quiet for a while as Aaron tried to take in what Spencer had told him, probably just like Spencer was trying to digest what Aaron had told him. Finally, a message popped up asking Aaron if he needed the notes from that day's lecture he'd missed, and the awkward silence was over. Aaron and Spencer talked for a few more minutes about class and their projects, but after the emotionally draining, edited baring of their souls, it just didn't seem like the time to get into their project.

Aaron set his chat client to away, tossed his laptop to the foot of the bed, and sat back against the headboard. As he relaxed, he noticed the faint smell of garlic and something tomato based. It took him a minute, but then he placed the robust smell of his mother's homemade spaghetti sauce. Her spaghetti had always been his favorite, ever since he'd been a toddler and begged her to make him "bisketti." For the first time in years, he felt a burning in his throat and a tightening in his chest. He didn't cry, but he sat there, on the very edge of tears, for a long time, thinking about what it would be like for him to lose his mother. After everything he'd gone through over the last few years, that would have killed him; there was no doubt in his mind.

Spencer had never even known his mother, never felt her arms around him when he woke from a bad dream, never had her blow on his scraped knee, never even brought her dandelions from the yard, totally unaware they were weeds because she treated them like prized roses. Aaron got up off the bed, rubbing his face with his hands before grabbing the now empty plate his mother had brought up earlier. Carrying it down the stairs into the kitchen, he set it down on the large island in the middle of the room. He watched his mother's back for a few minutes while she stirred the contents of a large pot on the stove. Then she used a wooden spoon to take a taste.

"Mom, can I have a taste?" Aaron asked quietly, and his mother turned to smile at him before dipping the spoon into the sauce. She held it aloft with one hand, her other hand underneath to prevent it from dripping onto her clean floor. Leaning forward, Aaron opened his mouth, allowing his mother to feed him from the old, worn wooden spoon.

"Man, that is really good," Aaron said, and took pleasure in her beaming smile at the compliment from her usually stoic son.

"Thanks, it will be even better later." She chuckled and tossed the spoon into the sink behind her.

"I love you, Mom," Aaron admitted quietly. He was sure the sentiment had come from the pain in his chest at the thought of what it would mean to lose her. His mother froze at the sink for several seconds and then turned to face her son. Aaron saw her eyes were bright with unshed tears.

"I love you too, Aaron, so much."

# ELEVEN

SPENCER watched the interpreter relaying the content of Dr. Mayer's lecture without really seeing her. He registered that her hands were moving, caught a few of the signs, but mostly he sat and wondered how to ask Aaron to come to his house to work on their project. His father had asked about Aaron again over dinner the night before, verifying his last name and asking strangely detailed questions about Aaron's behavior at school. He could tell his father was interested, but had no idea what would happen if he brought his friend home.

His heart raced as he drummed out a tuneless song on the desk in front of the lab computer's keyboard. He concentrated hard on not tapping too hard so he didn't disrupt class. Mr. McCluskey had taught him that hard lesson in his freshman year of high school by making him sit in detention, bored senseless, until he learned to stop fidgeting. It took many, many long hours to break him of the habit.

God, he hadn't thought about that in years.

AARON: You look bored.

It took him a minute to look over at the computer and away from the interpreter, but when he did he shrugged at Aaron. Well, he had his friend's attention, so that seemed like the perfect opportunity to ask the question, only he couldn't force his fingers to type it out. He drummed for a minute more before deciding this nervous shit was for chicks, and hit send before he could change his mind.

SPENCER: Not bored, just thinking. Want to come over to my house today and work on the project?

There, he'd done it; he'd gotten the words out. Aaron took his hands off the keyboard and stared in the opposite direction from Spencer, apparently trying to work out his feelings on the invitation. As Spencer watched, he put his hands on the keyboard and then took them off again and sat back, still never looking to his left, at Spencer. Crossing his arms, Aaron balled his hands tightly into fists. Spencer considered rescinding the invitation, but just sat still and waited to see what Aaron would do. Finally, he put his hands up to the keyboard again and started to type.

Spencer looked back at the interpreter so he could delay the rejection.

AARON: I can't. I can't do that.

*Shit.* He knew the answer was coming, but it still stung. Aaron didn't trust him. After the hours of talking, after telling each other their horror stories, after all the code they'd written during late night chats, Aaron still didn't feel comfortable being with him. It hurt more than he could readily define to himself, and he couldn't really figure out why. Aaron was the first person in a long time to look past his hearing impairment and actually see *him.* That meant more to him than he could ever articulate. He wanted Aaron to know he saw *him* too, not just the scars or the anxiety.

SPENCER: Okay, how about if I come to your house?

He had to build up Aaron's trust; he knew that. By going to Aaron's house, at least a few times in the beginning, maybe he could get his friend to come over and visit. The logistics of getting his father and Aaron together were just boggling. It shouldn't have to be that hard.

AARON: I think I could do that. Right after class, or?

SPENCER: I have another class after this one today. I can be there by 4:00.

Aaron pulled out his cell phone, completely ignoring Dr. Mayer's ban on them in the classroom, and sent a message to someone, probably his mother. A minute later, he saw Aaron look at the phone again and smile.

AARON: I'll send you my address. My mom invited you to stay for dinner too.

SPENCER: I'd love to.

Spencer smiled, and the expression felt tight, almost foreign on his face. After months of worrying about his father, it was weird to be happy. He liked Aaron, though, so being with him did make him feel better.

Minimizing the chat window, he turned his attention back to the interpreter, who looked irritated that he wasn't paying attention. He tried to focus on the lecture, but his mind drifted to a half daydream of what would happen later at Aaron's house.

"MOM, what if I freak out while he's here?" Aaron asked his mother as they stood at the kitchen counter making a salad. His mother chopped up the vegetables and put them in the salad bowl while Aaron tore up lettuce and spinach leaves and tossed them in with the radishes and cucumbers she'd already done. He couldn't admit it aloud, but Aaron didn't like knives. He didn't like them at all.

"You said you told him a bit about what happened, right?" she asked as she dumped a cutting board full of diced tomatoes into the bowl and mixed up the salad with two huge salad tongs.

"I told him the generic version, yeah." Aaron threw more lettuce leaves into the bowl, almost halfheartedly.

"Then if he's really your friend, honey, he'll understand."

"And if he isn't?" Aaron asked as he reached for the core of the lettuce and banked it off the wall into the kitchen garbage can in the corner. He grinned sheepishly when his mother looked at him, but then she went back to the salad.

"If he isn't, then you'll finish the project and move on to the next class."

"I want him to be," Aaron said almost too quietly for his mother to hear.

"So do I, honey."

AT TEN minutes to four, the doorbell rang. Aaron's head jerked around in the direction of the living room, though he couldn't see the front door from his seat at the breakfast bar.

"Don't you move. You keep stirring that cake," his mother ordered and then added in a louder voice, "Allen, can you answer the door and let Aaron's friend in?" She wiped her hands on her apron and pulled a glass baking dish from under the cabinet. Aaron watched her as he listened for his brother to open the door. Spencer was his first real friend in so long; his hands shook a little as he waited.

"Hi, Spencer," Allen shouted, and Aaron cringed. He looked at his mother, pleading silently to take over with the cake. She rolled her eyes, more at his brother's handling of Spencer's deafness than Aaron's nerves, and took the spoon from him. She picked the bowl up and started pouring the batter into the pan just as he rounded the corner out of the kitchen.

"He's deaf, genius. Talking louder isn't going to make any difference," Aaron told Allen as he shuffled into the living room. His courage failed just as the kitchen tile phased into living room carpet, and he stopped behind the couch as Spencer lingered near the front door. Spencer looked almost nervous as he took in the dainty couch and matching wingback chair that stood around spindly little end tables his family had never used. They spent all their time in the family room near the back of the house, where the television hung on the wall. The living room was mainly just for guests.

"Just leave your shoes by the door and come with me," Aaron said slowly, but more quietly than his brother had. With a glance at Allen, Spencer nodded and toed out of his shoes. He didn't speak; he just waited silently for Aaron, who wondered if maybe he didn't want to talk aloud in front of his brother. Aaron made a "come on" gesture, and Spencer followed him into the kitchen.

"Mom, this is my friend Spencer," he said, making sure he was turned toward Spencer so his friend could see his lips. "Spencer, this is my mom."

"It. Is. Very. Nice. To. Meet. You.," Spencer told her in his slow, purposeful cadence, even as he leaned against the doorframe almost out of the room.

"It is very nice to meet you too. Aaron has told me so much about you." His mom took off her apron and gave Spencer a little wave. He waved back with a quiet smile and looked relieved he didn't have to talk anymore. “Aaron, why don’t you take Spencer up to your room, and I’ll come get you when dinner is ready?”

They didn’t need to be told twice. Aaron could feel Spencer’s awkward tension and led him up the stairs. He understood exactly how Spencer felt around his family, because strangers were a source of anxiety for Aaron too. In fact, his heart stuttered in his chest as they reached the top. He didn’t like Spencer behind him. He didn’t like everything so close. He thought the air might solidify in his lungs. With the plush carpet of his room under his feet and the open space around him, the feeling dissipated almost as fast as it started. Aaron dropped down into his desk chair and powered on his laptop while Spencer dropped his stuff on the bed but didn’t bring out his computer right away. Instead, he looked around Aaron’s room, lingering at the soccer trophies collecting dust on a high shelf.

Aaron had never bothered to take them down. It was almost like they belonged to someone else. They could have, for all he cared about them. He waited as Spencer took a long, slow inventory of his room. What the hell was he looking for? Aaron’s skin crawled at the scrutiny, and he scratched absently at one of the scars on his arm underneath the long-sleeved polo shirt he wore. No one except his family had been in this room in years, but even then, he didn’t feel judged by it as he did with Spencer.

Finally, Spencer turned around and Aaron could see his face. More importantly, Spencer could see his.

“What?” he demanded. The blood rising in his face made it feel like it glowed with embarrassment. *Did you find what you were looking for in the freak cave?* Aaron could not meet Spencer’s eyes, choosing instead to focus on his own hands. The trailing end of a deep knife scar peeked out of the sleeve, mocking him, and his fists tightened around each other in helpless anger.

“You. Are. Not. Like. Anyone. I. Have. Ever. Known.. You. Are. Kind., Sensitive., And. Thoughtful.. I. Want. To. Know. More. About. You.. I. Thought. I. Might. Find. That. Out. By. Looking. Around. Your. Room.. But. None. Of. This. Stuff. Seems. Like. It. Would. Belong. To. You.. It. Surprised. Me..” Spencer jerked his head up to indicate the trophies. It was the longest conversation they’d ever had aloud, and Aaron reeled from the compliments. He had misjudged Spencer's intentions so badly. Shame crept up the back of his neck, replacing the embarrassment.

"I'm sorry. I'm not used to having… friends in my room. But you're right. This stuff doesn't have anything to do with my life now. It belongs to the old Aaron, the one that died."

They stood facing each other for a few long, tense moments. When Aaron didn't say anything else, Spencer sat on the side of the bed and grabbed his laptop.

"Want. To. Get. Started.?" he asked, and even with the slow cadence, Aaron heard the trepidation. A part of him wanted to tell Spencer it wasn't a good night, but a deeper part of him, the selfish part that was so desperately lonely, that part wanted Spencer to stay. That part of him wanted to tell Spencer everything, all his secrets, just to get the poison out. Instead, he just nodded.

Aaron brought up the chat window on his computer first, and left the development environment closed. He wanted to talk to Spencer more than he wanted to work on the project. His fingers hovered over the keys on the laptop even as his wrists rested on the bottom edge. Glancing over at Spencer, who typed furiously on his keyboard, he envied Spencer's focus. A "ding" on his computer caught his attention.

SPENCER: I wish you would stop saying that. You did not die. You are right here in front of me, and I am very grateful for that. Not many people see past my deafness and want to be my friend anyway. You did.

AARON: I'm so out of practice at talking to someone. The shrinks try to get me to talk. My mother tries to get me to talk. Whenever I try, something inside me locks up, and I can't get the words out. With my mom, I think it's because she already has to deal with so much because of me. I don't want to add any more to that. With the shrinks, I guess it's because they don't give a fuck about me. They don't want to help me. They just want to get paid and move on to the next schmuck with a problem. See how many they can fit in a day before they drive home in their Lexus to play golf.

SPENCER: Not all shrinks are like that.

AARON: The ones I've met are. Did you have to see a shrink?

SPENCER: I've had to talk to psychologists. I had some behavioral problems in school. Mostly, I acted like a dick because I was sick of getting bullied. See, the school administrators never saw that part. They just saw me fucking up. I was so glad to get out of high school.

AARON: I was homeschooled my last two years of high school. After what happened, I couldn't stand being around other people, so my mom kept me home. She figured out everything she needed to know to get me through the requirements. She bought me books and videos. She sat with me every day and went through every subject with me.

SPENCER: Your mom sounds amazing.

AARON: She really is. I couldn't imagine growing up without her.

SPENCER: I had dad and my aunt Nelle. My dad was everything to me growing up, mom, dad, interpreter, everything. He and my aunt Nelle learned sign language with me. They studied everything they could about ASL so that they could help me. It took me a long time to realize how hard that must have been for my dad, taking care of a premature deaf baby on his own after his wife had been murdered.

AARON: What happened to her? You said she was mugged.

AARON: I'm sorry. You don't have to talk about it.

SPENCER: No, it is okay. She was a nurse. One night as she was leaving the hospital where she worked, a guy attacked her in the parking garage. He raped her, and then shot her and left her for dead.

Aaron's insides froze, and he was thankful Spencer couldn't hear the pained sound that came out of his chest. In his mind, he saw Juliette's face, contorted in pain as the man with the mole on his cheek violated her on the floor next to him. He could almost feel the body on top of him as it pinned him to the floor. Adrenaline screamed through him, filling his body with fear. His hands shook on the keyboard, and every rational thought disappeared like a flash of lightning. A deep throbbing he recognized as his heartbeat echoed through his head until there was nothing left.

The computer beeped with another message, but he couldn't force himself to look. Shocked into horrified silence and nearly incapacitated by the mention of the word "rape," Aaron stared unseeing at his desk and tried to will the panic attack creeping up his spine to wait… just wait until

Spencer left. Another long, deep breath and his frantic heart slowed enough for him to stay upright.

"Aaron.." Spencer's voice, clear and strong, filtered through the fog of panic and pain. Aaron raised his head to meet Spencer's message on the screen.

SPENCER: What did I say? Please tell me so I do not say it again. I do not want to upset you.

Aaron stared at the screen as his throat closed around the breath trapped in it. No force in heaven or on earth could make him utter those words to Spencer, even electronically. He could not talk about it—ever—not to Spencer, not to anyone. His parents knew; he could see the shame in his mother's eyes. They'd found… well, evidence when they'd taken him to the hospital. She asked him about it exactly once and decided his reaction wasn't worth getting him to talk about it. It was the closest he'd ever come to ending his own life, and his mother would never take that chance again.

AARON: I can't.

AARON: I can't talk about it.

AARON: Please.

Before Spencer could respond, his mother stuck her head in through his bedroom door. Something in Aaron's face made her pause, and she looked at him for a long moment and then glanced at Spencer.

"Boys, dinner is ready," she said quietly, making sure to look at Spencer when she said it so he would understand. Aaron closed his laptop, and Spencer did the same. They both sat quietly as Aaron's mother left, unsure what to say to each other in the awkward silence. When Aaron looked into Spencer's face, he saw the pity he hated so much.

SPENCER'S chest ached. When he'd looked back through the conversation to see what he could have said to set Aaron off, one word stood out among all the others—raped. His father had been right. Aaron's sympathy aside, only that word would have caused his extreme reaction to the story of his mother's death. God, he felt sick.

Aaron unfolded himself from the desk chair and walked over to the bedroom door like he was going for his last meal. Spencer wanted so badly to hug his friend and take away every bit of his pain. The depth of it remained in his eyes, those fathomless blue eyes that hid nothing from the world. Not as eloquent as his father nor as empathic as his aunt, Spencer said nothing as Aaron wrapped his frail arms around himself.

He followed Aaron downstairs to an open dining room situated between the kitchen and family room. Two boys sat on the couch just beyond the dining room table and played a video racing game with tiny little characters in primary colors. Steering wheels in their hands, they held them out like weapons, crashing into each other on particularly wild turns. Their smiles and silent laughter made Spencer envious.

He turned to watch Aaron help his mother set up platters of hamburger patties, packages of buns, a bowl of fries, and a load of other serving dishes on an island in the center of the kitchen. It looked like a tiny buffet, with plates and silverware on the counter across from it. Spencer saw Aaron's mother call the other two boys for dinner just as their father, who looked remarkably like an older Aaron, came into the room.

"You must be Spencer. Aaron has told us so much about you," he said as he held out his hand. Spencer took it tentatively and had to swallow hard before he answered. Meeting this many new people in one day made his fucking skin crawl.

"It. Is. Very. Nice. To. Meet. You.," Spencer repeated, just as he had with Aaron's mother, giving the minimum his aunt would allow him to get away with. He hovered in awkward silence near the table as the family milled about in the open space. Aaron's father wandered over to grab the boys, who, heedless of their mother's instructions, continued to play their game. His whole life, it had been just him and his father. Spencer never played sports, wasn't in band, and had few real friends, so his house had been calm and quiet growing up. He never had the rowdiness and chaos of three boys and two active parents. He wondered what it was like.

A hand touched his arm, and he jerked from his thoughts.

"Here, honey, just fill this right up and take a seat next to Aaron," Mrs. Downing said as she handed him a plate. He looked over to see Aaron drop into a chair on the far side of the table with a plate half full of food. A harsh growl rumbled through his stomach, and he wondered briefly if Aaron's mother heard it. In his family, cookouts were reserved for family get-togethers and Dad's professional friends. They didn't even own a grill. Spencer took the plate over to the island, which nearly overflowed with food, and began to fill it.

"It's good to see a boy with a healthy appetite," Aaron's mother said after tapping him on the arm to get his attention. He could tell by the way she looked at her son that the comment was more directed at Aaron than at him. Aaron glanced up at the comment but didn't say anything. The pain still lingering in his eyes from their earlier conversation tore at Spencer. Carrying his plate carefully with both hands, he set it down at the place next to Aaron on the far side of the table.

"There are drinks in the refrigerator. Take whatever you want," Aaron told him as he looked up briefly from his plate to make sure Spencer could see his mouth. Aaron's brothers and father came in from the other room, and Spencer squeezed in around them to grab the first soda he could from the refrigerator. The shorter boy elbowed the taller one in the ribs and said something Spencer didn't catch, but the older boy moved out of his way with an apologetic grin. The camaraderie between them made his heart ache for Aaron, who sat alone at the table.

He sat next to Aaron and pulled his plate closer just to keep an arm from going around his friend, who looked so lost Spencer couldn't bear to see it.

"Hey, Spencer, are you…." The rest of the older boy's statement was lost to Spencer as he crammed a handful of french fries into his mouth. He looked at Aaron, who studied his food like he had an exam on it later that night.

"Allen, for God's sake, swallow before you talk," Mrs. Downing said after setting her plate at one of the heads of the table. Mr. Downing put his plate at the other and affectionately bumped his middle son on the head with his hand.

"Allen, he has to read your lips. He can't understand you if your mouth is crammed full of food. Show some respect," Aaron admonished and finally looked up, and for a long moment the entire family stood perfectly still, frozen in place as they stared at Aaron. He had no idea what was happening, but remained quiet until the moment passed.

"I'm sorry. I just asked if you were a programming major like Aaron," Allen said with an empty mouth and a glance at his older brother.

Aaron didn't talk much during dinner, but he did put in a few words every now and then, mostly in response to something Spencer had said. Even Spencer could tell he was making a sincere effort to be social. It made things so much easier. While he still felt a little self-conscious when he spoke, no one at the table batted an eye at the way he must have sounded. Living with Aaron and his panic attacks, they must be used to people being different.

They had accepted him effortlessly into their lives, and he couldn't tell them how much that meant.

After dinner, Allen and Anthony went back to their game, but not before reminding Aaron they had four controllers and asking if Spencer and Aaron would play too. Spencer took one look at Aaron's tired and drawn face and decided maybe he should go. He didn't want to leave. He wanted to stay and play games with Aaron and his brothers, but he could see Aaron had hit his social limit for the day.

"Maybe. I. Can. Come. Back. And. Play. Sometime.," he told Allen with a meaningful look at Aaron, who was staring passively at the floor.

"You're welcome anytime," Mrs. Downing told him with a hand on his shoulder and a quick look at her eldest son. The longing in her face was unmistakable. *Please come back. Please be a good friend to him. Please, just... please.*

Spencer followed Aaron to the front door, away from the boisterous activity of the house. Picking up his shoes, he sat on the stairs leading up to the second floor as he put them on. Aaron shifted his weight from one foot to the other as he waited with Spencer's book bag in his hand.

"Thank you," he told Spencer as he handed him the bag. Even through his deafness, Spencer heard so much in those two words, and he understood. Friends were hard for him too, and he knew he had made one of the best of his life that night, simply for knowing when not to push.

# TWELVE

AARON: No, we need to turn this into an object and use an instance. We can reuse it for other kinds of messages.

SPENCER: How?

AARON: By making the API names and local file names properties of the object.

SPENCER: That's fucking brilliant! Have you heard anything from Mayer?

AARON: Oh yeah, he e-mailed me earlier, and we have a green light. He said he's "intrigued."

SPENCER: Hell yeah!

AARON: The e-mail he sent you is probably sitting in your school account. You know, the one you never ever check?

Aaron laughed, which he had done more and more often over the past week. In fact, it was starting to feel normal rather than foreign. Spencer was a great partner, bright and efficient, and was turning out to be a great friend as well. They hadn't talked any more about their pasts after dinner with his family, but they were starting to learn each other's eccentricities. Aaron knew, for example, that Spencer got very frustrated having to sit in the back of the class. His interpreter was a distraction to the other students, and he favored lip reading anyway. He felt like a spectacle, but the school administration had forced the interpreter on him in an effort to avoid any appearance of discrimination. What he really wanted was for the instructors to use voice recognition software, but the school said they weren't going to burden their professors with the time it takes to train the software with their voices, not when there were interpreters available.

After all—it was Spencer's problem, not theirs.

Spencer, on the other hand, had learned that if it looked like rain, he needed to take careful notes for his friend. He'd once asked Aaron about it, but Aaron couldn't adequately explain why he just couldn't get out of bed when it looked like it could storm.

Aaron felt their project was going very well so far. They had coded all the back-end classes, error handling, and security. It had been accessed through a very simple command line interface, but they were to the point now where they needed to work on a pretty user interface. After that, they could put it on the Internet and start beta testing.

AARON: We're going to have to do this part in person. Do you want to stay in the lab for a while?

SPENCER: We can't. There is another class after this one.

AARON: I don't want to go into the main lab. Do you want to come over to my house?

SPENCER: Well, my house is quieter, and my desktop is better for interface work. It will be easier to see the design on my huge monitors. There's more space to work than on a laptop.

Aaron looked at his friend as he sat next to him in the lab. This was a big step for Aaron, and they both knew it. What if something happened? Spencer was right about his computer at home, though. It just made more sense to go to Spencer's. Aaron could bring his laptop and work from anywhere.

AARON: Okay, give me your address and I'll see if my mom can drop me off there.

SPENCER: I can take you, and I'll bring you home. It's not a big deal. Then your mom doesn't need to bother.

AARON: I thought your dad dropped you off at my house. You can drive? How can you do that if you can't hear?

SPENCER: I'm deaf, not blind.

Spencer chuckled and shook his head as Aaron grabbed his phone from his laptop bag. Sending a quick text message to his mom, telling her that Spencer would bring him home later, he was unsurprised when she asked him to e-mail the address. He had Spencer send the e-mail, and he forwarded it to his mom, who told him to have fun. She was probably beside herself knowing Aaron had a friend and he was going someplace that wasn't home or school. The fact that he was comfortable enough with Spencer to go to his house spoke volumes about their relationship.

Aaron followed Spencer out of the building and across the parking lot to a shiny midnight blue two-seater sports car. Aaron, who knew little about cars, just stood and gaped at it as Spencer hit the button to unlock it.

"My. Dad. Is. Loaded.," Spencer said with a smirk, walking around the car and getting in on the driver's side. Aaron got in on the passenger side after setting his laptop bag carefully behind the seat. Buckling up, he grinned at Spencer, who looked absolutely at home behind the wheel of his car. He could tell Spencer cherished this car by the way Spencer caressed the leather-encased steering wheel as he started the engine.

"See. This.?" Spencer asked, pointing to a small display on the dashboard. Aaron nodded, and Spencer honked the horn to make lights flash on the little box. "It. Is. A. Sound. Sensor.," Spencer explained, and honked again. Aaron saw the display light up again, and then faced Spencer so his friend could see his face.

"So, if there is a loud noise like a horn or a siren, it will light up?" Aaron asked in a slow, enunciated way so Spencer would have little trouble reading his lips. His natural inclination was to talk louder, but that just seemed silly since Spencer couldn't hear him no matter how loud he talked. Spencer nodded and looked carefully behind him before pulling out of the space.

"Most. Deaf. People. Do Not. Use. This., But. My. Dad. Wanted. Me. To. Have. One.," Spencer said, threading his way carefully through the parking lot. "Most. People. Are. Just. Really. Careful.." They drove for about twenty minutes in the opposite direction from Aaron's house, until they came to an obviously affluent subdivision. Spencer pulled into the gated community. The gates were open and there didn't seem to be any sign of a guard, which made Aaron wonder why there were gates in the first place. Winding through curved roads and bypassing cul-de-sacs,

Spencer finally pulled into the driveway of a huge copper-colored house with floor to ceiling windows in the front and a large two-car garage. It seemed Spencer wasn't kidding when he said his dad was well-off.

Aaron trailed behind as Spencer grabbed his bag and headed for the house. Completely out of his element for the first time in a long time, he was reluctant to go in. There was no way for him to know who was in the house, and he really wasn't up for meeting new people today, not after being in a strange place. Spencer noticed his hesitation and stopped halfway up the drive.

"Just. Me. And. My. Dad.," Spencer said as he waited for Aaron to join him. Slowly, Aaron walked forward and followed his friend as Spencer unlocked the door and entered the house. The foyer was easily the size of his brother Anthony's bedroom, and twice as grand. The polished marble floor, which seemed to go on forever, was hidden only slightly by a small oriental rug just in front of the door. Spencer stood on the rug as he removed his shoes and set them just inside the coat closet to his left. As Aaron looked around at the stylish table, huge gilded mirror, and umbrella stand that occupied the space, Spencer looked at him pointedly. Aaron furrowed his brow at Spencer's expression, but then realized he needed to take his shoes off too. The vulnerability made him shudder inside, but he did it anyway.

Spencer took Aaron on a silent tour of his home, starting in a grand parlor room with beautiful antique furniture, through the spacious kitchen that Aaron's mother would probably give him up for adoption to cook in, and then to his father's study. This was probably the most impressive room Aaron had ever seen, with the floor to ceiling bookcases under glass, the huge mahogany desk, and the leather sofa along the back wall. It looked like the study of a bestselling author or a college professor. Finally, Spencer led Aaron to a rec room at the back of the huge first floor, where he found a giant flat-panel TV and a rack of video game systems. Next to the rack, he saw a variety of video game accessories, including band equipment. Aaron thought it was a really odd thing for a deaf kid to want to play, but if it made Spencer happy, it was okay with him. Aaron loved to play video games. Or at least, he had. Aaron hadn't picked up a guitar, or even a controller in so long, he'd probably lost the ability to play.

As they walked into the room, Aaron saw a messy desk along the right-hand wall, underneath a huge bay window. The computer sat to the side of two large flat-panel monitors and a sophisticated-looking microphone. He noticed with mild surprise that there were also speakers on the desk. Spencer walked up to the desk and turned the machine on, pulling up a chair from a nearby table for Aaron. Aaron sat down and pulled his laptop out of his bag. As he did, Spencer handed him a piece of paper with a handwritten code.

AAVER-1681A-HH5H-87892-HRNB

"Network. Key.," Spencer said, and Aaron quickly configured his laptop for Spencer's home network. Then he logged into his chat client.

AARON: Okay, did you have anything in mind for the interface?

SPENCER: Something eye-catching and easy to use. We can check out that control set Dr. Mayer told us about. They have some really nice free controls.

AARON: Black background with some neon, I think—purple, or blue?

SPENCER: Cool.

They spent the next hour structuring an interface and building the controls on screen until they both agreed on the design. It was lightweight, flexible, and visually appealing. Aaron and Spencer were both very pleased with the way their project was progressing. They would be finished far ahead of the deadline, and thought they might score extra points by actually offering the capability to download and use the program in a production environment. They were about to send their first test message from the interface when a chat window popped up on Spencer's screen.

DAD: Can you help me with dinner? Your friend is staying, right?

SPENCER: We are having pizza, and he needs for me to make the crust. Do you want to come hang out in the kitchen with us?

Aaron hesitated. He really wasn't up for much more excitement today. He had pretty much reached his limit for new experiences and didn't want to have to face Spencer's dad. It seemed that Spencer understood.

SPENCER: You don't have to. You can hang out in here and work on the program. We can eat in here too. He'll want to meet you at some point because you're my friend, but it doesn't have to be today.

AARON: Thanks for understanding.

SPENCER: No problem. I'm not keen on meeting new people either. What do you want on your pizza? I'm sure we have sausage, pepperoni, mushrooms, green pepper, and onion. Anything else, I'll have to scrounge for.

AARON: Sausage and pepperoni would be fantastic.

SPENCER: Okay, I'll be back in a bit.

Aaron's gaze followed Spencer as he left, and then traveled around the huge room. It seemed that everything a teenage boy could possibly ask for resided in this room. He moved over to the leather couch and considered turning on the gaming system, but his eyes were starting to hurt from staring at the screen for so long. Leaning back into the plush leather, he closed them for a second, trying to stave off the headache he could feel coming. The aquarium set in the wall behind the couch was massive, and the sound of water bubbling soothed Aaron's nerves. Listening to the soft, melodious aquatic sounds, he turned, sitting sideways on the couch so he could watch the dozens of fish swimming carelessly through the predefined space. He wished he could be one of those fish, with no fear, no expectations, just swimming and eating and enjoying life.

Staring at the aquarium, he had no idea how long it had been since Spencer left the room, but he was content. The brightly colored rocks and plants that lined the bottom of the tank contrasted with the brilliant blue water. It appeared blue, at least, but Aaron was pretty sure there was a blue lining on the back of the tank and the water was actually clear. It didn't matter. He watched as a bright yellow and white fish swam down behind one of the plants.

Then someone clamped down on his shoulder, and he screamed. His mind spiraled, and he tried to jerk away from his attacker. Falling sideways off the couch to get away from the person who wanted to hurt him, he slammed his head on the corner of the coffee table and went into a full-blown panic as blood began to pour down his face.

He heard yelling and footsteps, but the blood was on his neck. It was coming from his neck. This time he wouldn't survive. He was going to die.

"Aaron!" a strong voice commanded. It was a voice he did not recognize. He looked up and, through the haze of the garage, saw Spencer huddled against the wall, terrified. No, that wasn't right. He hadn't met Spencer until after. How could he be in the garage? How could he be there while they were trying to kill him?

"Aaron, do you see what is in this room? There is a big TV, an aquarium, a desk. Do you see these things, Aaron?" the voice asked sternly. Aaron stared around wildly and wondered what kind of a question that was. Of course he could see what was in the room. "Tell me what you see."

"Computer… guitar… couch…." Aaron choked out, confused. He just wanted to huddle into a ball, just hide until his mother came. His mother always came. But the garage had faded, and the flashback started to recede back into the vault of memories from whence it had come. He was back in the present with a T-shirt pressed against his head and a man crouched on one knee in front of him. It was the fastest Aaron had ever been able to recover from a flashback. He looked at the man, who was remarkably like Spencer. Spencer's father didn't have Spencer's soft curls. In fact, his graying brown hair was cut in almost a military fashion, but his eyes were the same. They were just as warm, just as enigmatic as Spencer's hazel eyes.

He didn't know what to do next, so Aaron just asked simply, "How did you know?" The question asked so many different things at once. How did he know about Aaron's flashback? How did he know what to do to help him? How did he seem to know so much about Aaron's condition if they'd never met?

“I. Told. You. My. Dad. Was. A. Shrink.. Right.?” Spencer asked rapidly, his face reddening with guilt as he moved a little closer to where Aaron sat bleeding on the floor.

Well, that explained a few things for Aaron, but for some reason that automatic skepticism that usually came when he considered therapy or shrinks was strangely absent. Spencer’s father moved back now that Aaron was calm, and sat on the coffee table watching him.

“Can I look at the cut on your head first, and then we can talk?” he asked, pulling the T-shirt away from Aaron’s forehead. “It doesn’t look deep. Let me clean it up and put a Band-Aid or two on it. I’m going to guess you’re not too fond of hospitals or doctors?”

Aaron shook his head, amazed at the man’s insight. The problem, as Aaron saw it, was, how was Spencer’s father going to clean up his wound and bandage it without touching him? He couldn’t stand for his own mother to touch him, let alone some strange man.

“Are. You. Okay.?” Spencer asked slowly, sitting next to him on the floor as his father left the room to get what he would need to clean the cut. The concern in those soft hazel eyes touched Aaron. This guy, the one who had never met the pre-attack Aaron, had really become someone Aaron could rely on. Spencer was his first real friend.

Looking right into Spencer’s face so he could be sure Spencer could understand him by reading his lips, Aaron said, “I’m okay, thank you.”

“Thank. Me.? Why. In. The. Hell. Would. You. Thank. Me.? It. Is. My. Fault.. I. Forgot.. I. Forgot. And. I. Touched. You.. I. Was. A. Fucking. Idiot., And. You. Got. Hurt..” Spencer shook his head and then stared at the floor.

Aaron couldn’t speak to get his attention and try to argue, because Spencer wouldn’t hear him. Without thinking, Aaron put his hand on the side of Spencer’s face and tilted it up. Holding it still, he spoke again so Spencer could see him.

“You are not an idiot. I am broken, Spencer. That is not your fault. You are my friend, and you treat me like I’m normal, like I’m not a scarred freak. No one else does that for me.”

Spencer had stopped breathing for a moment, but then he took a deep breath.

"I. Do. Not. See. The. Scars. Anymore.. All. I. See. Is. You.," Spencer replied quietly, and continued to stand perfectly still as Aaron touched his face. Spencer's expression was wistful, maybe, full of wonder.

The doctor came back into the room then, and without a comment about the boys' position, sat back down on the coffee table in front of Aaron. With the presence of a third person in the room, whatever spell had been cast was broken, and Aaron sat back slowly, his mind strangely blank.

"Spence, can you hold this mirror for me?" Dr. Thomas said for Aaron's benefit as he signed to his son. Aaron could only imagine he did it out of habit, saying what he signed aloud. Spencer took the mirror from his father and held it up in front of Aaron.

"Okay, Aaron, I want you to take the peroxide and clean the area around the wound. Then I'm going to have you put on this gauze and tape," Dr. Thomas said, folding a piece of white gauze into a smaller square, maybe two inches by three inches, and applying medical tape to either end.

Aaron looked in the mirror, momentarily panicky because of the blood he saw on his face. Then he looked up into Spencer's face, and his friend smiled down at him, and he did what Dr. Thomas asked. It took just a few minutes before the cut was bandaged and Spencer's father was putting away the supplies. He came back into the room and sat back down, not on the coffee table this time, but in a leather chair farther away from Aaron. Aaron continued to sit in a small ball on the floor, his knees pulled up to his chest. Spencer had moved to sit on the couch next to him, careful not to touch.

"To answer your question, Aaron, I had the idea how to help you because I am a clinical psychologist that specializes in severe stress disorders. The method I used with you was called grounding. By grounding you in the room and in the present, it helps to keep you from slipping into your traumatic memories when they are triggered," Spencer's father said, settling back into the plush leather and crossing his long legs.

Aaron studied him for several minutes before responding. He took in the relaxed manner, the man's steady confidence. It seemed he knew everything there was to know about Aaron, or….

"You think you can help me?" Aaron asked quietly. They all thought they could help him. Every shrink his parents had sent him to thought they could help him, but they were wrong. The hope that had been building in his chest started to deflate, because Aaron really wished someone could help him. He was really starting to get sick of being broken.

"No…. However, I might be able to help you to help yourself."

Aaron looked up at that, meeting the man's gaze. He rarely looked anyone in the eye, but the answer was just so unexpected. What the hell did that mean, he could help Aaron help himself? Wasn't Spencer's father the shrink? How could Aaron fix himself, and if he could, why hadn't he done it already?

"What exactly does that mean?" Aaron asked, trying not to formulate any kind of hope or plan in his head, only trying to get clarification.

"It means that I can teach you coping mechanisms, relaxation techniques, and other ways to deal with your trauma. You are never going to be the boy you were before you were attacked, but…."

"How do you know what happened to me?" Aaron demanded. He could feel the anger, the uncontrolled rage building inside him, and for no good reason. Spencer's father could have read it in the paper or seen it on the news. There weren't many people around here who didn't know who he was—poor little Aaron Downing. The room was suddenly warmer, and his heart beat wildly in his chest, fueled by the adrenaline. Aaron could almost feel his face flushing with anger, but before he could really build up a head of steam, Spencer's father cut him off.

"Spencer told me what you had told him because he wanted to know if there was anything he could do to make things easier, being your friend. He cares very much about you. I dug up the press clippings and other things that I could find about your case because, like today, I wanted to be able to help you if my help was warranted."

He was calm and controlled, and Aaron could feel his anger deflate. Apparently, Dr. Thomas knew that trying to placate him would only make him angrier. The calm, detached, unemotional explanation was so much better than telling him to calm down, or backing off as his other therapists had done when he got angry. He was different from anyone Aaron had ever seen. Adding in that Spencer had only done it because he cared about Aaron helped to diffuse things as well.

"Can you really help me?" Aaron asked quietly, completely unable to stop the note of desperate hope that had crept into his voice. Aaron didn't believe much in therapy—he had absolutely no reason to. All the other therapists that his parents had sent him to had pretended like they wanted to help him, but everything they had tried failed miserably, so they just kept him calm and medicated and said that was the best they could do.

"I can help you control it, yes, but only if you want to. It's not going to be easy, and you will really have to commit yourself and work at it," Dr. Thomas cautioned, and Aaron nodded. It wasn't as if he had much of a life anyway. What did he have to lose? Deep down in the darkest places of his mind, he started to see a very small, very faint light. It was the merest shadow of hope.

"I don't know any of my parents' insurance information right now, but I could get that for you if you need it," Aaron said shyly, wanting to get that one little piece of business out of the way because he was anxious to start.

"I'm not going to charge you, Aaron." Spencer's father told Aaron firmly, adamant about that point.

"Then, if you don't mind me asking, what are you getting out of helping me?" Aaron asked, skeptical but curious. He had found out in life, usually the hard way, that very few people did things if there wasn't something in it for them.

"Two things, really. I'm going to get the love and admiration of my son for helping his friend, and I'd like to publish a paper on what we accomplish together, to help other therapists treat patients with stress indicators similar to yours."

Aaron nodded. If Dr. Thomas could really help him start being a more functioning member of society, he could publish ten papers.

"Spencer," Dr. Thomas said, moving his hands to get his son's attention. "I need to talk to Aaron for a while alone."

Spencer nodded and stood up. He had turned to leave the room when Aaron's arm shot out, and he grabbed his friend by the wrist. Spencer looked down at him, and, for the second time, Aaron didn't seem to realize that he was touching Spencer.

# THIRTEEN

"PLEASE don't leave," Aaron said slowly and plainly, looking up at Spencer. Then he turned to Dr. Thomas. "Please, can't he stay?"

Spencer's chest tightened at Aaron's plea. He thought he would walk to the ends of the earth just to feel the warmth of Aaron's fingers around his wrist. The monumental significance of Aaron touching someone else only slightly outweighed how good it felt. Even if Aaron were gay, Spencer knew he wasn't capable of that kind of relationship, but that didn't stop Spencer's heart from wanting him.

"Spencer, do you have any problems sitting in on Aaron's therapy session?" His dad looked at him and waited for an answer.

He wondered how Aaron would handle him hearing the most intimate details of his life, but the anguish in Aaron's eyes made him shake his head and sit back down.

"Okay, let me grab a few things from my office and check on the pizza. I'll be right back," his father said as he got up from his plush leather chair and left the room.

"Are you sure you're okay with this? It won't be pretty," Aaron asked Spencer with a sigh.

Spencer nodded.

"I. Want. To. Help. You.. You. Are. My. Friend., One. Of. My. Best. Friends.," Spencer said, and the tension in Aaron's shoulders melted as he relaxed back against the couch. He liked that Aaron could be so comfortable with him, more comfortable than anyone else he'd seen his friend around.

"You have seen the scars other people haven't seen and didn't run. I feel the same way, man," Aaron said, and leaned his head back on the couch, waiting for Spencer's dad to return.

Spencer watched Aaron and started to second-guess his decision to get his father involved. What if he was beyond the good doctor's help? What if his father's alcoholism made him unreliable? He didn't want his father to flake out on Aaron just when his friend needed him. Aaron was such a good person. Spencer wanted to see him take control of his life again, even if nothing else could happen between them.

His dad returned a few minutes later with his hands full of pizza, paper towels, and sodas. Spencer wondered why he didn't want to take Aaron into the office to talk. They set the cut pizza down on the coffee table with the sodas, and Spencer handed each a paper towel to use as a plate.

"My mom would have a fit if I suggested eating on the floor of the living room off paper towels. In fact, she might even do herself bodily harm," Aaron said with a chuckle, betraying the comfort he felt with Spencer and his father.

A smile crept onto Spencer's face as he accepted a piece of pizza and dropped down next to Aaron on the floor in front of the couch.

Before his father sat, he pulled a digital tape recorder and a small notebook from his pocket. It appeared playtime was over, but it still didn't feel much like a therapy session, sitting on the floor eating pizza. Maybe that was the intent, to make Aaron feel more comfortable.

"Aaron, are you currently seeing a therapist?" his father asked, setting the tape recorder on the table. Spencer noticed there was a piece of tape over the little red light, muting it almost completely. Apparently, he didn't want Aaron to feel like he was being interviewed, or he didn't want anyone to focus on the little red light.

"Not really," Aaron replied, taking a long pull from the soda.

"Can you define 'not really'?" Spencer's dad asked, in full "Dr. Thomas" mode, even though to Spencer, he looked slightly amused.

Aaron took another bite of pizza and appeared to contemplate his answer carefully.

"There is a doctor that prescribes my medications, antianxiety pills, tranquilizers, and stuff, but I stopped talking to him in sessions a while ago. He doesn't care. He gets paid no matter what my progress or lack thereof."

It looked like Aaron waited for a rebuke from the doctor, but none came. They talked for a little while longer about his therapy attempts, his flashbacks, and his medications. After nearly an hour, they got into the heart of things.

"You have several tactile, auditory, and visual stimuli for hallucinatory flashbacks which your doctor and parents have chosen to medicate. How do you feel about that?" Spencer's father asked, his eyes not leaving Aaron's and his pen poised to jot notes on the answer.

Aaron sat back, and sweat beaded on his temples, and he took several long drinks of his soda while he contemplated his answer.

"I feel socially retarded. I can't get a job, I have problems at school, and lately it seems like simple things have started to provoke reactions in me. The only way I can think of to deal with those reactions is to medicate myself into oblivion, and I hate that." Aaron looked down at his plate rather than looking at Spencer or his father.

A blush rose in his face, making him look even more awkward, and Spencer wanted to tell his father to give Aaron a break, but he sensed they were close to the end. He didn't want to undermine Aaron's confidence in the therapy or his new therapist.

"I'd like to end our talk here because there are some things we need to decide on before we go any further. First, I want to work with you on a professional basis, so you need to decide if you want to transfer yourself to my care. If you do, I'd like to start weaning you off the medication that has been prescribed for you. I can't do that until we have been working together for a while on the tools you will need to work through your crises rather than medicate them. You are legally an adult, so all I need is your consent to transfer your therapy records to my office, but I would strongly suggest you discuss the change with your parents. We would start off with three sessions per week plus exercises for you to do on your own," his father said, and Aaron's eyes widened. His breathing accelerated wildly, and for a second, Spencer feared that maybe he would have another panic attack.

"You want to take me off my meds?" Aaron asked, looking a little shell-shocked. "Do you really think I'd be able to handle my… my issues without them?"

"In time, yes, I think you will," Spencer's father confided. "There are a lot of different techniques you can use, like the grounding which we used successfully earlier, in order to deal with flashbacks and other psychosomatic crises."

"What kind of exercises would I need to do at home?"

AARON was excited. God, for the first time in years, he thought maybe he could see a light at the end of a very dark tunnel.

"Journaling, breathing exercises, meditation, and other techniques we find for you to use," Spencer's father listed.

Aaron knew these were all things he could do in the privacy of his bedroom. For some reason, he didn't want to share Dr. Thomas with his parents. This was the first therapist he had selected on his own, his first adult decision. He was also a little afraid his parents would disagree, maybe stop him from going to sessions. Aaron's gut told him trusting this man was the way to go, but then, his gut had steered him horribly wrong before.

"I'd like to start working with you," Aaron told him, making the decision without any hesitation. If this man believed he could help Aaron start to function like a normal human being again, then the least Aaron could do was give him the opportunity.

"Okay, I'll get the paperwork together to have your records transferred from your current therapist. The first thing I'd like for you to do is start a journal. You can do it in a written book you'd bring with you, or maybe on your laptop," Dr. Thomas instructed, taking a few notes in his notebook.

"Is it something you're going to look at?" Aaron asked, his mind racing through the possibilities of what kind of program he'd want to use. There was no doubt this would be something he'd do on the computer, because he hated writing longhand.

"Yes, at least parts of it," the older man said, watching Aaron's face closely.

Aaron thought about that for a moment and then nodded.

"I will give you directed exercises to write about, or you may want to write about things we've talked about in our sessions. This will give you an outlet for that."

*A blog.*

"I can put up a blog and set it so only friends can see the entries. That way, I can also make some of the entries private so no one can see them but me," Aaron told him with a shrug. The thought of keeping a diary, even an electronic one, wasn't all that appealing to him, but that glimmer of hope had started to rekindle in the back of his mind. He'd seen that glimmer once or twice before in the first few shrinks, but it soon became apparent they were completely inept when it came to helping him become human again. The hope had not resurfaced again, no matter how many shrinks his parents found for him.

Until now.

It wasn't just Dr. Thomas that made him feel hopeful; it was also Spencer. As Aaron looked up at his new friend, who smiled, Aaron felt the last vestiges of his panic and fear subside. It was strange how Aaron seemed to feel calmer with Spencer here after the flashback he'd experienced.

"I think that would work out well," Spencer's father said and followed his son into the kitchen, taking plates and glasses. Aaron looked around the large, comfortable room while he waited for them to return. He liked this room. It was light and airy, not oppressive like his bedroom. More than once, he'd wished for the same floor to ceiling windows that covered an entire wall of this room, just to get away from the dark.

Finally, taking longer than Aaron had expected, Spencer and his father came back into the room. Spencer's father was watching him, making Aaron feel a little uncomfortable. Spencer, however, looked almost… happy.

"Aaron, I have decided on your first directed exercise for the blog," Dr. Thomas said carefully. "Once Spencer has taken you home, I want you to create the blog and send me a link. First, write about how you feel about starting therapy with me, and second…." He paused for a long moment, looking back at Spencer, who smiled. "Second, I would like for you to describe how you believe you were able to touch Spencer immediately after your flashback, when you are seemingly unable to have anyone else touch you."

Aaron was stunned, and at first he considered the possibility Spencer's father was lying to him, and then… he looked at Spencer. Where he expected to see pity in Spencer's eyes, he saw only hope and something he didn't quite understand. It was the kind of look his mother gave him when he expressed any kind of interest in anything.

"Wait, what? I…." Aaron didn't need to finish the sentence, because Spencer nodded at him enthusiastically. Closing his mouth, he realized he was still staring at Spencer, who merely smiled at him, affirming he had in fact touched Spencer. It was something he had no conscious knowledge of, and he couldn't wait to get Spencer in the car so he could ask him about it.

"SO, I just reached up and touched you?" Aaron asked in utter disbelief. He had absolutely no memory of it. Vaguely, he recalled he wanted Spencer to look at him so he could make his friend feel better. It had been Aaron's fault, not Spencer's, that he'd had a flashback. Normal people can tolerate being tapped on the shoulder; there was no way Aaron could let Spencer feel guilty. Spencer was looking down, and that frustrated Aaron because, not only did that cut off their communication, but he found he liked looking into his friend's face. His eyes expressed every emotion, every reaction, just as if he'd spoken them aloud.

Spencer nodded, and the barest trace of a smile pulled his lips up at the corner. Aaron smiled in spite of himself. Deep down, he had to admit he liked the idea of touching Spencer's face. He just wished he knew how it had been possible.

As Spencer drove, silence fell over the car, and Aaron became lost in his thoughts. So much had changed about his life in the last few hours, which was strange to him since he still felt like the same damaged person he had been when he left for school that morning. Doctor Thomas had given him so much to think about, including, it seemed, his very first breakthrough.

His mother stopped him with questions about his forehead, startled that something had happened to him. He tried not to think about the last time he'd been hurt when she hadn't been there. With more patience than he knew he had, Aaron told her he'd cleaned it and dressed it himself. No, he didn't need her to check it. Yes, he'd put on antiseptic. Finally, he told her he had homework just so he could get away.

When he got up to his room, Aaron quickly pulled out his laptop and sat on his bed. There were hundreds of sites he could use for his blog, but a quick search of his favorite technology reviews narrowed down his options. What he really needed was a site where he could choose to publish some of his entries to registered users and some only for himself. There were just some things Aaron was sure Dr. Thomas would have him write about that the good doctor didn't need to see.

Aaron found a site that matched his requirements, and it didn't take long to create the address. It actually took longer to come up with a title and a subtitle than the address. "A Fucked up kind of life," that just about summed it up. It felt a little strange to use that kind of language when the blog itself was for Dr. Thomas, whom Aaron considered an authority figure, but if it was going to help him, he had to make it his own.

The first blog entry, the one where he got to be poetic and introspective, came rather quickly, so he created a new post and started to type.

---

A Light in the Darkness

Posted by Aaron at 8/28/2010 6:43 PM | Add Comment | Personal

Darkness pervades my every thought, my every action. There is nothing, not a single reprieve from the horror that lives inside my head. It has ensconced itself, as surely as if it had been born there. Maybe it had.

Had there always been a dark place inside of me, and it merely took that one unspeakable act of violence to unleash it?

But what of the light?

---

"How did your study session with Spencer go?" Aaron's mother asked him as she came up that night to call him for dinner. Feeling immensely guilty about not sharing his flashback or his talk with Dr. Thomas, he merely replied it had been fine. Her face lit up, and she seemed genuinely pleased he was able to socialize with a friend. Aaron didn't have any concrete reason to hide his new relationship with Dr. Thomas, but deep down he held onto the belief that seeing this new therapist under his terms without any involvement from his parents would make a difference. That maybe because it was something he was doing for himself rather than something they were doing for him, there would be a positive outcome.

"I'm glad you two had a nice day. Why don't you wash up and come down for dinner. I made tacos," she told him, smiling as she picked up his laundry hamper and left the room. For the first time in his life, he felt a little guilty about allowing her to wait on him like that, and resolved to take it down to the laundry room next time and get his brothers to do the same.

It was about time the Downing boys started carrying their weight.

"Allen, could you hand me the cheese?" Aaron asked his brother as they sat at the dining room table just a little while later. While his mother watched, stunned, Aaron dug into his third taco. He hadn't eaten very much of the pizza at Spencer's, and he found to his delight he was rather hungry. It didn't happen often, and he was going to take full advantage. Allen looked at him for a minute and then set the bowl of shredded cheddar cheese between them. Anthony, who sat across from Aaron, was on his fifth taco.

"Okay, if you boys are going to eat like this every night, you're going to have to get jobs," John Downing commented as he watched his sons, completely delighted. Between them, the boys had eaten well over a dozen tacos, and it didn't look like they'd be stopping anytime soon. Aaron looked up just in time to catch the glowing look his parents exchanged, and it made him smile. His parents hadn't smiled, hadn't looked happy like that, in a long time.

"We should have a cookout this weekend," Anthony thought out loud between huge mouthfuls of food. "We haven't done that in, like, forever." Looking up hopefully at his father and then his mother, he smiled, and then at Allen's loud guffaws, picked the lettuce off his face.

As his mother started to answer, Aaron laughed, while she stopped midsentence and looked on in amusement.

For just one evening, it was almost as if nothing had happened, like he was normal. Aaron wished he knew how to make that last. He was almost reluctant to let it end and go upstairs to work on the blog. Shattering the good feeling hurt his heart, but after a few minutes, he trudged up to his room and sat down at his desk.

---

A Touch of Magic

Posted by Aaron at 8/28/2010 9:12 PM | Add Comment | Therapy

When Dr. Thomas told me I had touched Spencer, not once, but several times during the course of my episode, I didn't believe him. It wasn't until my eyes found Spencer's and I saw, not the pity I had expected, but hope, that I decided it must be true.

But why?

My own mother, the person I love most, who is closer to me than anyone else, can't touch me. This boy, whom I have known but a few weeks, has broken though when no one else could. How is that even possible?

My whole life, even when I was a child, people told me I had an analytical mind. I suppose that is why I always excelled at debate. Lately, my intellect has been completely overshadowed by fear and emotion, except when I am coding. It is only then, lost in the logic and the syntax, when my mind is fully engaged, that I feel any kind of connection to the boy I had been. When I code, I don't feel helpless.

Is that the key?

It can't be. There are other people, the instructor and other students, that I associate with programming. I didn't reach out and touch them. Those people aren't friends, though. Spencer is the first friend I have made since Juliette was killed. No one had ever approached me, had ever extended that hand of friendship.

Is that the difference?

How can kinship with a friend outweigh the relationship I have with my mother or my brothers? I've never reached out and touched my mom or Allen. A simple pat on the shoulder or just grabbing my hand causes an immediate panic. Even before their hand reached me, my whole body would tense, making my heart race.

With Spencer, I didn't even think about it, I just reached out for him.

Maybe that is the point.

I reached out for him. I controlled the touch. Could it really be that simple?

---

His hands shook as he typed the last word. Shifting in his desk chair, his back protested from being so tense for such an extended period. Time seemed to stop while he wrote, but his computer clock told him it had taken an hour just to write those simple paragraphs. He reread the last few lines. Maybe that was the secret—it was contact he initiated. But somehow, he didn't think that was the entire reason for success. Deep down, he believed he could touch Spencer not only because it was something within his control, but also… because it was Spencer. Aaron didn't want to admit this in a blog entry Dr. Thomas would read, but he couldn't help but feel there was something special about Spencer that allowed the contact to happen. Either because he was so understanding of Aaron's problems, or because he was such a great friend.

In his whole life he'd never felt closer to anyone, not even Juliette, and it had happened so quickly.

"I think you made very good progress with the blog," Dr. Thomas said a few days later, as Aaron sat cross-legged on the floor of the rec room eating Chinese takeout. Spencer and his father had mastered the art of chopsticks, but Aaron ate with a fork, much to Spencer's amusement.

The doctor had read Aaron's blog post aloud at the start of the session, so he felt relieved that he hadn't put in anything about how close he felt to Spencer. Neither Spencer nor his father needed to know that bit, especially since he wasn't really sure what it meant.

"Thanks, I'd never really thought about doing a blog before. The shrinks always wanted me to keep a diary, but it felt kind of girly. The blog makes more sense to me because I can configure the security on it, and keep the things I want private from ever being seen. I feel more comfortable with that than with a little heart-shaped lock that wouldn't even keep out my twelve-year-old brother." Aaron took another long drink of soda to wash down the spicy noodles. His parents didn't like Chinese food, so he'd never had it before. Too embarrassed to admit that, he ordered the same thing Spencer got, and to his surprise, he really liked the chicken and noodle dish.

"I'm glad you feel comfortable with it. I think it's going to be invaluable when you start analyzing some of your behavior patterns. I have a few more questions I want to address before we get to today's session. Do you self-medicate?" Dr. Thomas asked as he set his Chinese takeout box on the table and picked up the notebook he used for their sessions. A pen appeared almost out of nowhere, and he looked up at Aaron expectantly.

"I don't know what you mean. Like do I take the pills myself without following the directions or something?" Aaron asked as he pulled another forkful of noodles from the container and popped them in his mouth.

"That, or do you drink?"

"I only take the pills when I get really stressed out, like when I have a flashback or something bad happens and I can't deal with it. I used to drink, a lot," Aaron admitted and then wished he hadn't said it. His parents could get into trouble if anyone knew their underage son drank.

When he stopped talking abruptly, Dr. Thomas grabbed his soda from the table and popped open the top.

"Aaron, I'm not here to judge you for drinking. In fact, I'd honestly be surprised if you didn't after what you went through. It's a horrible thing to cope with, and alcohol is a pretty effective way not to think about it anymore. Of course, it's not a long-term solution by any means, but I need to know all of the elements of your situation in order to be able to help you."

"I did drink. I'd sneak liquor from my parents' cabinet, only… after a while, I don't think it was much of a secret anymore. I think they were at a loss about how to help me. They never said anything about the missing booze, but they had to know. At least they could get some sleep at night too," Aaron finished in almost a whisper, ashamed he'd forced his parents to condone underage drinking just to be able to sleep.

"And when did that stop?" Dr. Thomas asked quietly.

"When I met Spencer." The words were out of Aaron's mouth before he could stop them.

Spencer looked up, chicken and noodles suspended in midair from frozen chopsticks. Aaron's face heated as he studiously avoided Spencer's gaze, and he felt the blush radiate, lighting up the room. Aaron caught the look Dr. Thomas gave him, and then Spencer, and wished he could melt into the carpet.

Dr. Thomas continued to question Aaron, who answered the best he could. Spencer became unnaturally quiet as he watched from the corner, and Aaron would have given anything to know what was on his mind. If only he had the balls to ask.

# FOURTEEN

SPENCER: Okay, I've been looking at this for an hour! WTF!?! I am taking a break. Please tell me what I am missing?? Please???

SPENCER: public static class StringExtensions

```
{
Public static DateTime ParseDateTime(string dt)
{
string dayOfWeek = dt.Substring(0, 3).Trim();
string month = dt.Substring(4, 3).Trim();
string dayInMonth = dt.Substring(8, 2).Trim();
string year = dt.Substring(10, 4).Trim();
string dateTime = string.Format("{0} - {1} - {2}", dayInMonth, month, year);
DateTime returnValue = DateTime.Parse(dateTime);
return returnValue;
}
}
```

Aaron laughed a bit at Spencer's frustration because he knew exactly what that felt like. He'd just gone through it a few days ago when he screwed up and forgot the base index on an array was 1, not 0. So, his entire loop was off by one value. It drove him crazy until he finally found it. Copying Spencer's code into his .Net development environment, it took him about ten minutes to create a quick program to instantiate the class and bounce data off it. Isolating the problem code made troubleshooting easier than keeping it in the entire application, if at all possible.

The first date he sent into the instantiated object worked fine; so did the second and the third. *Okay, you want to be difficult then.* He thought back to what Dr. Mayer had taught them just the other day about testing their applications—always test the extremes, the boundaries, and anything it's not supposed to be. If a user *can* enter something into an interface, they *will*. So, he took the lowest and highest dates that the DateTime type would accommodate. They were fine. With all the specific substring functions Spencer used, maybe it had more to do with the format of the date when it came into the class. Not to mention he had no error trapping and no formatting tests within the class. It was almost like he wanted a user to fuck it up. So, instead of entering a date with the standard format, he dropped the first digits on the month and day and entered 1/1/2000 instead of 01/01/2000. *Bingo*

AARON: Fuck yeah!

Aaron minimized the chat window and went to work on adding some testing to the class for different date formats while he waited for Spencer's response. He was surprised when the computer dinged almost immediately. Spencer must be done with his break and back to coding. When he brought up the window again, his breath froze in his lungs.

SPENCER: Fuck! You make me so hard.

*What. The. Ever-loving. Hell?* He pushed the desk chair back, distancing himself from the shocking words on his screen. Panic choked off his lungs, and his heart threatened to leap from his throat. Aaron couldn't believe, after everything they'd talked about, everything they'd been so careful *not* to say, how Spencer could say that to him. A vibe must come off him that just says *fuck with me*. God, he couldn't do it. He couldn't be friends with Spencer if that was the expectation. He couldn't.... He just... he....

SPENCER: Oh my God, I'm so sorry. That was not meant for you. I was talking to someone else in another window, and when yours came up, I didn't check the name.

Aaron couldn't breathe, he couldn't answer, he couldn't do anything but just stare at the words on the screen and try to stop the images that flooded his mind. As he pulled back up to the desk, his hands shook on the keyboard. His throat burned as the words came back to him and assaulted his mind.

*Suck me good, that's right, kid, make me hard so I can fuck you.*

*You make me so hard.*

SPENCER: Please, Aaron. I am sorry. Please say something.

AARON: I found your error. I'll send the code in an e-mail.

SPENCER: Not about the code, I could give a fuck about the code right now.

AARON: What the hell kind of conversation were you having that you would send that to me by accident?

Anger, humiliation, fear, it all swirled and burned in his chest. Damn it, he hated feeling like that, so out of control, and all over a few words on the screen. No wonder his parents wanted to dump him off somewhere.

SPENCER: I was talking to someone online about sex, getting off while we talked. I never meant for you to see it. I don't get a lot of action since people think I'm retarded. I have to take it where I can get it.

Aaron didn't go online much, and he certainly didn't socialize when he did. He couldn't even socialize with people standing in front of him, much less people all over the world. Though, maybe it would be easier to talk to someone he would never see. He had no idea. Everything had been so screwed up for such a long time, nothing seemed real anymore, nothing but the fear.

AARON: Do you do that a lot? Maybe we shouldn't talk over chat.

SPENCER: No, I don't do it a lot. Just sometimes.

AARON: Why?

SPENCER: Why don't I do it a lot, or why do I do it at all?

AARON: Both, I guess.

SPENCER: I do it because I am sick of being alone. It feels good to be wanted, even by someone I will never see. I don't do it often because it just feels empty.

Aaron didn't know what to say to that, but he didn't want Spencer to feel empty, and he didn't want Spencer to feel guilty about screwing up the screens for his chat. Yes, it had shocked Aaron, and he hated the way it scared him, but Spencer hadn't done it intentionally to hurt him or torture him. Somewhere deep inside, he knew Spencer wouldn't. A quick but confusing image of Spencer lying back on a nondescript comforter with his hand wrapped tightly around his cock flashed through Aaron's mind, and he jerked his hand away from the keyboard as if he'd been burned. It was the first sexual thought he'd had in such a long time. Fear boiled up, bubbling from his stomach to his chest, and filled him with such conflicting emotions he had a hard time processing them. *Fear, attraction, guilt, lust... panic.*

AARON: I have to go. I'll e-mail the code.

Before Spencer could send another reply, Aaron slammed his laptop shut. He could almost hear the drugs from his parents' medicine cabinet calling to him, offering him a way to forget the image of Spencer on his bed, of the rapists on top of him, and of Juliette—always of Juliette begging him to make them stop.

The pills were in his hand before he could change his mind.

"FOR this exam, you have the entire lab period of three hours, but I doubt it will take any of you that long. When you're finished, you can leave," Dr. Mayer told the students, and Aaron decided he would text his mom after he got out of the exam. While he didn't think Dr. Mayer would think it was cheating if he texted her now, he didn't want to have any problems with anyone else. He looked at Spencer, who gave him a smile, and he returned it tentatively. It was nice to have someone look at him and smile instead of cringe.

As he expected, the exam wasn't even really a challenge for him. He missed having Intellisense to finish the code when he started typing so he didn't have to remember all the methods and properties. For example, he knew the default event handler for the text box was ontextchanged, but it took a second to remember if the listbox was activeitem or selecteditem. He had no problems explaining the difference between mousedown, mouseup, and click.

Spencer turned to the next page on his exam, surprising Aaron, who had just started the last question of the first page. The competitive streak in him that reared its head shocked him. There had been nothing resembling ambition or the desire to win at something since his attack. With a grin, he finished up the question and sped on to the next page. When he flipped to the third page first, Spencer smirked and flipped his page seconds later. It seemed Spencer had caught on with his little game and decided to give him a challenge.

For the first time in a long time, Aaron felt good.

Spencer startled him by standing up suddenly and putting his backpack on. Aaron was on the last page of the exam, and he chuckled under his breath at his loss to his friend. *His friend.* He watched Spencer hand in his exam and wink at him as he walked out of the lab. Glancing back down at his exam, he found he only had the bonus question left. *Explain how to use a third-party application programming interface within the Visual Studio development environment.* He snorted quietly. That was exactly what he and Spencer were doing in their project. He wondered if Spencer skipped the question, and that's how he'd beaten him. Making a mental note to text Spencer and ask him if he'd answered the bonus question, Aaron began to write, because he never knew when a few points would mean the difference between a pass and a fail. He had to do the best he could on his good days in order to make up for the bad.

Today was a good day.

Finishing up his answer, he grabbed his laptop bag and carried the exam down to Dr. Mayer, who was looking up at him smiling.

"Not too difficult, I take it?" the instructor asked, and Aaron saw that Dr. Mayer was pleased he'd finished so quickly.

"No, not too hard at all," Aaron said, handing him the exam paper.

"Good. I think your partner in crime is waiting for you, so I'll see you in class next week," Dr. Mayer said, tilting his head toward the door. Aaron looked over, and, sure enough, Spencer was standing in the doorway waiting for him. Rather than being upset or feeling cornered as he normally would if someone were waiting to talk to him, he was pleased.

"See you next week, Professor," Aaron told his instructor and moved toward the door. They walked down the hall a bit so they didn't disturb the other students taking the test.

"Lunch.?" Spencer asked in his slow cadence. Aaron looked at his watch. If he didn't text his mom, she wouldn't be there for another two hours. Normally, he went straight to class and straight home afterward. With the exception of the bookstore, the dean's office, and the library, Aaron hadn't seen any other parts of the school. He wasn't even sure he knew where the cafeteria was. He almost refused, not wanting to take the chance that something could happen to set him off. Someone could bump him in line for food, or recognize him from high school like that girl from the bookstore. In the end, his desire to be close to Spencer won out.

When they reached the line for the hot food, Spencer allowed Aaron to go in front of him, and put himself between his friend and the people who had come behind. Very careful not to touch Aaron, he put an effective barrier between Aaron and the rest of the line behind them. Aaron was careful to stay a little away from the person in front of him, and he relaxed. Spencer had known almost instinctively what Aaron needed, and he'd done it without a second thought.

"What looks good?" Aaron asked Spencer as the person in front of Aaron placed his order.

Spencer said quietly, glancing behind him, that he was just going to get a burger and fries. Aaron looked over the board and decided to get chicken strips.

"What'll it be?" the bored woman on the other side of the counter asked loudly as the boy in front of Aaron moved away.

"We'd like chicken strips and a cheeseburger, both with fries," Aaron told her, with a smile at Spencer, who relaxed next to him. Aaron understood exactly what it was like to feel self-conscious. He noticed the woman's stare linger on the scar on his face as he placed his order. If Spencer could keep people from touching him, he could certainly keep Spencer from having to talk out loud to people who would think he was retarded because of his slow speech. It pissed Aaron off, because Spencer was one of the smartest people Aaron knew.

As Aaron had learned in a most brutal way, life wasn't fair.

Spencer pulled out his wallet and paid for their lunches before Aaron could protest. Spencer signed something at him, but since he didn't know anything about sign language, he didn't understand. Then Spencer held up one index finger, indicating that he should wait a minute as they walked to a deserted table near the far wall of the open seating area. As they sat across from each other, Spencer opened his bottle of water and took a long drink, then said, "Sorry., I. Forgot. You. Do. Not. Sign.. I. Said. Thanks.."

"Would it make things easier if I did? I…. Could you teach me? I mean, if it would make things better for you," Aaron rambled, embarrassed by his inability to get his point across. He used to be a damn fine public speaker, but since he rarely spoke to anyone but his mother since that night, the ability seemed to be lost.

Spencer smiled across the table, a quiet, shy kind of smile, and though he looked down for just a moment, Aaron could see it lit up his face.

"I. Have. Never. Had. A. Friend. Offer. To. Learn. To. Sign. For. Me.," he said quietly over the muted conversations all around them in the cafeteria, conversations that wouldn't so much as register for Spencer, but distracted Aaron.

Hyperaware of everything around him, he glanced behind him every few seconds to make sure no one stood there… watching… waiting for someone to burn him, or… or worse. All of a sudden, Spencer stood up.

"What?" Aaron asked, jerking all the way around in his seat.

"Trade. With. Me.," Spencer said as he pushed his tray to the outside seat.

"What?" Aaron asked again.

"Trade. Places. With. Me.. You. Are. So. Jumpy.." Spencer pulled Aaron's tray across the table to the seat he had vacated just in front of the wall. Aaron moved out of the way so Spencer could take his seat, keeping far enough away so not even their fingers touched. Though, if he were completely honest with himself, Aaron wanted to let them. He wanted to see if he could touch Spencer like he had that first night of therapy. He missed the comfort and encouragement that could be found in someone else's touch. The idea shocked him.

Spencer probably would have been horrified.

Aaron ate in silence, his mind spinning around the image in his head. In his mind's eye, he could see himself reaching out to touch Spencer's hand. The murmur in the room ceased to register with Aaron, and time stopped as his hand almost itched to move. He could feel the warm, soft skin of Spencer's hand under his fingers, and it made his pulse race. A fine sheen of sweat covered his face and rolled cold down the back of his neck.

"Hey. Man., Are. You. Okay.?" Spencer asked, breaking the spell of his daydream, and Aaron flushed.

Humiliated and ashamed, Aaron closed his hand tightly into a fist around his empty pop can and pushed his tray away, suddenly nauseated. What the fuck had he been thinking? The dull tabletop, the rubbery food, the chaotic chatter in the room, nothing had changed, but Aaron felt like his world had tipped on its axis. All he'd done was think about touching another boy's hand, and he could no longer function. He couldn't bring himself to contemplate what that meant, but it broke his heart nonetheless.

"Aaron.?"

Aaron looked up, tears trying to form at the corners of his eyes. The burn in his throat told him that his body wanted to let loose and sob right there at the lunchroom table. He could feel the ache in his chest threatening to burst from him, but something held it in. Careful not to touch him, Spencer pulled the soda can from Aaron's hand before the sharp edges of the crushed aluminum cut his skin.

"You. Know. You. Can. Talk. To. Me. Too., Right? I. Will. Not. Tell. My. Dad. If. You. Do. Not. Want. Me. To.." Spencer's face showed such care and concern that Aaron nearly told him about wanting to touch his hand, but then couldn't force the words out. What did it say about him that, after being brutally raped by a group of guys, he wanted to then touch one? Getting morning wood made him want to throw up. He shook his head, almost violently, and pushed his food away, unable to get the image of touching Spencer from his mind, no matter how much it nauseated him.

# FIFTEEN

THERAPY with Dr. Thomas was different from anything he'd ever experienced with another shrink. It felt like, since his therapist put the ownership on him to get better, Aaron just seemed to try harder. Dr. Thomas wanted to make him better for Spencer. Though he had to admit Spencer's father had him intrigued about the different methods the man could teach him to control his freak attacks.

"I can't believe part of my therapy involves playing video games," Aaron said as the game loaded on Spencer's huge flat-panel television. Spencer continued to look directly at him as his leg bounced against the couch cushion beneath it. Music came on for the game, and Aaron looked up, but Spencer didn't turn his head, and it took a second for Aaron to remember that he couldn't hear it. He selected a character, and after a minute, Spencer did the same.

"Having. Something. To. Distract. You. From. Your. Head. Helps.," Spencer said as he picked the mushroom car, which sucked for speed but worked well on the rainbow course because it was less likely to throw you off the side.

Aaron had picked up all the tricks over the last few days playing with Spencer. He thought maybe he could even go home and kick his brothers' asses at it after a while. Playing with Spencer was so easy because, while he lost as often as he won, Spencer took everything in stride. No gloating when he won, and no tantrums when he lost. Aaron liked that Spencer was so even-tempered; it made his "therapy" easier.

Dr. Thomas had also suggested movies, books, surfing the web, and something Aaron hadn't really considered—doing something he enjoyed before the attack. The one thing he thought he might be able to do was soccer. With no physical contact, it might be easy to get Anthony to go in the back yard and kick around the ball with him for a while. Aaron liked the sunshine, and playing soccer gave him a reason to be outside. Before the whole world changed around him, Aaron used to love the outdoors.

"Damn. It.!" Spencer cried suddenly, and Aaron tried hard not to laugh as his friend went over the side of the track. "I. Always. Fuck. Up. On. That. Part.."

With Spencer's attention on the screen, Aaron couldn't tell him he had the same problem. The only thing Aaron could do was slow quickly and round the same corner, narrowly staying on the track to take the lead. The steering wheel slipped in his sweaty hands as he crossed the line and started the second round with a huge burst of powerup speed and a weapon in his arsenal. He hated using the shell torpedo things against Spencer, but that was all part of the game.

"You. Just. Wait. Until. I. Get. That. Spiked. Shell.," Spencer warned, and even though he knew his friend couldn't hear him, Aaron laughed.

He felt freer than he had since that dark night, and for once, he was okay with it. For whatever reason, Dr. Thomas thought playing video games would help him, so he'd allow himself just a little slack. In the end, maybe he could take some of the pressure off his mother by being a functioning human being.

The game continued for the next several minutes, Aaron and Spencer sharing first place all the way though the game. When the final flag flew, Aaron stood victorious, but in the overall standings, Spencer took first place for the cup. He tossed the controller off to the side of the couch and fell back against the cushions. Turning his head, Spencer smiled at Aaron.

"That. Was. Fun.. I. Usually. Have. To. Play. By. Myself.." Even with the slow timbre, Aaron could still hear the sadness in his friend's voice. He wondered what life must have been like for Spencer growing up, always being different, not having brothers or sisters. In school, Aaron had had a lot of friends. His high school wasn't big, so he knew most of the people in his class, and there were always friends at his house. Aaron hated that he'd taken that away from his brothers. Because they could never be sure what would set him off, they never brought friends home.

The house used to be full of light and laughter, but after his attack, it was all darkness, fear, and anger. At least, that's how it felt to him.

*Distraction.*

"Did you go to a special school for deaf kids?" His voice shook slightly, and he wondered if Spencer sensed the desperation in it. Grabbing one of the throw pillows from the couch, Aaron wrapped his arms around it. It didn't replace the feeling of someone holding him, helping to hold all the emotions in, but the knot in his chest loosened just a little.

Spencer held up one finger, asking Aaron to wait just a moment, and left the room. The silence enveloped Aaron, and his leg bounced so hard he actually heard his socked heel hitting the carpeted floor. It was a nearly inaudible thumping, which reminded him of a wild heartbeat. He focused on the sound, and nothing else. The thoughts slamming into his brain about how much better his parents and his brothers would be without him were pushed aside so he could narrow in entirely on that sound. He sped up the bouncing and heard the sound speed up too. He forced himself to slow it down, and the sound slowed as well. He controlled the movements, making a kind of song, distracting himself until Spencer came back. His friend had only been out of the room for a few minutes, but the room seemed to have no air in it.

"I. Put. In. Some. Egg. Rolls. To. Snack. On.." Spencer said as he walked back through the door. He couldn't see the way Aaron had to force himself to breathe, or that the throw pillow was dangerously close to an early demise in the boy's trembling hands. He didn't see the droplets of sweat bead down the side of his face in the otherwise cool room. Spencer simply picked up their laptops from the desk and went back to the couch. Handing Aaron's to him, Spencer opened his and logged on.

SPENCER: It is easier to talk this way.

He looked up to see the distress on his friend's face, and Aaron saw him catch his hand as he reached for Aaron.

SPENCER: You need to breathe, Aaron. Just like Dad taught you. Slow, deep breaths.

Aaron closed his eyes and forced the image of himself hanging from the garage rafters from his mind. Opening them again, he focused on

Spencer's face and noticed that Spencer was breathing very slowly, trying to encourage him. Aaron took a deep breath and lost himself in Spencer's pale skin. He didn't think he'd ever noticed that Spencer had tiny little freckles over his nose and the tops of his cheeks. The green in his eyes stood out more than the specs of brown with the hunter green Grateful Dead T-shirt he wore today. Other colors were prominently featured in the shirt, but the collar and shoulders were a deep green. He found it interesting that Spencer's eyes changed color. Aaron's eyes were always exactly the same color of blue, or so he thought. He didn't look at himself anymore.

SPENCER: No, I did not go to a special school. My dad thought it would be better to mainstream me with other kids. In some ways, he was right. I was forced to live life like a hearing person, which gave me skills I needed, but no one wanted to be friends with the deaf retard.

AARON: That had to be hard.

Talking to Spencer helped because his death seemed to be harder to see. The rope wasn't gleaming white in the otherwise darkened garage. The bluish tinge to his skin had faded.

SPENCER: I was in an afterschool program for deaf kids at the community center off Grand Ave., so I had friends there. We felt more comfortable with each other, much more comfortable than hearing kids felt with us. They were not all mean. A lot of them just did not know how to approach me, or what questions they could ask.

AARON: I know what it's like to have no friends. Before, I had a lot of friends. I guess I was one of the popular kids, whatever that means. But after, I couldn't stand for people to look at me. It freaked me out completely when Mayer said I'd have to have a project partner this term. I figured I'd get a Barbie doll who would have to go puke every time she looked at me.

SPENCER: Fuck, Aaron. I never thought that about you, and I bet you are imagining most of the reactions you get. When I saw you that first time, I wondered what the hell could have happened to you to make you act like that just from a hand on your shoulder. I wanted to help you.

AARON: It could just be because you are more empathetic than most.

SPENCER: It could. But it does not matter, because you are stuck with me now.

AARON: Oh no.

Spencer laughed, loud and long, which made Aaron smile.

AARON: How do you know how to laugh if you can't hear other people laugh?

SPENCER: It is like sneezing, I guess. It just comes out. For a long time when I was a kid, I felt self-conscious about it and about other sounds that I would make because I never knew if they were right. My aunt worked with me for a long time until I felt comfortable with things like laughing, clapping, word pronunciation and dialect, and even belching. Social niceties are learned, and a lot of them are learned through sound. It is amazing what hearing people take for granted.

AARON: You've worked really hard to compensate for being deaf.

SPENCER: Which is surprising, since I am totally lazy. ;)

"You are not lazy," Aaron said through his laughter, and without thinking about it, pushed Spencer's shoulder. When he caught sight of Spencer's surprised face, he jerked his hand back. "Sorry."

Spencer shifted on the couch and pulled his leg up beneath him so he faced Aaron.

SPENCER: Do not be sorry. I do not know why you can touch me without having problems, but I think it is some kind of breakthrough for you.

AARON: I think it's because I'm doing the touching. When people touch me, it just takes me back to that place. When I touch someone else, it's under my control. I just never thought about doing it before, and I really never thought I'd like it.

Aaron realized what he'd just admitted, that he wanted to touch Spencer, and his stomach tied in knots. Spencer wasn't gay, and straight guys didn't like other guys touching them. While he didn't think Spencer would beat the crap out of him for it, he couldn't imagine that Spencer would invite him to just rub on him whenever he wanted. His thoughts were confirmed with Spencer's next instant message.

SPENCER: I am going to go check on the egg rolls.

He nodded at Spencer because there wasn't really anything to say. When Spencer came back a few minutes later with a plate full of egg rolls, soy sauce, and a couple of sodas, Aaron didn't bring up the subject again. Content just to be in Spencer's company, he ate quietly. Spencer wouldn't be able to read his lips while he had a mouth full of food anyway.

"Do. You. Want. To. Play. Another. Game.? I. Have. Tons.. Dad. Seems. To. Think. Stuff. Compensates. For. Being. Deaf.," Spencer told him with a shrug, causing him to look around at all the shiny toys in the rec room with a new perspective. Aaron's father did well and provided the family with what they needed, but he didn't think they had the money for all the extravagant stuff sitting around in Spencer's house. Just in this room alone, Spencer had every gaming console on the market, a state of the art desktop computer, a laptop, two huge flat-panel televisions, an iPad, and his iPhone—and that was just in plain sight. The furniture, lush and expensive, looked practically brand new. Aaron wondered if they had just bought it, or maybe if they never used it. The room had a stiff, unlived-in look, even with all the toys. Even the house itself was an extravagance. Spencer had taken him on a tour the last time he was over, and they had five bedrooms for just the two of them.

"It's so quiet here. With my brothers, our house is always total chaos," Aaron mused.

Spencer's expression turned wistful.

"What?"

"I. Wish. I. Had. Brothers.."

"So, next time, let's play at my house. My brothers would love to play." Aaron's voice swelled with his excitement. His mother would be ecstatic. She liked Spencer, and she'd love for Aaron to have someone over just to hang out. His brothers liked Spencer and had already invited him back to play.

"I. Would. Like. That.. It. Gets. Really. Lonely. Here.."

"Your dad never seems to be home. Is he gone a lot?"

"He. Goes. To. A. Lot. Of. Conferences.. He. Is. Saving. The. World.," Spencer said with a snort, but something about his demeanor seemed off. Aaron wasn't sure if Spencer was outright lying or just holding something back, but he decided to let it go. Spencer grabbed his laptop and started typing.

SPENCER: It has been like that for the last year or so since he stopped taking clients. He is gone a couple of weekends a month, and sometimes for a few days around them. That is why he keeps having to schedule out your therapy sessions around his stuff. Like you don't have a life too.

AARON: I don't have a life. The stuff he's teaching me, like the video games and the breathing exercises, they're helping. I haven't had a bad trigger lately, but the little stuff I'm able to breathe through.

SPENCER: Good. You know if there is anything we can work on together, all you have to do is ask, right? I want to help.

AARON: You are helping. I honestly feel better since we became friends. I'm getting out of the house. I'm living, even just a little bit. It's been so long since I had something to think about other than what happened.

SPENCER: Think your brothers would be up for a bit of play this weekend?

AARON: I'll ask them, but I know I would.

"THIS app is fantastic, boys," Dr. Mayer told Spencer and Aaron as they all stood huddled around Spencer's laptop, playing with the new interface. "The Twitter API isn't all that user-friendly, but you've even worked in their native security module. You're definitely getting an A, but what are you going to do with it now? I haven't seen anything like this on the free download sites."

"We've been talking about putting up a download site and then linking to it from all the major free download services. At least it will be something for Spencer to put on his resume. Especially if it takes off and becomes kind of popular," Aaron commented as he flipped to the next screen to show Dr. Mayer the interfaces he'd built for pulling random songs or files worked on for tweeting.

"What about your resume, Aaron?" Dr. Mayer asked, his voice quiet but kind. Aaron didn't look up immediately, but his fingers stalled on the touchpad of Spencer's laptop. Spencer looked between them with confusion clear in his face. He hadn't seen what Dr. Mayer said because he'd been watching the screen.

"I'm not capable of working, Dr. Mayer," Aaron said, and then let his voice drop to a whisper. "I can't be around people."

"What if you didn't have to be around people? I was thinking about asking you to TA for me next semester. I could e-mail you the stuff you need to grade or set up. You wouldn't need—" He stopped abruptly as Aaron began to back away from the small table where they all stood. A look of hopeless fear crossed the instructor's face, and Aaron could only imagine the expression on his own. The room had started to get smaller at the very mention of the job, but as Dr. Mayer tried to coax Aaron into accepting, something pulled the air from it as well. He couldn't breathe and it was hard to think with the blood pounding in his ears.

"Aaron?" Spencer asked, but Aaron just shook his head.

"Ask Spencer, I can't… I just… I…." He turned around and smacked headfirst into a tiny Asian boy coming into the room for the next class. Aaron screamed, and the other boy's face went from angry to frightened in an instant. He knelt quickly to grab his fallen books as Aaron's legs gave out and he fell to his knees. Spencer knelt right beside him on the classroom floor. Reaching for Aaron, his hand froze in midair when his friend cringed away like Spencer would hurt him.

"D…. Don't…. Don't touch…." Aaron stammered, and Spencer, whether because he could read Aaron's lips or just assumed, moved back several inches to give his friend space. Aaron stayed in the room enough to see the hurt flicker through Spencer's eyes before everything changed and he was in the garage.

"What a freak," a voice said somewhere outside the perimeter of the echoing, empty garage. The voice, however, didn't echo, and neither did the next voice.

"Clear the room, right now. Everyone out."

"Aaron. It. Is. Okay.." Another voice said, and that voice took the edge off the blinding fear. He was scared. So scared. But the feeling seemed to warble, like an out of tune radio.

"What. Do. You. See.? Aaron., Tell. Me. What. Is. In. The. Room.." Some part of Aaron's mind recognized that Spencer was trying to ground him, but he could see nothing but the garage. Insulation peeled and hung down from the ceiling in ragged sheets above his head. Water damage stained the brick walls which had once been painted white. The blue trim had faded long before he and Juliette lay helpless beneath it. His body ached, and the concrete under his mostly naked body chilled him bone-deep. He tried to look around, to answer the voice's question, but the shoe on the back of his neck made that impossible, so he answered the only way he could.

"Blood. All I can see is the blood."

"I. Do. Not. Know. What. To. Do.." Spencer's voice sounded helpless, just like Aaron. Soon, the knife would slice across his neck, and the end would come. Juliette's agonized screams echoed though his memory and broke his heart all over again. "Please., Aaron., Just. Breathe.." The sound of exaggerated breathing reached him, even in the garage, but he couldn't feel the breaths on the back of his neck. Throughout the whole horrible ordeal, he could feel their breath on the back of his neck when they were on top of him. He always felt their hands as they held him down; he couldn't feel them now. As he took deep breaths, matching the ones he could hear from Spencer, the flashback started to recede back into the darkness.

It took several minutes before he understood with absolute certainty that he was in a classroom.

Humiliation burned in his face when he saw not only Spencer, but Dr. Mayer sitting on the floor with him. If he reached out with his right hand, he could touch Spencer. Dr. Mayer sat a little farther away against the wall near the door. Thank fucking Christ it was Friday, and he wouldn't have to face either of them again until Monday. He wanted his mother with the fiery need of a five-year-old lost at Disneyland.

"Careful," Dr. Mayer said as Aaron sat up and put both hands on his throbbing head. The look his professor gave him in that moment slid down the scale from concerned to pitying, the longer Aaron sat there. He couldn't stand their pity—especially Spencer's. The look on his friend's face made hot coals fire up in his stomach. Bracing most of his weight on the wall, he slid up into a standing position.

"Maybe. You. Should…," Spencer started, but before he could finish, Aaron had burst through the door and taken off down the hall toward the parking lot where his mother would be waiting for him.

He just wanted to go home.

# SIXTEEN

"WHY do you think the grounding didn't work?" Dr. Thomas asked him as he sat curled in a tight ball in the supple overstuffed armchair in the rec room. The chocolate leather almost swallowed his tiny frame, but it made him comfortable. He couldn't say he felt safe, exactly, but usually he felt content. He couldn't quite muster contentment right then, because Spencer had been extraordinarily quiet throughout class, on the ride to his house, and as he sat on the floor in Aaron's therapy session. He couldn't help but feel that Spencer was angry with him for some reason, or maybe he just didn't want to hang around with the freak anymore. Aaron could certainly understand that. It had taken every ounce of self-determination to overcome the humiliation of what happened on Friday and walk back into the classroom. He hated facing Spencer and facing Dr. Mayer feeling so fucking weak, so inferior to every other person on the planet.

"I don't know," Aaron said automatically, shrugging and pulling his arms closer around his body. If he pulled in on himself tight enough, maybe he would disappear. He wanted to disappear—especially if it meant he could be away from Spencer's gaze. He lived in a huge spotlight, and the bright intensity of it highlighted his every flaw.

"Today I want to work on identifying some of your triggers. If you can learn to avoid those triggers or at least control your reaction to them, you'll have less of these debilitating episodes," Spencer's father said as he sat back on the couch and wrote something down in his little notebook. The tape recorder, ever present, sat in the middle of the table in front of Aaron. It pointed at him accusingly. "Now, walk me through what happened just before the event."

Aaron sighed. He'd tried so hard all weekend not to fucking think about it, and now Dr. Thomas wanted a play-by-play. Every time he thought about what happened, he only saw Spencer's frightened face.

"Dr. Mayer had just told me he wanted me to TA for him." He couldn't look up at them, the shame of his setback burning in his stomach. "He kept hounding me about it. The room got really small, and I had to get out of there. I didn't know what else to do. When I turned around to leave, I ran into someone. I felt the pain as we collided. A pain shot through my head, and it started. All of a sudden the classroom kind of melted away and I was back in the garage. Juliette was screaming. The men were there." Aaron closed his eyes, trying to block out the images he saw in his head.

"Okay, stop there. What do you think triggered the flashback? Was it the pain, or running into the person? What are some other factors? Were you tired or stressed at all?" Dr. Thomas asked as he scribbled furiously on his little pad.

Aaron tried to think back to that moment and remember with perfect clarity the classroom where he and Spencer showed Dr. Mayer their project. Things had been going so well until Dr. Mayer brought up the subject of being a TA.

"I think it started with the stress and humiliation of the conversation," Aaron reasoned. "A normal person could have talked to their professor about working for him, but all I could think about was how horribly I would fail. I couldn't be trusted, couldn't be counted on. Rainy days leave me incapacitated in bed, and then what would he do?"

"So, it started with a fear of failure."

"It started with me being a coward," Aaron argued and sunk deeper into the chair, trying to get lost in its depths.

"You. Are. Not. A Coward.!" Spencer cried, and Aaron looked over at him, startled. He noticed that Dr. Thomas was also watching his son. "You. Are. So. Brave. Just. For. Living.. I. Do. Not. Know. If. I. Could.."

"That isn't bravery, Spencer. I don't have any other choice," Aaron clarified. Spencer rocked back and forth slightly in his position on the floor but didn't make any move to get up or move closer to Aaron.

"Have you had thoughts of suicide?" Dr. Thomas asked, and Aaron hesitated. He had—many of them, but he didn't trust the good doctor enough to voice these episodes aloud. He knew that if Dr. Thomas thought him a danger to himself, he'd have no choice but to lock Aaron up somewhere. He'd be in a cell away from his family, away from Spencer. His throat constricted around the answer, but he couldn't lie.

"Doesn't everyone from time to time?" Aaron answered evasively.

"That. Is. Not. An. Answer.," Spencer said quietly, and Aaron saw the desperate sadness in his friend's face. Aaron traced the creases in the arm of the leather chair with his fingers, staring intently at his progress. He didn't have an answer they wanted to hear, so he decided on the truth.

"Sometimes," he whispered. A long line in the leather near the edge of the chair took an inordinately long time to draw with his finger while silence stretched in the rec room. All Aaron heard was the ticking of a clock somewhere in the room. He counted along with the seconds, trying to distract his mind from the dark thoughts that threatened to invade it.

*1... 2... 3... 4....*

"Have you ever tried?" Dr. Thomas asked.

*8... 9... 10... 11....*

"No."

"Do you have a plan of how you would do it? A time? A place?"

*15... 16... 17... 18....*

"I've thought about hanging myself in the garage, but I can't stand the thought of one of my little brothers finding me, or my mom, or really anyone in my family. I've put them through so fucking much. They don't need that in their heads forever. I have enough in my head for all of us." Aaron's voice cracked with the weight of just exactly what was in his head.

*24... 25... 26... 27....*

"Aaron, while I don't think it's healthy for you to have these thoughts, it's not unreasonable given what you've been through. You don't have a concrete plan. You don't have a history of suicide attempts. You're starting to form a support network. You're working through your emotions in therapy. I'm concerned, but not to the point where I would have any legal basis to admit you for observation. That scares you, doesn't it?"

Dr. Thomas dropped his notepad on the couch and sat forward with his elbows on his knees. His hazel eyes, so like his son's, were intent on Aaron's. Aaron nodded. Glancing over, he saw the concern and fear in Spencer's eyes and for a moment forgot about counting the seconds with the clock to distract him. An overpowering need to hug Spencer took hold of Aaron's heart. He couldn't think of anything else.

In the next second, it was gone.

"Let's get back to your triggers. Your flashback at the school appeared to be caused by a combination of stress and bumping into the other student," Dr. Thomas said as he picked up his notebook again and began writing. "What about a flashback you've had before that. Do you remember your last one?"

Aaron thought back. The subject made his skin crawl with unpleasant anxiety. He remembered seeing Allen standing in the living room with his date. He remembered with horrifying accuracy the look of rage on his brother's face as he lost control. God, he hated ruining Allen's first date, one of his first real chances at normalcy since Aaron had fucked up his life.

"What is it?" Dr. Thomas asked, no doubt having read the flickering emotions on his face.

Aaron took a deep breath.

"Whatever it is, you're safe from it here. Nothing is going to hurt you."

He snorted. The good doctor didn't understand that Aaron wasn't safe anywhere, not from the men who had stolen his life because they were still roaming free, not from the screaming in his head, and certainly not from the crash he'd experience if Spencer decided Aaron wasn't worth the effort. Aaron blinked, unsure where the last thought came from. Trying not to revisit that idea, he answered Dr. Thomas.

"I'd taken a nap in the afternoon and experienced a really bad nightmare. As I woke, I heard someone knocking on the door or ringing the bell—I don't remember exactly." Aaron closed his eyes, concentrating on the memory so he could relay it accurately. "I went downstairs because I thought the men had come back for me. I didn't want them to hurt my family. Allen was standing at the door with a date. He wore his letterman's jacket, just like the one I'd been wearing. I freaked out and had a complete meltdown in the living room. I'm pretty sure the poor girl hasn't spoken to Allen since."

"So you'd woken from a dream and were already vulnerable and stressed. You saw someone that looked like you had the night you were attacked. So stress was a factor, just like in the flashback in the classroom, and there was also a visual reminder." Dr. Thomas's voice was thoughtful as he wrote. "That's enough to work with for today. We're coming up on an hour, and I don't want to take on too much at a time. Tonight, I want you to find a safe place in your house and try to think of other triggers. You can write them on a piece of paper or put them on the blog, but make sure you're not alone when you work. Tomorrow, I want to work on a few stress reducing exercises, because that is usually a common trigger for individuals suffering with PTSD."

"I can do that. My mom will love it if I do some homework at the kitchen table. I haven't done that since we worked through my homeschool stuff together. I think she feels like what I'm doing now is out of her league."

"Do. You. Want. To. Play. A. Game.?" Spencer asked as his father gathered up his stuff and wandered out of the room. Aaron wasn't sure if he wanted to give them some time to talk or if he had something else to do.

"No, Joshua," Aaron said with a smirk as Spencer stared blankly at him. After a minute, the smile faded from Aaron's face. "It's from *Wargames*."

"I. Know. Where. It. Is. Fucking. From.." He slammed the lid on his laptop and shoved it across the table. Turning away from Aaron, he walked stiffly to the side table near the rec room door and grabbed his keys. "People. Have. Made. Fun. Of. The. Way. I. Talk. My. Whole. Life.. I. Did. Not. Think. You. Would. Be. One. Of. Them.."

Aaron's face flushed. He hadn't been making fun of Spencer at all. Unmoving, Spencer just stood waiting, but Aaron could see his friend's hands were shaking. Walking around to stand in front of Spencer, he waited, but the other boy wouldn't look up.

Aaron held out one hand just inches from the bare skin of Spencer's arm, but couldn't make himself touch—no matter how badly he wanted to.

The flashback still floated just beneath the surface of his mind, and he felt incredibly vulnerable. Breathing deeply in and out for nearly a minute, he pulled his cell phone from the pocket of his jeans.

AARON: I wasn't making fun of the way you talk. I don't even notice a difference. It was WHAT you said. Please don't be mad at me. I can't take it today on top of everything else. Please?

Aaron heard the phone buzz in Spencer's pocket and watched with growing apprehension as he checked the display. Then, almost too slowly, Spencer looked up, and Aaron felt a rush of warmth over his face, like he'd stepped into the sun. Spencer opened his arms, and without the hesitation Aaron expected, he stepped into them and rested his head on his friend's shoulder. A tentative hand rested on his back, but the comfort wrapped itself around him, and he sighed just as he heard Spencer's voice in his ear.

"I. Could. Never. Stay. Mad. At. You.."

# SEVENTEEN

*SPENCER stood in front of Aaron, soft chestnut curls spiraling around his downcast eyes, his manner so pregnant with supplication, so tempered by defeat, that Aaron's heart ached with it. When he could not stand it even one moment longer, Aaron did not stomp his foot as others might to get his attention. Instead, he reached out with no thought other than Spencer's comfort and touched his face. A tingling sensation, as if his hand had suddenly gone to sleep, startled Aaron, but he didn't pull away.*

*The warmth of his hand on Spencer's cheek caused Spencer to look up. An unreadable expression, shock maybe, flitted across his handsome features, and Aaron smiled. As their eyes met and Spencer held his gaze resolutely, Aaron had a wild impulse to kiss Spencer's slightly trembling lips. In fact, his stomach burned with the intensity, the need of it. A white hot tingle of anticipation tore down his spine in a violent shiver.*

*Was it Aaron's imagination, or were their faces closer?*

*He didn't know if he had moved closer or if Spencer had, but neither of them, it seemed, were willing to pull away. Aaron couldn't mistake the momentary look of longing that passed over Spencer's face or the way his eyes darted subtly to Aaron's mouth. Then Spencer leaned forward slightly in silent invitation.*

*Tilting his head almost imperceptibly, the sweet surprising sting of hope coursed through him as Aaron felt Spencer's breath on his face, hot and unsteady.*

*His lips touched Aaron's, soft and subtle….*

Aaron's heart raced as the dream clung to him and refused to recede into the dark part of his mind where hope lived. His breath came in short, quick pants as he sat straight up in bed, disoriented at being alone. Spencer had been right there with him, so close that the other boy's presence loomed large in the room. With mounting fear, he half expected Spencer to come back from the bathroom to crawl into bed with him. His cock ached in his sweats, harder than it had ever been, and Aaron could feel nothing but confusion. The room, almost unbearably warm, seemed different in the diffused light from his window. The monsters that normally loomed in the shadows were harder to see, the angry scars on his face and body slightly diminished by the image of Spencer in his mind.

Throwing his legs over the side of the bed, Aaron sat on the edge, holding tight to his sheet, trying to stop his world from spinning. Not once in two years had he dreamed of wanting to have any kind of physical or sexual contact—with anyone—and he had no idea how to handle it. Panic rose in his chest, and he took a deep breath in through his nose and blew out hard from his mouth just as Dr. Thomas had taught him. In through his nose, and out through his mouth. The panic swelled higher, like an ocean storm, and for a moment, he couldn't breathe. Then he closed his eyes and tried again. In through his nose and out through his mouth. Again and again he breathed, slowly and deliberately. The tightness in his chest lessened, and he could have wept, if only he were able.

"Aaron, honey, are you okay?"

Aaron looked up to see his mother standing in the doorway, her oversized pajamas making her look like a teenage girl, the way she pulled her hands into the sleeves and stretched the material as she stood nervously at his door. The way she bounced just a little on the balls of her feet told Aaron how much she wanted to come into his room and comfort him, but she kept her distance.

"I'm okay, Mom, it was just a dream," he said quietly to the floor, and breathed in slowly through his nose. She came in then, no doubt drawn to the fear and pain she heard in his voice. Making sure to keep a good foot between them, she sat down on the edge of the bed. He didn't look up, but simply blew out hard.

"Do you want to talk about it?" Her voice sounded small and quiet in the dark, not like her usual call-to-attention mom voice. Normally, she had a way of making three nearly grown boys and one man do whatever she wanted merely by changing the inflections of her tone. Aaron knew she expected him to say no, and he nearly always did, but the confusion and the pain in his heart made the words tumble out in a rush.

"I dreamed that I kissed someone," Aaron whispered into the darkness. The deep breathing exercise stopped, and he blushed, though he hoped his mother wouldn't see.

"Was it a good dream?" she asked, and Aaron's hand ached to sit, even for just a moment, on top of hers, but he didn't allow himself to move. His head had started to ache from the stress, and his throat, bone dry at the idea of saying it out loud, rasped as he answered.

"I don't… I don't know…. It just…. It feels so wrong to think about… about kissing someone. I can't… not after…." Aaron's face flushed further, and he was sure she could see it glow. If she did, she gave no indication.

"There isn't anything wrong with kissing someone, sweetheart. It scares me sometimes that because of what's happened, you wouldn't meet someone that made you look past the attack. I couldn't stand that, because you are so special, you deserve to find a person that loves you like I love your father." She hesitated, no doubt trying to decide what, if any, questions she could ask without closing the window on a really good chance to talk to her son. "Honey, have you ever kissed anyone?"

Aaron shook his head, and even in the dim light, he saw her nod.

"Does this person have a name?"

The blinding fear returned in an instant. It didn't even immediately register that she didn't say "Does this girl have a name?"

"I…," Aaron started, the lie forming on his lips, but he found he just couldn't do it. For so long, his mother had loved him despite his scars and sacrificed her time and sanity to care for him. She deserved better than to be lied to. "It… it was Spencer, Mom."

"Your friend from school?" she asked with a neutral expression.

He couldn't tell if the idea that he'd dreamt about kissing a guy surprised her or not. Maybe she figured, with the attack, he'd have to be gay.

"Yes, my friend from school," he whispered as his nerve failed. The words "I'm gay" wouldn't form in his throat so he could articulate them. With everything else he'd put her though, he couldn't say them aloud.

"Aaron, look at me." His mother's voice was soft and reassuring, so he did as she asked and noticed the small upturn of her mouth. It was hard holding her gaze while he had this conversation with her. It felt like they were shining a huge spotlight on everything wrong with him, and he'd been in the dark for so very long. She took a slow, deep breath before continuing. "I'm your mom. Did you really think I didn't know, honey? Even if I hadn't had years to come to terms with it.... Aaron, I almost lost you, my beautiful boy. I don't love you any less because you're gay. Neither will your father or your brothers. We thank God every single day that you're still in our lives, baby. That's just not something we would get upset over."

For the first time in two very long years, Aaron Downing began to cry.

"I thought they picked me because I was gay. If I'd been straight, Juliette would be alive, and you wouldn't have to take care of me like I was some kind of huge baby. And... and it was just one more thing for you to have to deal with on top of everything else. I hated it. I thought it was so stupid because I'd never meet anyone that would look past the scars and the spastic freak-outs, so what difference did it make? I don't know why Spencer is different, Mom, I don't even know if he's gay," he managed through heaving sobs. Tears ran down his frightened face in the darkness.

"Oh, honey, they picked you because you were there. Your father and brothers have lived with you all your life, and I'm sure they don't have any idea. Those... those men could not have known that you were gay. It was never your fault. Ever." She rubbed her hands on her knees, and it looked like it took every bit of willpower she had not to reach for him. "But as for your dream, have you talked to Spencer at all about being gay?"

"No. I mean, even if he is, why would he want me? I'm broken, Mom. I'm about as fucked up as you can get. He's such a—" He cut himself off, not willing to reveal every part of his heart, not yet. "He deserves someone whole."

"Two years ago, we never would have been having this conversation. You weren't rational enough to deal with it. I'd have given you a tranquilizer, waited until you were doped up enough, and kissed your forehead before going back to my room for a sleepless night, scared to death for you. I know that you feel fucked up"—Aaron gasped at her choice of words, but she didn't pause—"but, Aaron, you really are healing more every day. The progress you've made just since you've met Spencer is astonishing. I think his friendship is really good for you, but I think if he is gay you should take anything else between you very slowly. We can try another doctor if you think you're ready to talk to someone," she hedged.

Aaron still couldn't bring himself to tell her about Spencer's father. He knew she was right, and the time he spent with Dr. Thomas helped him. It felt like telling her, like sharing his secret, would ruin it. Becoming Dr. Thomas's patient was the first adult decision Aaron had ever made, and he wanted to hold onto it just a little longer, maybe until he had something substantial to share.

"I started a kind of journal," he replied, trying to give her something without revealing the whole truth. "It's helping me to sort out some of my feelings." The blanket caught every bit of his interest as he avoided her eyes.

"That's a good way to work things out," she replied just as a yawn escaped. "I'm glad we got to talk tonight. It's been a long time since we could just sit and talk." Reaching to pat Aaron on the shoulder, his mother drew back when she saw him flinch.

"Are you going to tell Dad what we talked about?" The underlying question screamed through the subtle wording. *Are you going to tell him I'm gay? Is he going to think everything is my fault? Will he hate me? Will he send me away?*

"I'm going to tell him that we talked and you're starting to cope better. Do you want me to tell him that you're gay?" Her voice was soft and understanding, like his answer would be okay no matter what it was. Aaron nodded, unable to voice the words. "I can do that. Anthony is a little young yet, but I think you should tell Allen. You two used to be so close. I want to see you have that kind of relationship again."

"I will, Mom… later," Aaron reluctantly agreed. "I think I'm going to try and sleep some more before I have to go to class. It's easier to deal with when I'm not tired." With a long, deep yawn, Aaron crawled back under his blankets. His mother pulled them up for him, careful not to touch him as she let go.

"I love you, Aaron," she said quietly as she stood.

He looked up and caught her gaze.

"I love you too, Mom."

*AARON hated it when Spencer looked down. Usually it was accompanied by a look of consternation or shame on his face. It made his heart hurt. Other people might have stomped on the floor, trying to get Spencer's attention as one might do with a dog, but he couldn't. Some force, some overwhelming need compelled him to touch Spencer's face. When he did, Spencer looked up and he smiled. Very slowly, as if gauging Aaron's reaction, Spencer leaned toward him, and he felt Spencer's warm, soft lips touch his in his very first kiss.*

*The panic he expected to well in him at the intimate contact never came. The only thing he felt in that moment was fire. Spencer's kiss was like an inferno, engulfing and burning off his fear, leaving only a residual heat. Tentatively, wary of his own ingrained reactions, he put his hands on Spencer's shoulders and was shocked by his reckless need. Spencer's fingers snaked up the back of Aaron's shirt, stroking his bare skin, and Spencer's lips moved to his neck. He let his head fall back. Not feeling the tight pulling of skin from his scars, he finally realized it was a dream. The weight of this crushing disappointment took him by surprise. He had thought that even in a dream, the reprieve from his damaged skin would have been a cause for joy, but it meant he wasn't really with Spencer.*

*Leaning into the kiss, knowing he was safe in this dream with Spencer, Aaron took this one unique opportunity to play out all his conscious and even repressed fantasies. Barely sixteen when his life changed, he had only just started to come to terms with being gay. He'd never had any kind of relationship with anyone, much less kissed or touched another boy. He'd fantasized about it, almost constantly, just as any other boy his age would have, but that horrifying night even took those from him. Whenever he thought about another boy after that, all Aaron could think about was pain and shame.*

*Aaron could almost feel Spencer's soft, gentle lips opening and closing in a soundless rhythm as he left tender kisses across his chest. Looking down, he saw the unruly mop of light brown curls contrasting beautifully with his own pale skin, which, to his heart-wrenching delight was smooth rather than scarred. Aaron's back arched, begging silently for his touch. In the dream, he could be the man Spencer deserved, unbroken and beautiful, the man he would have been. Spencer's warm, sensuous mouth closed over Aaron's nipple, licking, sucking, and in that moment he was filled with a desperate craving for Spencer's affection, and he felt the low, ragged moan that was forced from him.*

*Aaron's fingers entwined in Spencer's hair as his lips moved lower, causing the muscles in Aaron's abdomen to tighten under his attention. Pulling Spencer up on top of him, he found they were both naked.*

He woke up sweating.

"AARON, you seem a little distracted, a little edgy today. Is there something you want to talk about? Did something happen?"

Aaron squirmed in the chair, uncomfortable remembering the dream in front of Spencer's father, incredibly glad Spencer was studying for a midterm in the other room.

Dr. Thomas pressed gently. "I want to help you. In order to do that, you need to be able to confide in me. I won't push. That's not my way. Pushing you to talk about something you don't want to disclose will only lead to resentment and distance between us, and that isn't helpful."

"I… I had a dream last night. It was… disconcerting," Aaron blurted.

"Was it about the attack?"

Aaron shook his head and looked down at his knees. "It was… sexual."

"Aaron, that isn't anything to be ashamed of. I hadn't planned to start that aspect of our talks until you felt more comfortable with me, but I don't want for this to upset you." He looked thoughtfully at Aaron for a moment, as if contemplating his next question carefully.

"Aaron, I know this is a very personal question, but it's something I need to know in order to help you."

"I'll tell you if I can," Aaron offered.

"Have you had any kind of fantasies about sex since you were attacked?"

Aaron shook his head quickly.

"Was this the first dream you've had like that?" Dr. Thomas asked, his voice very gentle.

"No, I've had one other, but it was just… just a kiss."

"It's not uncommon for people who have been assaulted, especially with such violence, to disconnect from sex, even to be scared to think about it because they think it means they wanted the assault to occur. I'm not going to try to invalidate those fears, because they are very real to you."

Aaron looked up then, surprised. Other shrinks had kept telling him there was no reason to be afraid; it was all over now. Not one of them told him it was okay to feel what he was feeling, that it was okay to be afraid.

"I'm going to ask you a few more questions to get a better background, a better understanding."

"Okay."

"Was the dream about someone you know?"

Aaron flushed scarlet from his hairline, down his neck. With his normally pale complexion, he felt almost like his face was glowing. He had no idea how to explain to his doctor he'd had sexual dreams about his son.

"Yes," he whispered.

"Someone you're close to?"

He nodded.

"Now, again this question is foundational. There are no right or wrong answers, no judgments. Anything you tell me in these sessions is strictly confidential unless I feel you are in danger."

Oh God, he already knows, Aaron thought.

"Was it a man or a woman you dreamed about?"

At that, Aaron stood and walked over to the window.

"A guy," Aaron said flatly, not turning back. He liked the Thomas family's huge rolling lawns and the flowers that even now were still visible, intermingled with the other landscaping. It was calm and peaceful here, not like his house where the neighbors were just a few feet away and his brothers were everywhere.

"Were you attracted to the man in your dream?"

"Yes."

"Are you attracted to men in general?"

Aaron couldn't stop the helpless tears that formed in his eyes. Talking quietly to the trees outside rather than to the shrink who sat waiting for his answer, he said, "I figured it out about a year before the attack." He noticed neither he nor Dr. Thomas ever called a spade a spade and used the term "rape." It was always "the attack" or "the assault." "That's why they picked me; somehow they knew. Maybe it was the way I walked, or some other mannerism they considered effeminate. Because I'm gay, Juliette lost her life."

"I don't think that's true, actually," Dr. Thomas said quietly, and Aaron turned around from the window.

"What do you mean?" he asked, moving toward the chair in front of the man.

"I have done a lot of research, read hundreds of case studies about violent rapes, because helping to treat the survivors of these kinds of attacks is what I specialize in. Statistically, an overwhelming majority of gang rapes on a male and female victim are on couples. I'm almost positive you and your friend were targeted because that group of men thought you were a couple. Rape isn't really about sex; it's about power and humiliation. Assaulting you in front of a girl they thought was your girlfriend, and hurting her in front of you when you were powerless to stop them, gave them a sense of power."

Stunned, Aaron sat back and thought about Dr. Thomas's explanation. For well over two years, he had assumed they had been targeted because of his sexual orientation. Could it be possible he was wrong?

"As for you having a sexual dream about another guy, particularly one you are close to, there isn't anything wrong with that. In fact, I would take that as a positive sign. What did you do when you woke up?"

"I went to take a shower. I felt… dirty."

"You didn't masturbate?" he asked in a clinical tone, which made Aaron feel slightly less embarrassed, but he still blushed as he answered.

"I haven't done that since before…."

"Okay, I think that's enough for today," Dr. Thomas said, taking note of Aaron's agitation and embarrassment. "Please consider that sexual dreams and masturbation are normal and healthy, Aaron. There is no reason for you to feel ashamed or guilty. I do believe that you beginning to rediscover your sexual self is an improvement. You are starting to work past your fears and take your life back."

IT WAS the first time in over two years that Aaron had taken a shower before bed. Normally, because of his desperate need for routine and structure, he took one as soon as he woke to wash away the vestiges of his nightmares. As steam rose above the curtain, he removed his clothes, folded each piece, and set them neatly on the sink. His hands trembled with the fear of what he was about to do. Dr. Thomas said that masturbation was healthy, that reclaiming his sexuality would help in his recovery. He couldn't stand the thought of anyone walking in on him while he jacked off in bed, so a shower was his only other option. Making sure he'd locked the bathroom door, he turned and pulled back the curtain. The water felt pleasant on his naked skin in a way he didn't quite remember feeling before.

Stalling, he grabbed the shampoo and washed his hair. Nothing about the situation felt sexy. It felt forced and uncomfortable, like he was doing it just to prove to himself that he could. With a growl of frustration, he grabbed the bodywash from a ledge in the back and let a bit pool in his palm. Foregoing the washrag, he rubbed his hands together to lather them and ran his hands over each opposite arm. Closing his eyes, he drew in a shaky breath as his fingers slid across his bare chest. The jolt of arousal when his fingers trailed across his nipple surprised him. He hadn't expected to ever feel that spark again.

Still soft, he closed his eyes and conjured an image of Spencer in his mind, but it wasn't the Spencer from school. Rather, it was the Spencer from the dream, the one who wanted to kiss him. He replayed the dream kiss in his mind, embellishing and adding little pieces of fantasy. His cock started to get hard at the thought of Spencer's tongue in his mouth, fencing with and teasing his own. With a longing he didn't know he could achieve, he wanted to feel Spencer's lips against his.

A quiet moan, lost in the shower mist, escaped his parted lips.

He trailed his fingers lightly down ribs visible through his skin, though he didn't look. He knew each and every scar. Sliding along the concave shape of his stomach, the touch tickled as he hesitated just below his navel. *Could he really do this?* Still focused on Spencer's face, Aaron toyed with the coarse hair that haloed his penis, too scared to take it in his hand. Half-hard from the anticipation alone, he concentrated on how it would feel for Spencer to be in the shower with him, touching him. Spencer would be so gentle, loving in a way he'd rarely seen in life. Aaron needed gentle. He needed it so badly.

A soapy hand wrapped around Aaron's dick, and for one fleeting moment, he wanted it to be Spencer's hand. As the desire and power washed over him, he put Spencer on his knees in the shower before him. His cock strained forward in his hand, desperate for the feel of a hot mouth. Aaron had no idea how that would feel, but if the hand twisting over the head of his hard cock was any indication, he wanted to find out.

Resting his other hand on his stomach, Aaron let his head fall back and savored the wonderful, erotic decadence of masturbation. Before the attack, he'd jacked off a few times a week. He had almost forgotten how good an orgasm felt, how relaxing it could be. God, how he'd love to be able to sleep without drugs after a nice hot come in the shower. Hot and slick, he glided his hand effortlessly over his skin. Chasing that perfect feeling, he stroked harder.

The voice came from nowhere.

*You like that, don't you, faggot?*

Aaron's hand jerked away from his body as if he'd been burned by it. He could feel the breath on the back of his neck as his tormentor spoke. The smell of beer and sweat was just a memory, but it was potent in the stifling air. An echo of his screams filled his ears as he remembered that first violent penetration. They were on top of him—ripping, cutting, and ruining his body, forcing his face into the oil-stained floor.

He reached back and slammed the shower from hot to cold. The erection he'd managed to achieve was long gone, but with the freezing water, his memories seemed to recede as well. Aaron forced them back into the glass box where they lived, transparent so they could always watch him and come out at his most vulnerable. Such as when he stood naked in the shower, horrified by his own sexual self.

A violent shiver wracked his body as he turned off the water and grabbed a towel. Even at room temperature, it was warm against his blue-tinged skin. His shoulders heaved, and tears streamed down his face as he reached for the clothes, still folded neatly on the sink, as if he hadn't just broken into pieces. The shirt trembled in his shaking hands when he pulled it over his head. He relaxed marginally with the modesty it afforded.

After throwing on his briefs and sweats, he grabbed his laptop and sat back on his bed. With a heavy heart, he opened his blog and started to write.

# EIGHTEEN

SPENCER: I got hosting through Hostcast and put it on one of my dad's cards. He was thrilled to support blah blah blah.... Anyway, they have some templates we can use for the basic site. We just have to finish the installer and we can put the app up for download.

AARON: Spaaron.com was a good name for the site, very clever. Very techy. Anyway, I can finish up the installer tonight, and we can load it up from the lab tomorrow during class.

SPENCER: No way, you have homework to do for my dad tonight. I'll finish the installer tonight. I have the most recent code changes anyway.

AARON: Fuck, I was hoping you'd forget.

SPENCER: Just set up an account on one site and look around.

AARON: You really think I'm going to find an online support group for people as fucked up as I am?

SPENCER: You are not fucked up, but yeah, I think you can find a way to make some friends without having to leave the safety of your house.

AARON: Maybe if they never meet me in person, they won't know what a mess I am.

SPENCER: Yep, you're just a hot mess.

Spencer looked at Aaron, who sat at the desk beside him in the midst of an explosion of laughter. Red-faced, with his head down almost on the surface of the desk, Aaron's shoulders shook violently, and Spencer couldn't help but laugh with him.

AARON: OMG, I can't believe you just said that. I'm actually blushing.

SPENCER: You crack me up. I'm going to head to the john. You want to go ahead and add the code for the new security changes to the API?

AARON: Yeah, I'll just work on your desktop rather than synching the code to my laptop.

SPENCER: Cool. I'll be back in a few.

Spencer headed out of the room, still chucking under his breath, and walked into the downstairs bathroom. It was more of a half bath, really, with just a sink and toilet. The bathrooms upstairs were huge, and his had a whirlpool, which he happened to love. Seeing Aaron let go and laugh like that meant so fucking much to Spencer. Little by little over the last three months since they'd started working on the project together and had become friends, his heart had let Aaron in.

He washed his hands and noticed, to his annoyance, that neither he nor his father had put a towel up. Wiping his wet hands on his jeans, Spencer stopped by the refrigerator to pick up two sodas and a bag of chips on his way back to the rec room. He was pretty sure his dad would be asking about dinner soon, because when Spencer got home at two in the afternoon, his father was still passed out in his room.

The first thing he noticed when he came back was that Aaron wasn't typing. The second thing he noticed was that Aaron was white as a ghost.

"What. Is. Wrong.?" he asked as he dropped the sodas and chips on a table and approached Aaron very slowly. Aaron startled easily, and Spencer didn't want to make any sudden movements.

"I didn't mean to read it…. It came up while… while… I…." Aaron stammered, pushing back from the desk. He stumbled a little when he stood, and Spencer looked past him to see a second chat window.

DAD: You want pizza or tacos for dinner?

DAD: Spence?

DAD: Look, I know you're upset with me about Aaron.

DAD: Yes, he told me he was gay, and I know you want to be with him, but I don't think he's ready to explore that, not after what happened. You need to give him time.

DAD: Spencer, will you just talk to me?

SPENCER: I was in the bathroom, Aaron got your messages. Give me a few minutes.

"Aaron., I. Do. Not. Know. What. To. Say.," Spencer said quietly, trying to look anywhere except Aaron's terrified face. God, he couldn't even imagine what Aaron must be thinking. They'd never even talked about anything remotely related to sex. He didn't want those damn messages to change their relationship. He didn't want to lose his friend. Aaron walked over to the couch and sat down, so Spencer followed and sat at the opposite end, facing him.

"What did he mean about wanting to be with me?" Aaron asked and pulled his knees up to his chest. He looked so much like a scared little boy that Spencer longed to hug him, but he didn't dare. In his head he scrambled for an explanation for the messages, but they were pretty damn clear.

"I. Am. Gay. Too., Aaron.," Spencer started, and then stopped. It was so much harder than he thought it would be. "I. Did. Not. Want. You. To. Find. Out. That. Way.. I. Am. Sorry.. I. Do. Like. You., But. I. Do. Not. Want. That. To. Get. In. The. Way. Of. Our. Friendship.." Aaron looked around the room, apparently at a loss for what to say. Spencer understood how he felt. Rather than rambling on with another apology, Spencer decided to do just what his father suggested and give Aaron a little time to digest what he'd said. He could see the struggle in Aaron's furrowed brow, the doubt and pain in his eyes. God, what Spencer wouldn't give to take it away. Then Aaron spoke, and Spencer nearly missed what he said because he spoke to his knees.

"I like you too."

Speechless, Spencer took a chance and very slowly reached out to put one finger under Aaron's chin. Aaron went very still but didn't move away. When his finger connected with Aaron's skin, his heart skipped.

Lost in the sea of Aaron's eyes, the perfect clear blue of the ocean at midday, he found it hard to breathe.

Aaron's face moved closer, just a fraction of an inch, and Spencer wanted to bridge the gap, but he couldn't move. If Aaron wanted something, he'd have to take it. Spencer wasn't going to push or even ask for anything. One wrong move with Aaron could set back everything he'd accomplished over the last few months.

"I had a dream about kissing you," Aaron admitted. "I've never kissed anyone, but I… I think… I think I want to."

"You. Have. To. Do. It., Aaron.. I. Do. Not. Want. To. Take. Anything. Too. Far.. Please.," Spencer whispered.

Aaron scooted forward on the couch and then stopped. Spencer could feel his heart pounding in his throat. Aaron's eyes closed, and he took several long, deep breaths before his lips turned up into a smile. He opened his eyes again, only briefly, and watched Spencer's face until they were too close.

Spencer felt Aaron's soft, sweet lips against his. With trembling hands, Spencer grabbed the edge of the couch cushion so that he didn't wrap his arms around Aaron and trap him in his grasp. He couldn't predict how Aaron would react to being held like that. But he did let his lips fall open. He couldn't help it; he wanted more.

The first frightened touch of Aaron's tongue against his made his cock throb against the unforgiving fly of his jeans. Their long, slow, sweet kisses were almost too much for Spencer to bear. He couldn't breathe. He couldn't think. He felt as if his chest might explode with the emotion welling in it.

And then it was over.

Aaron sat back and stared wide-eyed at Spencer. A shaking hand came up to cover his lips as if he were afraid Spencer might kiss him again.

The pride and love in Spencer's heart faltered, making it plummet into his stomach. *Please don't let him be upset. Please, God. He's been through so much.*

"Aaron., I...," Spencer started, but nothing else came to him. Embarrassed, he sat there with his mouth hanging a little open. He wanted to tell Aaron he didn't expect anything from him. He wanted to know what Aaron was thinking. He wanted to kiss Aaron again.

AARON'S head was spinning. He'd just had his very first kiss, with a guy, and he wasn't freaking completely out like thought he would. The kiss hadn't triggered any flashbacks or anxiety, just a nervous kind of butterfly feeling in his stomach. The reality of kissing Spencer made his dream dull in comparison.

"Wow, that was—" *Amazing. Incredible. More than I dreamed it would be.* "—nice." Aaron felt stupid, stumbling over his words, but Spencer still appeared a bit shell-shocked.

"It. Was. Really. Nice.," Spencer murmured as he reached over to take Aaron's hand, where it rested on the cushion. He stopped just inches above, waiting for permission, waiting for Aaron to put his hand in Spencer's. With a tingling sense of fear and excitement warring inside him, Aaron lifted his hand, nestled it inside Spencer's larger one, and entwined their fingers. He'd held hands with Juliette more than a few times, just out of friendship and love, but holding hands with Spencer felt different. It felt more intimate, more personal—special.

"I. Do. Not. Know. What. To. Do. Now.," Spencer said to their hands. Aaron could understand his fear. He didn't know what to do either. He'd never been in a relationship and wasn't even sure he was capable of it. For God's sake, he couldn't even jack off in the shower. What kind of relationship could he offer someone? But he liked the way his hand felt inside of Spencer's. He didn't feel safe, exactly, but he felt content, like someone turned off the screaming in his head, at least for a little while.

"I think your dad is right. I don't think I'm ready for... for...."

"I. Am. Not. Asking. For. That., Aaron.. I. Would. Never. Ask. You. For. That.." Spencer turned so he faced Aaron completely, but didn't let go of his hand. "In. The. Last. Three. Months. You. Have. Become. My. Best. Friend.. I. Would. Not. Do. Anything. To. Hurt. You.. We. Can. Just.

Be. Friends., Or. We. Can. Do. Something. Else., Something. We. Define.. I. Will. Not. Take. You. Farther. Than. You. Are. Willing. To. Go.."

"That's just it. I don't know what I *can* do. I… I don't want to keep you from having a relationship with someone that can give you what you want."

"I. Just. Want. You.."

Spencer's sentiment made his heart race, and not in the normal terrified kind of way. The contrast made him dizzy. He needed to be away from Spencer for a little while to think about the monumental shift in their relationship. In two and a half years, he never considered he would ever want to date someone. The idea that he did, and more importantly, that someone wanted to date him, just knocked his whole world off balance.

"I can't believe this is happening. I never thought I would find someone to look past the scars. I want to try, if you do," Aaron told him, his voice full of hope that Spencer could not hear.

But his eyes lit up like maybe he understood what it meant to Aaron. Maybe something in Aaron's face showed it, or Spencer merely sensed it, because he smiled softly.

"Then. We. Will. Try.."

THE screen stayed resolutely blank as Spencer watched, hoping Aaron would come online. He felt alone, and couldn't even explain to himself why. Dad was upstairs in his study, and he'd just seen Aaron at school a few hours before. The empty feeling in his chest had grown steadily through the afternoon until he couldn't stand it and got onto the computer, hoping Aaron would be there. The solution stared at him from behind the laptop screen. He could just text Aaron and ask him to log on, and he knew he would end up doing that eventually.

The screen blinked and he looked up. A smile played at the edge of his mouth until he saw that the message was from one of his online fuck buddies. He couldn't have picked a worse time to start that conversation with Spencer.

[MARK]: Hello?

[SPENCER]: Hey, man.

[MARK]: Hey, there you are. You haven't answered the last couple of times I pinged you. Everything okay?

[SPENCER]: Yeah, I have been busy with school.

The screen stayed clear for a moment, and in the silence, Spencer considered talking to Mark about what bothered him. Mark was a friend, right? They'd exchanged pictures and fucked around online dozens of times. The next message made him sigh in frustration.

[MARK]: I've been hard for you for days.

[SPENCER]: I am not in the mood.

[MARK]: Maybe I can get you in the mood. My dick has been in my hand since you came online.

[SPENCER] Seriously, I met someone.

[MARK]: Really? He can play too. I'd love to watch you guys fuck.

Spencer slammed the laptop closed in disgust. He would go in later and clear out all the people from his chat list he no longer had any interest in chatting with. How could Mark even think he'd let that prick anywhere near Aaron? The thought nauseated him. Why did Spencer ever think fucking around on the Internet would make him feel better? He felt good with Aaron, even without the sex. What he had with Aaron was real, more real than anything he'd ever had before. He wasn't going to fuck that up by playing with guys on the net.

*SPENCER'S lips felt warm and soft on Aaron's as they kissed slowly but deeply on the couch in the rec room. He didn't know where Dr. Thomas was, but got the impression that he and Spencer were the only ones in the house. Aaron's arms rested lightly around his boyfriend's neck. His boyfriend—he never thought he'd use those words, but in his heart, and in the dream, that's what Spencer was. Spencer's shaggy curls tangled in*

*Aaron's fingers as he pulled and brought him closer. God, he wanted to crawl in Spencer's lap and never leave.*

*Somehow his hand wound up in Spencer's. Aaron pulled it down to the open fly of his jeans and rubbed. Never in his life had he been touched like that, with such love and tenderness. His cock dribbled drops of something onto Spencer's fingers, and then Spencer was gone.*

*Aaron looked down to see those sweet hazel eyes he loved so much looking up at him through a wisp of brown curls. Oh God, he wasn't.... Spencer's beautiful lips, the ones Aaron so enjoyed kissing, wrapped gently around the head of Aaron's cock, and for a moment, he couldn't breathe. The sensation, even just the idea of it, sent tingles through his body. He felt them everywhere—in his legs, his balls, his stomach. It was like nothing he'd ever felt before.*

*Spencer kept his eyes on Aaron's while he worked his mouth lower, taking Aaron deeper. Spencer's hand stroked the insides of Aaron's thighs, comforting him, relaxing him, and he felt desired. Aaron felt wanted in a way he'd never felt before. The tip of Spencer's tongue traced the contours of Aaron's dick, and he moaned. Spencer's free hand rested on his chest, and he wondered at it for a moment. Then Aaron realized that Spencer wanted to hear Aaron moan for him; he wanted to feel it in his fingertips. Aaron tightened his fingers in Spencer's hair and gave him what he wanted.*

Under the blankets, Aaron's hand rubbed his cock through the light cotton sleep pants. He listened intently, but didn't hear anyone in the hall through the closed bedroom door. Taking a chance, and without thinking about anything other than Spencer's face, he pulled the pajama pants down his legs just enough to let his dick pop free of the briefs that trapped it. He spit into his palm and kept his mind completely blank as he wrapped his fingers around the shaft. His harsh breaths sounded loud in the otherwise silent room, and he kept his voice quiet so no one would come to check on him.

The tingle in his cock spread quickly up through his stomach and down through his balls until he couldn't think of anything else. Twisting his slick fist around the head, he massaged back down to the base. With his other hand, he reached down between his barely spread legs to touch his soft sac, and the tingling promise of an orgasm intensified. *Please. I want to feel it. Just this once.*

The decadent image of Spencer on his knees, looking up at him, with his lips stretched around Aaron's cock, took him over that final edge and dropped him into freefall. Warm spurts of semen jetted onto the sheet as his hips ground up to meet his hand. Harsh cries were muted into ragged breaths as he tried to stay completely quiet.

His body seemed to melt into the bed, and he closed his eyes against the sheer pleasure of the way he felt: sated, relieved, triumphant. In that moment, he felt like maybe he could function like a real person one day.

Maybe, just maybe, there was hope.

# NINETEEN

"MY MOM is going to pick me up at three because we're going to dinner for my little brother's birthday," Aaron told Dr. Thomas as he tossed his bag next to Spencer's bag on the desk. He'd been working with Spencer for the last two hours on their new program, and would much rather be adding additional functionality to it than be down here baring his soul. Uncomfortable as it was, however, Aaron knew that this therapy was the key to him becoming a functioning individual. The final walls he had built to surround the deeply hidden hope that he would ever be remotely normal had fallen. While he knew he was setting himself up for a major disappointment if this failed, it had been so long since he'd even dared to hope. Believing in himself, in Dr. Thomas, and in his ability to heal was essential to the success of his therapy, and for the first time, he was going to embrace it. Dr. Thomas was the foremost expert in the country on his type of trauma. If he couldn't help Aaron, no one would be able to.

"That's fine. We should be done before then," Dr. Thomas said pleasantly. "I read your last blog entry, and I think you're making great progress in describing your reactions since the attack. Once you can really understand your triggers, you'll have more success in dealing with the more subtle ones. You recognize the obvious triggers, like being touched, the smell of gasoline, and the sight of blood. It's the smaller, less obvious triggers, the ones that bring up memories without being overt. The sound of the thunder yesterday prompted something, and we weren't even aware that was a trigger for you."

"Yes, that explains at least one reason why I don't like stormy days, and I honestly didn't remember the sound of the storm during the attack until you pointed it out to me here," Aaron said, and rather than being ashamed by his limitation, he was encouraged at its discovery.

"Aaron, let me ask you," Dr. Thomas said quietly, sitting back in his chair. "How do you feel you're progressing in therapy? I can tell you all day long what I think of your progress, but it isn't me that has to live with what you have to live with."

Aaron sat back in his chair as well. It had taken weeks of intensive sessions for him to feel comfortable with Dr. Thomas, but now, while he didn't think he could tell him everything about the attack, he felt like his therapist did truly care about him, about his recovery. That, as much as anything else they'd discussed, made Aaron want to work with the man rather than against him, as he had done with so many other therapists that didn't believe in him.

"The first therapist my mother took me to was so out of his element. I have a feeling he was used to dealing with stressed-out CEOs or couples fighting about money. He had no idea what to do with me, and even a scared sixteen-year-old boy could see that. The reason he had no chance of helping me is because he never believed that he could, and he never tried. Dumping antianxiety pills and tranquilizers on me was his solution, to make me so drugged-out that I wasn't freaking out, but I wasn't really conscious either. After that, I had a successive list of therapists, and with each one, my belief that I could ever be anything more than the broken shell of a person that I'd become, faded."

Dr. Thomas nodded, but didn't interrupt. That was one thing Aaron really admired about the man: he always heard everything Aaron had to say, and even some things he never said.

"You never put the ownership of my recovery on yourself. You always put it on me. You didn't try to hide my problems behind a regimen of drugs. I'm still all kinds of fucked up, but I think the difference now is I have hope," Aaron explained. Dr. Thomas nodded with a small smile, and then sat back in the chair. His expression changed to something more serious as he spoke.

"I want to try something different with you today. I was thinking about using a mind mapping diagram to chart out a memory and some of the things that might trigger it. It's pretty much a free association exercise."

Dr. Thomas wheeled out an impressive whiteboard from where it had been sitting along the back wall, waiting for their attention. In the center of the board he drew a lopsided oval, underneath which he wrote "memory." From the oval, he drew three lines, each in different directions. At the end of each line he added more ovals.

"I want you to think of a memory, and we're going to put it in the center oval. Then, we're going to map out things you associate with that memory. If we find a trigger, we can document it."

"That sounds easy enough," Aaron said and grimaced as Dr. Thomas shook his head and laughed.

"It may sound easy, but it's going to be very hard for you. It could also trigger a panic attack, but we know how to deal with those."

"Okay, so where do we start?" Aaron asked, even as his body tensed with the idea of remembering something from that night, purposefully, and with painful detail. As much as he wanted to forget every moment, he understood that working through the fear and the anger would be the only way to move on and have any kind of life.

"Think of a memory from that night, but let's start out with something manageable, like the abduction or the riding in the van. I want for us to be more comfortable with the process before we move on to something harder." Dr. Thomas stood next to the whiteboard and picked up one of the markers. "Just sit back on the couch, close your eyes if you want, and pick a memory to work with."

Aaron suddenly wished Spencer were down in the rec room rather than up in his room studying for his calculus final. In addition, he also had a paper due in freshman composition and another one in psychology. The only class he seemed to breeze through was programming. Aaron, having only taken the programming course, didn't have as much academic work. His therapy homework ended up being far more painful. Dr. Thomas waited patiently for him to come up with a memory, so he closed his eyes and waited for one to come.

*"Open your mouth," the taller man said as he stood in front of Aaron, who had been driven painfully to his knees on the oil-stained floor. His hands massaged the front of his dirty, faded jeans, and Aaron blanched. He could feel every bit of the blood leave his face, and soon his*

*entire body felt as cold as the concrete beneath him. Turning his head, he bit his lips together and shook his head.*

*"Pete, get him to open his fucking mouth." He opened the fly on his jeans and pulled out his semi-hard cock. The other man, the one not on top of Juliette, held a lit cigarette within inches of his chest.*

*"Do it now," he said and pressed the tip against Aaron's flesh. The white-hot pain ripped through his skin, and Aaron opened his mouth to scream. The first man choked off the sound, muting it by shoving his cock into Aaron's wide open mouth.*

"Okay, I have it," Aaron told Dr. Thomas as he pulled his feet up onto the couch and wrapped trembling arms around them.

"Can you sum up the subject of the memory into a few words?" The doctor popped the cap off a marker and turned toward the board.

"Burns," Aaron said, summarizing the entire horrific event into a single word so he didn't have to go into the excruciating detail. Dr. Thomas turned to look at Aaron for a long moment, concern written into his slight frown.

"Are you sure that's where you want to start?"

"It's less horrible than the other things they did to me, and it's the first thing that popped into my head. Go ahead and write it up there." Aaron shrugged and hugged his knees a little tighter to his chest. Dr. Thomas turned slowly, almost as if he were reluctant to do so, and wrote the word *burns* on the board in the center oval. Then, he drew a line up and to the right, away from the oval. He drew a circle at the end of that line and wrote the word *senses*.

"Put yourself back into that memory, experience it, and tell me what your senses are telling you: sight, sound, smell, touch, and taste." The words sounded as if they came out only by sheer force.

What Dr. Thomas didn't understand was that Aaron needed to do it. He needed to get that shit out of his head, for his mother and for Spencer. Heart slamming against his rib cage, he closed his eyes and let himself go back, back on his knees for the sadists who nearly destroyed him.

"My knees hurt," Aaron started as the memory took shape in his mind. "It's cold in the garage. I'm still dressed, but the floor is like ice.

I'm on my knees, and they are standing over me." He cracked one of his eyes open and watched Dr. Thomas drawing more little circles around *senses*, blurred through the wetness in his eyes. He filled them in with other words: cold, pain, and fear. Aaron closed his eyes again, forcing the hot tears that had welled in them to fall. "I can hear Juliette's clothes tearing. I can hear her pleading with the man on top of her. She's just out of my line of sight, but if I turn my head, I can see her. The guy in front of me is touching himself through his jeans. I know what he wants. He smells like piss and sweat, and I'm trying not to gag. My teeth are biting down hard on the insides of my lips to keep them closed as he's trying to nudge them open."

Aaron began to rock back and forth on the couch. *The burns... the burns are coming.*

"His dick is out now, and he's telling the other guy to make me open my mouth—"

"What the hell is going on here?"

Aaron's eyes flew open, and he looked around wildly at the sound of his mother's voice. Out of instinct, he kept himself wrapped in the ball as he found her face, which was red, shocked, and livid. Spencer stood next to her, looking confused and wary.

"Mom, I…." Aaron started as he wiped the wetness from his face and stood up. He couldn't think of anything else to say. His mother would be so hurt when she found out he'd been in therapy and hadn't told her. The last thing on earth he wanted was to hurt his mother. She'd been everything to him for so long.

"Aaron and I are in the middle of a session, but by your reaction, I'm guessing Aaron didn't tell you he started working with me," Dr. Thomas said quietly, and Aaron admired his calm confidence. At that moment, Aaron had neither calm nor confidence, but then Spencer's father hadn't just broken his mother's heart.

"Who are you?" she demanded, and strode into the room to put her five-foot-two frame between himself and Dr. Thomas, as if she were shielding Aaron from him. *Ever his protector.*

"My name is Dr. Henry Thomas. I'm a clinical psychologist specializing in severe trauma. I met Aaron when he came to spend time with my son," he explained and turned the whiteboard around to push it back against the wall. At that moment Aaron saw the other circles Dr. Thomas had drawn. Shame welled up inside him as he wondered how much his mother heard.

"Aaron, we're leaving. Let's go," his mother said with a venom that he rarely heard from her. It rang of disgust, anger, and contempt.

"Aaron is an adult, capable of making his own decisions. You can't force him to leave," Dr. Thomas said quietly, and Aaron's mother spun around with raw fury in her eyes. Aaron stood up with every intention of getting between them and reasoning with his mother, but her next sentence stopped him cold.

"I know all about you, Dr. Thomas. We researched you thoroughly when we were looking for a therapist for Aaron. I thought you were a savior until I found out you're an alcoholic and your practice closed because your partner was having sex with an underage patient. That's not the kind of help my son needed or deserved. Now I find out you've been treating him without my knowledge or consent. How are you getting paid, Dr. Thomas? I haven't gotten any kind of statement from the insurance company. Was that part of the plan to hide it from his family? What are you doing with my son?"

Spencer's eyes were wide as he looked between his father and Aaron's mother. He looked sick, but unsurprised by the accusations. Did he know his father was an alcoholic? Did he know about the underage patient? He lived with Dr. Thomas; he had to know something. Aaron didn't believe Spencer's father would hurt him or set back his recovery. He'd been helping Aaron.

"Mom," Aaron said after taking a deep, steadying breath.

She clutched at her handbag, and her wide eyes filled with tears.

"I… I need to talk to your father about this. I don't like him treating you. Maybe we can find someone else, someone who—"

"No," Aaron interrupted. "Dr. Thomas has done more for me in the last couple of months than anyone has ever done. He's taught me techniques to help control things that set me off. He's helping me work through some of the stuff in my head."

“Let’s go home and talk it over with your father,” she said, and her voice broached no argument. Aaron looked helplessly at Spencer and then at Dr. Thomas.

“Mrs. Downing, Aaron is an adult. If he wants to continue treatment, I will abide by his wishes.” Aaron’s mother started to interrupt, but he continued. “However, I did tell Aaron it would be better for him to include his family in therapy. I was under the impression you were at least aware of his choice. Why he’s not mentioned it, I can only make an educated guess. But this is *his* life; you need to take his wants and needs into consideration.”

“I have always made sure my boys had what they needed. All of them. You’ve known him for what? A month? Two months? How could you possibly know what he needs? Is your son getting what he needs from you?” Michelle’s face paled as Spencer stepped up beside his father, ready to defend him, but she stood resolute in her judgment.

Aaron saw the fight coming; he could feel it. Still shaky from the mind mapping exercise and the memory he’d had to conjure for it, he couldn’t take watching them fight. They, along with his father and brothers, were the people in his life who meant the very most to him. He also needed to work out what he’d heard about Dr. Thomas. Not about the partner getting caught with an underage patient, but about the alcoholism. The doctor really had no control over what his partner did, but he did make the choice to drink. With the memory of the men’s beer-laden breath still fresh in his mind, Aaron didn’t want to think about the atrocities men could do to each other while drinking.

“Mom, let’s just go home, please….”

With a soft look at her son, Aaron’s mother relented and turned to go. Only when they were in the car and safely out of the Thomas’s subdivision, did Aaron pull out his cell phone and send a text to Spencer.

AARON: I’m sorry I didn’t tell my mom about therapy. My parents picked all of my therapists, and none of them helped me a bit. It was the first decision I’d made on my own since that night. I didn’t want anything to ruin it.

SPENCER: It is okay. My dad is not angry.

AARON: Are you angry?

SPENCER: Me? Of course not. I just wish I would have gotten to spend some time with you today.

AARON: Me too.

"Mom, I'm sorry I didn't tell you about Dr. Thomas," Aaron said, breaking the awful silence that filled the car. She glanced over as she stopped for a red light, and he continued. "I… I heard you and dad talking a couple of months ago about… an… an institution, and—"

"Oh, Aaron…." She pulled over to the side of the road and into the parking lot of their local grocery store. God, he'd been there a million times when he was a kid, but he couldn't remember the last time he'd set foot in it. It was just one more part of his old life that seemed a million miles away. His mother turned completely in her seat so that she faced him, and one tear slipped down her cheek. "That night, your father was upset about Allen. He feels so helpless because he wants to make things better for you and he can't. I'm so sorry you heard it, because he didn't mean it. We never wanted you away from us."

"Allen heard it too. He had come in to apologize for yelling at me, and he stood in the hall and listened with me. Anyway, Dr. Thomas is helping me, Mom. I even…," he started, but couldn't quite finish. He wasn't sure that kissing was something guys talked about with their moms. But then, Aaron didn't have the same kind of relationship with his mom that most guys did. Theirs was closer.

"You even what, sweetheart?"

"A couple of days ago, I saw a chat message from Spencer's dad to him by accident. He was talking about how Spencer liked me. So I told him I liked him too." Nerves and embarrassment making his voice higher and faster, he took a deep breath and tried to calm down before he continued. He couldn't tell her about the kiss. He didn't want to make things worse. "It felt… normal, and right."

Aaron's mother watched him for a long time, until the silence became uncomfortable.

"We don't know if a relationship would work between us, but I just… I wanted to try. I really like him, Mom. He makes me feel almost… safe."

"Honey, when you get into a relationship like that, when anyone does, you never know if it's going to work out until it does. You just have to have faith in the other person and a little patience. Yes, you guys have a few obstacles in your way, but most couples do—they're just different ones."

"You really think we could make it work?" Aaron could hear the hope in his voice and did little to contain it. He wanted his mother's assurance that everything would be okay; the same assurance he'd gotten from her for as long as he could remember. If his mother told him they had a chance, he would believe her.

"I think you can do anything you put your mind to, Aaron. But I don't want you with a therapist who is going to do more damage than good."

The family decided to put off Allen's dinner for another night. Aaron sat at the breakfast bar after dinner while his mother loaded the dishwasher. She soaked the enchilada pan for far longer than she would normally take. She took the burners off the stove and scrubbed them down. He sighed when she went into the cabinet and pulled out oven cleaner.

"Mom, what's wrong?" he asked quietly, trying to sound casual. His mother had mentioned to his father they needed to talk about something later, something about Aaron. Allen and Anthony glanced up from their dinners as their father hesitated and then nodded. No talk about Aaron ever went well in their house. Allen shot a nervous glance at Aaron, who mouthed to his brother that it was okay. The entire family walked on eggshells where Aaron was concerned, and for the first time in a long time, Aaron wanted it to stop.

"Honey, I just… I don't know what the right answer is for this one. I'm hoping your father does."

"A right answer about what?" John Downing asked as he came into the kitchen, probably looking to see what was taking Michelle so long to initiate their conversation. He picked up a dish towel from the counter and started to dry the burners from the stove.

"Aaron, you should go up to your room so your father and I can talk," his mother sighed as she pulled the drain on the kitchen sink. He watched as she wiped her hands on a towel hanging on the handle of the oven door, and tried to figure out how to frame what he wanted to say. For most of his life, his mother had done everything for him, and he didn't want to sound ungrateful, but he needed to start taking ownership of his life, just like he took ownership of his therapy.

"Mom, this is really important to me. I think I need to be a part of the conversation," Aaron told her. He turned to look at his father, who stared at him. It had been a very long time since he'd had an opinion on anything that happened in the house. Usually, he simply took his medication and tried very hard to be something resembling human. He hadn't completely worked out what it meant that his therapist was an alcoholic, but he wouldn't stop seeing Dr. Thomas. It was the first time in two very long years that he had any hope. No one would take that from him.

"Okay, Aaron," his mother said, and it looked like she didn't think it would be worth the battle. She held a hand out in the direction of the kitchen table. Aaron led the way, followed by his parents, and sat, not at his usual seat in the back, but at the head of the table nearest the door leading to the deck, where his father normally sat. His parents sat next to each other on the front side of the table nearest the kitchen. He liked that they held hands.

"Could someone tell me what's happening, please?" John Downing asked, and to Aaron it looked as if he wasn't entirely comfortable not knowing what the conversation would be about. It was clear from their kitchen talk that he was the only one who didn't know what they'd be discussing.

Aaron's mother squeezed her husband's hand and began. "This afternoon, when I picked Aaron up from Spencer's house, I found out Aaron has been seeing a therapist and kept it from us."

It was probably the nicest way she could have said it.

His father frowned. "I don't understand. You haven't talked to any of the therapists we've met with. Why would you try to find one on your own? Why meet him in secret? Why Spencer's house? Did you think we wouldn't understand?"

His father's voice, hurt and confused, made Aaron's throat constrict painfully. He'd never meant to hurt his parents. He'd never meant to hurt anyone.

"John, he heard us talking the night of Allen's date. He thought we were going to send him to an institution," she told her husband with a flash of anger across her delicate features. His father blanched as his eyes, so like Aaron's, widened with shock and remorse.

"Oh, Aaron, I was upset, and I… we… it never… I'm so sorry." It was the first time in his life he'd ever seen his father stammer or search for the right words. Always so perfectly articulate and poised, he never fumbled.

"I told him that," Michelle assured her husband as he worked to pull himself back together. He didn't cry, but sorrow and remorse radiated from him—kind of the way Aaron used to be. After a few minutes of silence, he looked to his wife and asked the question that needed to be asked.

"So, why does Aaron seeing a therapist pose a problem? Just the fact that he's sitting here at the table, participating in the conversation, shows that something is helping. A few months ago, he'd have gone to his room and let us decide what should happen for him."

"The therapist he's seeing is Spencer's father, Henry Thomas," she said with a sigh, and when her husband didn't immediately show any sign of recognition, she elaborated. "You and I looked into taking Aaron to Dr. Thomas when he first came home. Then we found out his practice had closed because his partner slept with an underage patient."

"Oh, that's right. Wasn't he the alcoholic?" The smile slid from his father's face as he remembered, and suddenly, Aaron felt bad for Dr. Thomas. Was that all anyone thought of when his name was mentioned? Just like Aaron. The scars, the attack—that's all anyone thought of when Aaron's name was mentioned. It's like he didn't exist; only his reputation existed, and he had a reputation for something he hadn't even done. Just like Dr. Thomas and his partner sleeping with a patient.

"Yes, that's why I'm worried about Aaron seeing him. I'm also worried that he's been hiding his therapy," Michelle said with a glance at Aaron, who they were talking about like he wasn't sitting at the table.

"I didn't know about the alcoholism, but even if I did, it probably wouldn't have stopped me. I hid it from you because it was the first adult decision I'd ever made, and I didn't want anything to mess it up," Aaron said, but didn't add the unspoken *like what's happening right now* before he continued. "I don't care who his partner slept with. *He* didn't do anything wrong. In fact, he's done lots of things right. That first day I went to Spencer's house to work on the project, I had a flashback. Not only that, I hit my head on the coffee table and split it open so there was blood. Dr. Thomas knew exactly what to do, and he's been helping me ever since. He's teaching me ways to deal with the attack, helping me figure out what my triggers are for the flashbacks, and we've found some healthy outlets for my stress."

"Aaron, it's not that we doubt what's he's doing. I'm just worried about his intentions, and about his drinking problem. What if he's a violent drunk? What if he hurts you?" his mother asked.

Aaron hoped they could see what kind of progress he'd made over the last few months, hell, over the last few weeks, and understand that, whatever his failings, Dr. Thomas was a good influence.

"He never drank while I was there. I had no idea about the alcohol until you mentioned it today. Every session has been controlled and had some kind of purpose—like the one you saw today. He's been working with me to help identify the triggers that set off my panic attacks. You'll notice I haven't had a bad one in a while. Storms, blood, being touched unexpectedly, even the smell of gasoline—they all trigger memories in my head of that night. I have been learning to either avoid them, or manage my reaction to them. Stress makes them worse. Dr. Thomas has been teaching me ways to reduce my stress. I have an online blog I work out my feelings in. He had me start looking for online support groups so I could talk to other people who understood, because that helps me not be so isolated. There are, like, a million different things he's been doing to help me and…." Aaron held his mother's gaze and steadied himself before he spoke again. "And I'm not going to stop seeing him, Mom. I know you're trying to protect me, and I appreciate that, but I've felt more human in the past month than I have for two years. Spencer has been taking me to his house for therapy, and Dr. Thomas isn't charging me, so it doesn't go through the insurance. I love and respect you both, but you can't stop me from staying under his care."

“Aaron, we just want what is best for you,” his father said as his mother stared open-mouthed at him.

“Dr. Thomas is what’s best for me.”

Hours later, Aaron lay in bed and stared unseeing at the darkened ceiling. They’d talked for nearly two hours, always coming back to the same point about Dr. Thomas’s alcoholism. He couldn’t believe his parents wanted to take away the one thing in his life that made him feel human.

# TWENTY

"THEY haven't said anything else about it. Maybe they're looking for a psych ward to stick me in," Aaron said with a sigh as he let his head fall back onto the couch in the rec room and closed his eyes. Spencer held on tight to Aaron's hand, ignoring the blatant looks his father gave them from his wing-backed chair. The coffee table in the center of the room seemed to be the line in the sand. It had been a hard couple of weeks with finals, wrapping up the project, and Aaron's mother's epic meltdown.

"Aaron, they can't have you committed unless you are an immediate danger to yourself or to others. Nothing you have told me in the last several months leads me to believe you're either," his father told Aaron, apparently to keep him calm, but Spencer could feel, just by the lack of tension in his hand, that Aaron wasn't stressed. It felt more like he was resigned. Spencer had enough tension for both of them. In his heart, he knew the confrontation wasn't over, but he had no idea where things would go next.

"I. Know. They. Want. You. To. Stop. Seeing. My. Dad., But. They… Do. They. Like. Me.? Would. They. Make. You. Stop. Seeing. Me.?" He hated the vulnerability in his voice, but Aaron was the best thing that had happened to him in a very long time. His chest ached with the thought that Aaron's parents might talk him out of being with him. More and more each day, especially during moments like this, sitting on the couch just holding hands, he was growing to love Aaron. He'd fight for that, against his father or Aaron's parents, or anyone else that tried to separate them. They'd gone through too fucking much.

"No, I don't think so. Even if they did, I wouldn't care," Aaron said, and the corners of his mouth turned up into a soft, secretive smile. With a quick glance at Spencer's father, Aaron mouthed soundlessly *I'd miss you. You make me feel special. Besides, you're a great kisser.*

Spencer had never seen Aaron be so frivolous and flirtatious before. It lightened his heart, and he leaned over very slowly and kissed Aaron on the cheek.

His pocket buzzed, just as his father looked up toward the hallway.

*Doorbell*

"I'll get it," his father said and pushed up out of the recliner. Aaron rested his temple against Spencer's cheek. Spencer turned his head slightly and kissed Aaron's forehead. They sat like that for a minute, which turned to two, and then five before Spencer's father returned to the room carrying a manila envelope and some official-looking papers. He looked sad, almost resigned, when he sat back down in the chair.

"Dad., Is. Everything. Okay.?" Spencer asked and brought his head up from where it had been resting on the top of Aaron's. His father flipped through the paperwork, and Spencer saw that the front page looked like some kind of court document. It had the boxes in the top left and some kind of seal or stamp on it.

"Aaron, your parents have filed an injunction to prevent me from treating you. I'm sorry." He handed Aaron the bundle of papers, held together precariously by their fold, and walked back out to the hallway. Spencer had a feeling he would find his father in the kitchen, sitting at the breakfast bar with a drink.

Aaron already had his cell phone in hand when Spencer looked up into his reddened face to see the rage building.

"Aaron.. We. Should. Talk. About. This. With. Dad.," Spencer told him, and it felt like every word needed to be forced from his lungs, because he didn't want to talk things over with his dad. He wanted to do exactly what Aaron was doing—calling Mrs. Downing to yell and scream and rage about the way they had treated his father. Guilt roiled in his stomach like acid. He had brought Aaron and his father together. It was his idea to put Aaron in his father's path, so he'd try to help—and look what happened. He'd gotten his father into legal trouble.

"Mom, it's Aaron. No, I'm not ready for you to pick me up. In fact, I don't think I'll be ready to see you again until tomorrow. I'm going to stay at Spencer's tonight. Do I think it's a good idea? I think it's a better idea than serving his father with court papers and taking away the only thing in two years that's helped me feel like a real fucking person instead of a walking corpse. You didn't listen to me at all that night we talked about Dr. Thomas, did you? No, I don't want to talk about it anymore. I'll be home tomorrow. Yes. Bye, Mom." Aaron threw the phone onto the coffee table and put his head in his hands. Spencer looked up to see his father standing in the doorway. He must have heard Aaron's fight with his mother.

"Guess that means you're staying for dinner?" Spencer's father asked, and Aaron looked up, sorrow filling his face.

"I'm sorry, Dr. Thomas. I'm sorry about what my parents have done."

"Aaron, none of this is your fault. I offered to treat you and you accepted. Everything else is pretty much my own fault," he said and shrugged away from the doorframe.

"I should have told them," Aaron said. His body felt so tense, like a wild animal ready to spring. The remorse on his face and the sadness in his eyes broke Spencer's heart.

"If you had, they would have reacted the same way, and you wouldn't have made the progress you did. I will speak to my attorney and see what we can do to fight the injunction. Tomorrow, I'll speak with your parents and see if we can't work this out. Try not to worry," Dr. Thomas told him with a weary smile and went back to the kitchen.

"I guess I should have asked before I blew up at my mom, but would you mind if I stayed over? I can sleep down here in the rec room on the couch," Aaron asked, looking rather abashed as he caught Spencer's eye.

Spencer's imagination moved far past that, and had jumped to watching them making out in his bed. He shook it off immediately, because Aaron just couldn't deal with that yet. God, he'd spent more time whacking off in the shower since Aaron kissed him than he had his entire junior year of high school.

"Of. Course. You. Can. Stay., And. You. Do. Not. Have. To. Sleep. Down. Here.. I… I., uhm… Have. A. Queen.. It. Is. Big. Enough. For. Both. Of. Us.," Spencer told him, the naked, raw hope plain in his voice. His heart ached when Aaron closed his eyes.

Aaron didn't shake his head, but his entire body stiffened. "I don't know if I can do that. I have really bad nightmares sometimes, and if I wake up in bed with someone—"

"Then. We. Will. Deal. With. It.. I. Have. Seen. Your. Panic. Attacks.. But. If. You. Do. Not. Want. To., I. Will. Understand.," Spencer murmured like it was the last thing on earth he wanted to say. Aaron's body didn't relax as Spencer expected it to. "What. Is. It.?"

"It shouldn't have to be this hard." Aaron looked away, and it took everything Spencer had not to pull Aaron back against his chest. "I'm eighteen years old. I should be able to sleep in my boyfriend's arms without freaking out."

Spencer smiled; he couldn't help himself. The warm feeling bubbled in his chest like a laugh, but stronger.

"What?" Aaron asked.

"I. Liked. That. You. Called. Me. Your. Boyfriend.."

Aaron smiled, and the warm feeling in Spencer's chest grew just a bit more.

"I like it too," Aaron said and leaned over to rest his head on Spencer's chest.

"Come. And. Lay. Down. With. Me.. If. You. Want. To. Come. Down. Stairs., I. Will. Set. Up. The. Couch. For. You.," Spencer said into Aaron's hair. Aaron stayed quiet for several minutes, and Spencer was afraid he might have missed the answer when, finally, Aaron nodded. Spencer held Aaron for a long time, letting him get used to being held, before he took Aaron's hand and led him to the stairs.

SPENCER'S nerves were like live wires under his skin as he got undressed and ready for bed. He'd already brushed his teeth and then got out of the way to let Aaron into the en suite bathroom. He could almost see Aaron as he stood on the other side of the door to the bathroom and changed into a pair of Spencer's huge, baggy sweats and a long-sleeved thermal from his father.

"There. Is. An. Extra. Toothbrush. In. The. Cabinet. Above. The. Sink.," Spencer called through the bit of wood that separated them. Spencer climbed into the bed and slid back to the far side, next to the wall. He usually slept on the other side, but he didn't want Aaron to feel trapped in any way.

He turned on his side and faced away from the wall while he waited for Aaron to come out. It took far longer than he expected, and he wondered if maybe his friend was afraid, or if he was having a panic attack. Spencer slid over and had thrown his legs over the side of the bed when the bathroom door opened. Scrambling back to the far side of the bed, he threw the blankets over his legs as Aaron emerged. The sweats hung down at the ankles, and he had to roll up the sleeves on the shirt. He looked like a little kid in grown-up clothes, lost and alone. The frightened look on his face killed Spencer, and he nearly asked if Aaron wanted to sleep downstairs.

Avoiding Spencer's eyes, Aaron shuffled to the bed and sat down on the side. It took a few minutes before he would lie down next to Spencer.

"If. You. Want. To. Sleep. Down. Stairs., You. Can.. It. Will. Not. Hurt. My. Feelings.," Spencer told him, trying to make his voice as gentle as possible. It felt like his voice came out kind of soft, but of course, he couldn't tell. Aaron turned his head so Spencer could see his face.

"Just give me a minute, please."

Spencer watched as Aaron closed his eyes and did a few deep breathing exercises Spencer recognized from the sessions with his father. Slowly, almost reluctantly it seemed, Aaron's body relaxed. The tension in his shoulders and in his face loosened, and his hands unclenched at his sides.

"Okay, let's try this," Aaron said after a minute, and opened his arms. Spencer moved slowly to the middle of the bed, the blankets rubbing against his bare back, and rested his head on Aaron's chest. Closing his eyes, he relaxed to the feel of Aaron's heart beating against his cheek. He couldn't hear it, but the steady pulse felt comfortable and safe. God, he'd never done that before, just lain with someone in bed and felt strong arms around him.

His mouth captured Aaron's before he could stop himself. The sweet feel of Aaron's lips, soft and pliant under his, made his cock harden. When Aaron opened up to him and their tongues brushed against each other, they lingered just long enough to make Spencer crazy. The afternoon with the delivery guy seemed like for-fucking-ever ago, but he also knew he needed to be gentle with Aaron.

Aaron pulled away slowly, but Spencer moved forward instead, keeping no space between them as their kisses turned deeper. His fingers brushed through Aaron's short hair, and he felt a hand at the base of his spine, holding him gently. Overwhelmed by the emotion of the moment, Spencer couldn't articulate, even to himself, how deep Aaron's kisses touched him. It was as if someone had opened him up and shone a light into his soul. They took his breath away.

Spencer moved over Aaron, and they touched everywhere: chests, stomachs, legs, and everywhere in between. He could feel his erection pressing against Aaron's lower stomach, and groaned with the effort to master himself. The last thing on earth he wanted was to scare Aaron.

They kissed harder, and Spencer tried desperately to show Aaron how much he was needed, and wanted, and… loved.

AARON'S heart raced in his chest, and he tried to breathe as Spencer's weight pinned him to the bed. *I can't do this, I can't... I can't....* The memory formed in his mind of another body on top of him, pinning him to the garage floor. Only that body tore him in two and he couldn't get away from it. Spencer kept kissing him, heedless of the fact he was trying to push him off. Spencer's eyes were closed, and he couldn't see Aaron's face. Tiny, frightened whimpers broke from his throat that Spencer couldn't hear. He tore away from the kiss, shaking his head, trying desperately to stop the flashback from taking over his mind.

"Aaron.?" Spencer asked. Regret and disappointment filled his face.

Aaron couldn't breathe. Silent sobs filled his chest, almost strangling him with their intensity. His throat burned and he pushed Spencer hard, but with the spell broken, Spencer moved instantly.

"Aaron. I. Am. Sorry.. Are. You. Okay.?" Spencer touched his arm, and the rest of Aaron's body caught up with his heaving chest. Tears spilled down his face, and everything started to shake. Sitting up quickly, Spencer propped himself against the headboard and took Aaron into his arms. He made quiet shushing sounds and rubbed Aaron's head like a parent might comfort a child. Aaron wrapped his arms around Spencer's waist and nuzzled his face against Spencer's bare chest. It felt nice. That part felt so nice. He selfishly took Spencer's comfort, knowing he could offer nothing in return.

"We. Do. Not. Have. To. Do. That.. I. Just…. I. Did. Not. Think.." Spencer squeezed him tightly for just a second, and in that embrace, Aaron felt his love and his remorse. It gave him the strength to sit up and look Spencer in the face.

"It's not your fault," Aaron told him, and began to relax as the memory faded.

"Do. You. Know. What. Triggered. It.? We. Have. Kissed. Before.."

Spencer continued to rub his back, and it comforted him as he thought about the question. They had kissed before. He didn't think it had to do with the fact they were in bed, because he knew Spencer didn't expect sex. It wasn't Spencer's naked skin—he liked the way that felt against his face. It could have been the intensity, or their position. Yes, that was a definite possibility. He didn't like being trapped on the bottom. Of course, he'd also had that problem masturbating in the shower, so maybe it was sex in general.

*Only one way to find out.*

Aaron wiped his face on his borrowed sleeve and gulped down air as he tried to stop the shaking and the fear. His eyes held Spencer's, and he leaned forward very slowly.

Spencer pushed backward against the headboard and tried to get out of his reach. "What. Are. You. Doing.?" he asked.

Aaron's chest tightened at his hesitation. Spencer wanted to protect him, just like his mother wanted to protect him, but if he ever wanted to get any better, he needed to work through the pain, not hide from it.

"I think you being on top of me triggered it. Either that, or the intensity of the kissing. I want to test that theory," Aaron told him, surprised by how calm he sounded. His heart pounded in his ears. He had no clue if it was a good idea or not, but he knew he wanted to try again. Dealing with the flashbacks had become easier over the last few months since he'd been seeing Dr. Thomas. He would risk them if it meant having a few minutes of "normal" with Spencer.

"Okay." Spencer stopped trying to climb the headboard and held perfectly still as Aaron came forward and let their lips touch again. The fear and panic rose in him again, but not as strongly. He kissed Spencer deeper, losing himself in the feel of Spencer's mouth on his. Spencer hesitated at first, but then wrapped his arms very loosely around Aaron, and Aaron could have wept at his gentleness. Lying half on Spencer, Aaron's groin pressed against his unyielding body. Very, very slowly, he moved his hips and felt his cock rub against Spencer's, filling, hardening, and he felt dizzy with arousal. He couldn't tell if his heart raced from excitement or fear, but they needed to stop before things got out of hand again.

He broke the kiss reluctantly and buried his grin in his boyfriend's shoulder.

"DO YOU want to talk about last night?" Dr. Thomas asked as he placed a plate of scrambled eggs on the table. Aaron put the toast he'd just made next to it while Spencer set the table. *Did he?* He had already sent a text to his mother to let her know he'd made it through the night. She responded with a very curt *Okay*. God, she was probably furious with him, but the anger he'd felt the night before dissipated with the dawn.

"I thought you couldn't treat me anymore?" Aaron went over to the refrigerator and checked the door for jelly, happy when he found both strawberry and grape. Positioning them near the toast with a small feeling of triumph at actually having helped, he turned to look at Dr. Thomas, who was making sure everything on the stove had been turned off before taking his place at the table. God, the whole kitchen smelled like bacon, which made his stomach rumble.

"That doesn't mean I can't listen," he said, picked up his fork, and looked at Aaron expectantly. Aaron glanced at Spencer, who gave him a gentle, reassuring smile, so he tried to organize the jumbled mess from last night in his head. The legal thing his parents did made him angry, but he had to take a really hard look to figure out why. They'd been doing everything for him for the last two years, but something changed over the last few months. He wasn't with his mother as much as he had been in the beginning. He could go to Spencer's. He could go to lunch with him. He didn't feel that panicky feeling every minute of every day like he used to. It wasn't all due to Spencer, but Aaron liked being with him. He helped Aaron relax.

He made Aaron feel normal.

"I'm mad at my parents for what they did. I know they are trying do what they think is best for me, but they sat and listened to me that night and completely disregarded my decision to keep seeing you." Aaron picked up a piece of toast and spread grape jelly over it in a thick layer. No butter. Just jelly. It had been like that for as long as he could remember. Maybe there were some things about him that hadn't changed. Fundamentally, on some level, he was still Aaron—even if he didn't feel like it sometimes.

"I can see where that would make you feel invalidated. Have you talked to your mother since the phone call last night?"

"I sent her a text this morning to let her know I was okay. Last night was the first night I've stayed away from my house since I was in the hospital." The eggs were amazing. Light and fluffy with just the right amount of cheese, they melted in his mouth as Aaron ate. He noticed he always ate better at Spencer's house. Either because they made all his favorite things, or just because he felt more comfortable, he wasn't sure. Expectations were lower there, and the atmosphere more relaxed. That knot in his stomach about the institution seemed to loosen when he hung out with Spencer and even with his father.

"And how did that go?" Dr. Thomas asked, and while his voice remained casual, his eyes flickered to Spencer, who watched the conversation with interest.

"We didn't have sex, if that's what you're asking," Aaron said as his face heated. He took a serious interest in his eggs, and couldn't even glance at Spencer, who sat next to him without comment.

“That wasn’t what I was asking. What you and Spencer do in bed is none of my or anyone else’s business. I just wanted to know if you had any nightmares because of the sexual connotation of sleeping together or even from sleeping in a strange place.”

He didn’t look upset, which relaxed Aaron a bit, and he snagged another piece of bacon from the platter next to the eggs.

“I had a bit of a problem at first, while—” Aaron glanced at Spencer, who nodded that it was okay to tell his father they’d been kissing. “—while we were kissing. But we talked about it, and I took a hard look at what could have caused it. I think it was because… well… because Spencer was…. Do we have to talk about this?”

“No, but I’m glad you talked about and worked through the trigger. That’s very good, Aaron.”

The conversation turned toward school, which had ended the week before. Spencer had managed to get through his final exams without exploding. Aaron had gotten out of bed and made it to the college to take his. He’d e-mailed his advisor and agreed to take Freshman Composition along with the second programming course in the sequence since Spencer said they never had to read anything aloud. He made sure to schedule his programming course at the same time as Spencer’s. Dr. Thomas said he thought Aaron taking two courses the following semester was manageable. The discussion smacked of normalcy in a way Aaron rarely felt.

“Are. You. Going. To. Go. Home. Today.?” Spencer asked just before shoveling the last of the eggs from his plate into his mouth. Dr. Thomas looked up from his coffee and waited for Aaron’s answer.

Taking a long drink of his orange juice, Aaron contemplated the answer. Being with Spencer comforted him, but he needed to talk things over with his parents. If nothing else, he wanted to clear the air about the injunction against Dr. Thomas.

“Yeah, I need to talk to them.” Aaron shrugged and polished off the bacon from his plate. His stomach actually hurt, he’d eaten so much. In the last two years, he couldn’t remember a time when he’d eaten until it was actually painful. His first thought was to call his mother. She’d love that. “I love my parents. I just need to make them see that your dad is helping me.”

THE empty living room loomed in front of him as Aaron opened the front door. He dropped the grocery bag with his dirty clothes on the floor near the stairs. Closing his eyes for just a second, he gathered himself as he slipped off his shoes. There was no sound except a faint music, probably coming from the basement where his brothers slept. The scent of blueberry drifted in from the kitchen, so he decided to apologize to his mother and maybe start a conversation.

She sat at the kitchen table drinking coffee and stared at an untouched muffin on the table in front of her. The circles under her eyes and the sadness in her face made his heart hurt. He'd put her through so much in the last two years. Why couldn't she see that he was trying to make it better by seeing Dr. Thomas? He didn't want to be such a fucking burden on his family, on her. Though he'd eaten breakfast with Spencer and his father just a couple hours before, he grabbed a muffin from the counter as he walked into the room. His mother finally looked up as he sat down across from her at the table.

After several long minutes of being squared off, she broke the silence.

"Are you okay?"

Of course, it was always his well-being first. No matter what else happened between them, she always put his feelings above her own. He needed to get through to her that she didn't need to do that anymore; he just wasn't sure how.

"Yes. I was a little unsettled at first, but after that, I was fine." Aaron broke off a piece of the warm muffin, which smelled like heaven, and popped it in his mouth. The sweet tang of blueberry melted against his tongue, and he was startled by the sound of her chair scraping against the tile as she stood.

"Please don't go," Aaron pleaded. His mother looked down at him with wide eyes, obviously surprised by his request. "We need to talk about this, just you and me." His father would go along with whatever his mother decided, so he needed to convince her.

"I know that it may not seem like it right now, but your father and I want what's best for you. A therapist who can't take care of himself or his patients isn't a good choice for you. I know you care about Spencer…." She stopped when Aaron shook his head.

"This isn't about Spencer. Yes, he introduced me to Dr. Thomas because that's his father, but that's not why I want to see him. He helps me, Mom. More than anyone has in the last two years, except you. You got me to breathe again and move again, but he can get me to *live* again. After the attack, I used to wonder why God didn't just let me die like Juliette. I used to wish for it just so that I wouldn't have to be terrified all the time."

His mother looked stricken. He had never told her the truth about how he felt, choosing instead to dilute it to a half-truth or simply remain silent. She needed to know.

"Don't say that," she whispered and wrapped her hands tightly around the coffee cup.

"I have to say it. We never discussed it before because I was never able to. They took everything from me that night, including my ability to talk about what they did to me. On that freezing concrete floor, they broke me, they shattered me. They—" He stopped abruptly and grabbed the edge of the table. The room grew smaller as his breathing accelerated into panicked little gasps. "They raped me, Mom," he whispered, because he didn't have the strength to say it any louder.

The tears that had welled in his mother's eyes at the mention of his suicidal thoughts spilled down over her cheeks. She didn't try to stop them or even wipe them away.

"I know, honey," she said, and her voice shook with tears.

"I have to find some way to make peace with that or I'll never get my life back. Dr. Thomas is helping me find that peace."

"How do you know it isn't you finding that peace? Or having a friend? Or finding your attraction for Spencer? How do you know it's Dr. Thomas? Let's just try another therapist and see, okay?"

His mother's face pleaded with him, shining, so full of hope he almost gave in. It wasn't Spencer. It wasn't having a friend. It was Dr.

Thomas who had started to give him his life back—or at least lead him back to his life.

"Why did you file those papers with the court?" Aaron asked, trying to defuse the questions with a slight subject change to lessen their power. The debate skills came back to him easily, and he prepared to make his case. So much depended on his ability to convince his mother of the truth.

"Your father had a colleague file the injunction because we were scared Dr. Thomas might cause more harm than good with you. Your uncle Mark is an alcoholic, Aaron. It's destroyed his life, and the lives of just about everyone around him. I can't take the chance that this therapist will hurt you—psychologically or even physically. Think about it, honey. His alcoholism isn't even a secret. We found out about it when we talked to one of his former staff to get a reference. It has to be pretty bad in order for so many people to know about it. Please, Aaron, you're better now. I see it every day. Just try a different therapist," Michelle pleaded with her son.

"No. There is no reason for me to look for another therapist, when I have one that's helping me. In order for your injunction to work, you'll need to have me declared incompetent, which you can't do. I've seen a dozen shrinks over the past two years, and I know exactly how to play one. And by the way, that's the difference. I never even thought about playing Dr. Thomas. He wanted to make me better." Aaron stood up. Her eyes shuttered as he stood, and her posture tightened as he tossed the half-eaten muffin into the garbage can on the way to the stairs. He'd lived with her all his life, and knew that she wouldn't relent. If he wanted to continue to see Dr. Thomas, he had to find another way to reach her.

# TWENTY-ONE

"MOM, I'd like to invite Spencer and his father for dinner tomorrow," Aaron said that night at dinner as his mother stood making hamburgers at the stove. A covered baking dish with baked beans sat on the back of the stove to stay warm. The smell of bread and molasses and sunshine permeated the kitchen, making Aaron's stomach rumble. It had been so fucking long since he looked forward to food.

"Aaron, we just served him with legal papers. That's not a good idea." She didn't turn from the counter, but tensed as she pulled another finished burger from the griddle and put it on a plate for him. Allen and Anthony were already eating at the table as they watched the exchange. Aaron was glad for a moment that his father had a late meeting because it was easier to argue when they didn't gang up on him.

"All I'm asking for is dinner and a conversation." He took his plate to the table, where he sat across from his brothers, who were studiously eating their food and looking anywhere but at him. His mother sighed and turned off the stove before sitting down at the head of the table next to Aaron. She didn't bring herself a plate.

"I know, honey, but it's not going to make us change our minds about letting him treat you." She started to reach for his hand and then stopped herself. He wanted to tell her that it was okay, that she could touch his hand, but anger and pride stopped him. He didn't want to comfort her when she wouldn't even listen to something that *really* mattered to him. Nothing in his life had *really* mattered to him for so damn long.

"Then it won't be a problem to invite them over, will it?" he asked.

He tried to keep an innocent look on his face, but she didn't buy it.

"Yes, it will. It will be awkward."

"My whole life has been nothing *but* awkward." Aaron pushed his plate away, having finished the burger in several large bites. He drank his soda when he didn't get a response from her. The room remained quiet. Both Allen and Anthony ate slower than Aaron had ever seen before as they continued to watch the exchange. Finally, after a long, almost debilitating silence, someone spoke, but it wasn't his mother.

"Mom, Aaron found a therapist because we heard you and Dad talk about sending him away. I'm sorry, but it's not fair. Aaron should have a say in this doctor he found," Allen said quietly. After a moment, he looked up from his plate and into his mother's face. Aaron's mother turned to her youngest son.

"I guess you have an opinion too," she prompted.

Anthony looked at Aaron, and then Allen, and finally at his mother. "I just want Aaron to be happy again, Mom."

Aaron's mother took the empty plates from her three sons and stacked them next to the sink. She returned for the platters and then for the glasses, never saying a word as she gathered the dinner dishes. Aaron waited, undeterred by her silence. His brothers waited too, and Aaron appreciated their support more than he could say. She ran water into the sink and started rinsing the dishes. After a minute, Aaron joined her and put them in the dishwasher. Platters on the bottom, plates on the left, glasses on the top, silverware in the basket—they continued on, rinsing and laying them out in the dishwasher in silence. She didn't even look at him as she handed him each piece, but he would wait her out because he was far more stubborn than she.

He'd just forgotten it for a while.

When the dishes were loaded, he added soap, closed the door, and turned it on. He leaned against the counter and watched her wiping down the stove and the sink. His impatience got the better of him, and he nearly asked again about the invitation for Spencer and his father, but she answered before he could ask.

"Okay, invite them to dinner. It won't change my mind, but maybe we can change yours."

AARON spent most of the afternoon in his room trying to concentrate on a book Dr. Thomas had suggested he read. After the third time he read about gaining back his sexual identity, he dropped the book on the bed and checked the time on his phone. Spencer and his father would be there in about half an hour for dinner. He could smell something garlicky coming from downstairs, and his stomach snarled. Since he'd decided to stay in his room and read after breakfast, he hadn't thought about going down to get lunch, though he was surprised his mother hadn't forced the issue.

Changing his shirt for a nicer long-sleeved polo, Aaron brushed his hair and teeth, and decided to wait downstairs for his friend. Allen still hadn't gotten the hang of talking to Spencer. He still yelled or talked really slow. Sometimes, he even gesticulated wildly as he spoke, which usually embarrassed them all.

The doorbell rang as soon as Aaron reached the top of the stairs. They were early. He took the stairs two at a time and managed to get to the door before Allen, who detoured instead to the family room. With a silent prayer to whatever god happened to be listening at the time, he opened the door. Spencer stood just in front of his father, and Aaron could tell he'd made an effort. His hair, usually a wild mass of curls, had been tamed and loosely framed his face. Instead of his usual T-shirt, he wore a turquoise button-down that made the green in his eyes more prominent. Aaron stared for a long moment before he remembered himself and invited them in. As he stood back to let Dr. Thomas in the door, he noticed that the doctor had also put in an effort to impress his parents.

Finally, after spending the day stressing out about dinner, Aaron could relax just a little.

"My brothers are playing a game in the family room, or we could stay in the living room until dinner is ready," Aaron told Dr. Thomas, who looked at his son and shrugged. Glancing around the room, taking in the details, they looked uncomfortable, like plus ones at a wedding, asked to come but not exactly invited.

"Would you like something to drink?" Aaron asked, and noticed the strained smile on Dr. Thomas's face falter. So, quickly, he added "I think we have soda, juice, and water. Or, surprisingly, I can make coffee. I think we might have some tea…." Aaron counted off on his fingers as he rambled. Spencer grinned, and finally Dr. Thomas smiled again and asked for water while Spencer requested a soda. He left them on their own to retrieve their drinks.

"Did I hear the doorbell?" his mother asked as he pulled glasses down out of the cabinet.

"Yes, Spencer and his father are here." Filling the glasses with ice, he got water from the tap for Dr. Thomas and grabbed a Coke and a Sprite from near the back door. He'd learned a few weeks ago that Spencer wasn't a fan of diet or lemon lime. It surprised Aaron just how much he knew about Spencer. He felt like a part of Spencer's life, and not just because he knew what kind of soda Spencer liked without asking, but because of all the other little things he knew—like how Spencer put ketchup on one side of a hotdog and mustard on the other. He didn't know anyone else who put ketchup on a hotdog, not in Chicago.

"Okay, everything is ready, I just need to put the chicken fettuccini into a bowl. Can you put the garlic bread on the table?"

"Sure, Mom," he said, making an effort to show that he appreciated her inviting Dr. Thomas to dinner, even if she had no intention of listening to him. Together, he, Spencer, and Spencer's father would find a way to get through to her. They had to.

He dropped the basket of garlic bread onto the table and took the drinks into the living room. It irked him a little that neither of his parents came in to greet their guests. If it had been friends of theirs, all three boys would have to line up and make an impromptu receiving line. Ice clinked against the side of the glass as he handed it to Spencer, and he realized his hands were shaking.

"My mom is just finishing up," Aaron told Dr. Thomas by way of an explanation for their rude behavior. Just as he said it, however, his father came in from the kitchen.

"Dr. Thomas, this is my father, John Downing," he said, and let out a breath. *Finally*. His father didn't hesitate to shake Dr. Thomas's hand and then said hello to Spencer. The temperature in the room came down marginally, and it was easier for Aaron to breathe.

So many things in his life rested on that dinner—his hope, his happiness, and in large part, his sanity.

"Well, why don't we sit in here and chat while we wait for Michelle to finish up. She said it shouldn't be more than a few minutes or so," his father said and waved his hand vaguely in the direction of the living room furniture. Surprise showed on John Downing's face as Aaron took a seat on the couch between Dr. Thomas and Spencer rather than taking the other vacant armchair near his own. No one seemed to want to open up the conversation. The only sounds in the room came from outside it: video game bleeps from the family room, clangs and bangs from the kitchen, and even shrieks of joy from the neighbor kids playing out front. But the four men sitting in the living room looked around the room at everything but each other.

"We should probably just open the door and let the elephant in the room amble out," Dr. Thomas said as he set his glass of water on one of the coasters strewn about the coffee table. "I'm not angry about your injunction. I understand that you are trying to protect your son. As a father, I can appreciate that. However, as a therapist, I have to tell you that you aren't helping him. Just as you and your wife have been doing for the past two years, you are enabling him, and that's not what he needs."

"With all due respect, Dr. Thomas, it's for my wife and I to decide what he needs," his father spat back.

Arguing with a lawyer wasn't really a pleasant thing, but Spencer's father didn't back down. "No, Mr. Downing, it's up to Aaron to decide what he needs. He's the only person who knows exactly what's going on inside his head. I've consulted with my attorney, and in order for your injunction to succeed, you're going to have to have a judge declare him legally incompetent to make decisions in his medical care."

Aaron's face heated, and his hands clenched at his sides. They were going to go to court and have a judge tell them he was incompetent, all because he'd picked a therapist. Didn't that show he was capable of making decisions about his care? Damn it, Dr. Thomas was one of the best trauma specialists in the country. Aaron had made the right decision. He was sure of it.

"You would do that?" Aaron asked his father and faked a calm he didn't feel. They didn't need the conversation to descend into something angry, at least not yet.

"Aaron, it's just a piece of paper. It doesn't mean anything." His father's face was an open book, showing every emotion he felt. Right then, it showed Aaron that his father was placating him and that he didn't mean a word of what he said.

"Really? It just strips away my rights as a human being and puts me firmly under your control. Am I wrong?" Aaron felt Spencer nudge his leg and felt better. He wanted to reach over and hold Spencer's hand, but he didn't know if his mother had told his father he was gay. He didn't want to test the idea right then.

"Technically, but it's our job to take care of you."

"Because you think I can't take care of myself? Do you think the attack was my fault too?" Aaron asked and watched the blood drain from his father's face.

"Of course not, but that doesn't have anything to do with the situation at hand," John said, but was quickly interrupted by his wife standing at the doorway to the kitchen. She didn't greet Dr. Thomas or Spencer; she simply announced dinner was ready and asked that they move into the dining room.

With reluctance, Aaron stood, and felt Spencer's hand on his back.

"It. Will. Be. Okay.," Spencer whispered to him as their fathers passed. "No. Judge. Is. Going. To. Give. Them. What. They. Want.."

"Yes, but what will they do if they lose?" Aaron asked. He could just see his parents packing up and moving to New York or San Francisco just to get him away from Dr. Thomas. Then, not only would he lose his therapist, he'd lose his best friend and his boyfriend. He couldn't think about that happening, not when he'd finally found even a little bit of happiness.

"Come. On.. We. Will. See. What. They. Have. To. Say.."

Allen and Anthony were allowed the rare privilege of eating in their rooms, after leaving Aaron with matching supportive looks. Aaron sat with Spencer on one side of the table and Dr. Thomas sat alone on the other with Aaron's parents at each end. Plates were served, drinks were poured, and salad dished out by the time the conversation turned back to the subject of Aaron's therapy.

"I don't want to cause a rift between you and Aaron. That was never my intention. We talked about sharing his therapy with you, and I thought in time, he would. You asked me what I would get out of treating Aaron for free, and as I explained to him, I would use our findings to publish papers and help other therapists treat patients with similar indicators. The fact that he had not found a therapist to that point who could do anything more than medicate him and mask his symptoms tells me the information is sorely needed." Dr. Thomas took a long drink of water while he waited for a response.

Michelle looked at John and then at Aaron. "Dr. Thomas, while I appreciate what you're saying, it's not your intentions we're concerned about so much as your ethics. We found through careful research that you were a top-notch trauma therapist. At the time, we thought you might be the answer to all of our prayers. But then, we talked to Nancy Burgoff. Do you remember her, Doctor?" Michelle asked, her voice almost malicious with quiet triumph. Dr. Thomas's expression did not change.

"Yes, I remember Ms. Burgoff very well," he said, but didn't elaborate.

"She told us that your partner, Dr. Huehn, had an affair with a sixteen-year-old female patient. He is currently serving time for that indiscretion, is he not?"

"He is," Dr. Thomas said, but again, did not elaborate.

"Your practice closed soon after his arrest. She also told us you showed up to an APA function so intoxicated you could barely stand. Rumors started throughout the psychiatric community in Chicago that you'd become an alcoholic. Do you deny the rumors?" she asked point blank as she stared him down from across the table. The meal was forgotten in the showdown, and Aaron could do nothing but watch with a sick feeling in his stomach.

"I do not deny that I drink; however, I have never done so before a session or even when Aaron is in the house. What I do in my personal time is really none of your concern, and for the record, I haven't talked to Huehn since his arrest. He hid his affair from everyone, including the staff at the clinic. The only reason anyone found out about it was because of the girl's pregnancy. The LLC offered Emily and her family a very generous settlement, which I can't discuss because of a confidentiality agreement, but from what I understand she's doing very well with the female therapist I recommended for her. I am not a monster, Mrs. Downing. If I didn't care about your son's well-being, I wouldn't be here letting you take your anger out on me," Dr. Thomas told her, and sat back in his chair, taking another long drink of water. His dinner sat cooling on its plate on the burgundy placemat.

"And what is it that I'm so angry about, doctor? Are you going to do some dinner table analysis?" She laced her voice with sarcasm, and Aaron started to rise and say something to her, but a look from Dr. Thomas stayed him.

"I am not here to antagonize you, Mrs. Downing. I'm here to see if we can come to an amicable solution so that I can continue to help your son," he answered.

She snorted. "How have you helped him so far? I haven't seen any changes in him during the last few months that can't be attributed to his new friendship with Spencer, or working out his issues on his own."

"Mom, when is the last time I had a panic attack? When is the last time you had to feed me tranquilizers like candy? You want to know what Dr. Thomas has done for me? You want to know how he's started to give me my life back?" Aaron asked before turning to Spencer.

"Touch me," he told Spencer in a low voice. "Anywhere you want, just touch me."

"Aaron, this really isn't necessary," Michelle said in a high, panicked voice, no doubt steeling herself for one of Aaron's meltdowns in the middle of the dining room.

"Aaron, please…," his father said, his voice mingling with Michelle's in their fear and concern.

"Do it," he told Spencer while his parents looked on in horror. Spencer reached over and brushed Aaron's cheek with his fingers. Aaron's eyes closed for just a second as he felt his boyfriend's touch against his face, and then he lifted a hand and held Spencer's palm against his skin. The gasp he heard belonged to his mother, and he raised his head to see her eyes filled with tears. So, with his free hand, he reached along the table and took her hand.

The tears fell freely.

"How…?" she asked, completely at a loss for words as her tears turned to sobs. The free hand not covered by Aaron's flew to her mouth, and her quiet cries were the only sound in the room. A chair scraped the tile, and John stood up. He moved around the table to stand next to Michelle and put an arm around her shoulders.

"With Dr. Thomas, I found that my problem is with touches I don't control. If I reach out and touch you, or I tell Spencer to touch me, I'm controlling it. I still have some issues with being touched unexpectedly, but we're working on that. Well, we *were* working on that," Aaron said with a shrug and pulled Spencer's hand back down to the table, where he held it.

"What else are you working on?" she asked, and Aaron noticed that *she* didn't use past tense when talking about his therapy. The slip encouraged him. Spencer must have heard it too because he squeezed Aaron's hand gently. Aaron looked up at Dr. Thomas.

"I can't reveal the content of our therapy sessions, even to your parents, without your permission. Since I don't have any waivers with me, I can't divulge any information. If you want them to know, you'll have to tell them," he said with a small smile, and Aaron wondered how much of that was true.

"Well, we've been working on identifying my triggers for flashbacks and stuff. We found some that I had no idea of—like storms. I didn't remember that it stormed that night while I was there. So, when it storms, I have a problem leaving the safety of my room. The smell of gasoline, the sight of blood, being touched unexpectedly, all of these things can trigger an episode. Dr. Thomas has encouraged me to find an online support group for rape victims. I found one, but haven't talked to anyone yet. I just watch the other conversations and see that I'm not as alone as I thought. He showed me that I can distract myself using video games and escape what happened for a little while. That's just what we've accomplished together in the last two months. Imagine what I would have been like in a year, if I could have kept working with him," Aaron said, again being sure to use past tense so his mother would understand he didn't want his therapy sessions to be over.

“That’s…,” his mother started.

“Impressive,” his father finished, causing her to look up at him.

“Aaron, we want you to make progress, we do. I’m just scared. What if something happens and Dr. Thomas is no longer able to treat you. What will you do then?” she asked, and Aaron got the impression she was going to make that more descriptive, but decided to spare Dr. Thomas’s feelings.

“Then Dr. Thomas can refer me to another therapist, one he thinks I’ll work well with. I’ll continue using the blog to work out my issues. I’ll keep using the tools we’ve developed. But, honestly, I’ve talked to Dr. Thomas almost every day for the last two months, and I have faith in him. Please, Mom, call off the injunction. I promise to talk to you about what’s happening in my therapy and if I have any concerns about it. I’ll sign a waiver so you can talk to him too,” Aaron insisted, and felt hope well up in his chest. God, he felt like a little kid begging for a puppy, but if that’s what it took, he’d do it.

“I just… I don’t know,” Michelle said again, looking up helplessly at her husband for support.

“I started working with a colleague earlier this week, engaging in therapy myself,” Dr. Thomas offered. “We’re encouraged to have our own therapists for the stress of caring for patients. I haven’t had one for quite a while.” The way he leaned forward in his seat, it almost looked like he wanted to say more, but didn’t.

“Oh… I’m glad you’re going to be… feeling better,” she said lamely. It seemed to Aaron as if she were grasping for straws, but something in her expression changed and she looked up again at her husband.

“I’ll talk to Harry about pulling the injunction in the morning,” his father said, and Aaron squeezed Spencer’s hand tightly in his. A wide smile broke across his face, and Spencer’s father smiled back. The wonder in Michelle’s voice tugged at Aaron’s heart.

“There’s my son,” she whispered.

# EPILOGUE

TIME seemed to solidify. One moment rolled into the next as Aaron watched each passing second on the clock and waited. He had no idea what Spencer planned for their afternoon together; his friend had merely said they were going out. His fingers jumped rhythmically against his leg as he considered the possibilities. Spencer knew Aaron wouldn't want to be around people, so dinner or the movies were out. A concert or play was out because it would be even less likely if Spencer couldn't hear it, but for Spencer, he might try. *Maybe*. He didn't like uncertainty or surprises—not anymore.

Aaron didn't understand why they had to go out in the first place. Over the last few months since they'd made their relationship official, they'd watched dozens of movies—either in the rec room at Spencer's house or the family room at his house, always with his head on Spencer's chest—where they read the closed-captioning together. He liked just being alone with Spencer, talking or touching or kissing. Being around people would make him edgy and tense and they'd probably have a miserable time.

The doorbell rang, and Aaron nearly vomited.

He heard his mother greet Spencer as she let him in, asking him where his coat was. In his slow cadence, Spencer told her he'd left it in the car. Aaron couldn't help but smile, both at the reassuring sound of Spencer's voice and at his mother's caring nature. Some of the fear dissipated as Aaron upended his soda to drink the last few swallows before dropping the empty can in the recycling bin. Shuffling footsteps got louder as Spencer came up the hall and into the kitchen. He looked adorably windswept, his cheeks pink with the blustery February cold. The big gray hoodie, the one he wore everywhere, wrapped around him like a cloak, and his hands were shoved deep into the pockets.

Spencer's eyes lit up when they found Aaron's.

"Hey.," he said as he stepped right up to Aaron. He touched Aaron's face gently, as if Aaron were made of paper, something fragile but beautiful. It made Aaron feel special, and he leaned forward and covered Spencer's mouth with his own in a tender, welcoming kiss. Spencer's face was chilled but his lips warm as they molded to his again and again. Aaron pulled back just enough so Spencer could see his face.

"You have to tell me where we are going. I can't… I can't deal with it. Please…," Aaron said as he bored holes in Spencer's faded T-shirt with the intensity of his embarrassed stare. While he understood things were better than they'd been a year ago, or even six months ago, his insecurity still forced him to wonder if he would never be the guy Spencer wanted.

"It. Is. Okay.. I. Packed. Some. Stuff. To. Go. Ice. Skating. At. The. Lake. Behind. My. House.. We. Can. Get. Skates. At. That. Sporting. Goods. Place. On. Calumet.. I. Do. Not. Know. How., But. I. Want. To. Learn.," Spencer said, his face full of hopeful regret.

Aaron sighed. Spencer had never done anything to scare Aaron or hurt him, not on purpose. A day skating sounded nice. It sounded normal, something he and his brothers would have done before their world changed. He just hoped that, on a Tuesday morning, the place was going to be quiet, but with a jacket, scarf, and hat, he doubted anyone would be able to see his scars.

He could be just like everyone else.

"I know you're sick of being trapped in the house with me. We can go skating," Aaron said, and though Spencer couldn't hear the sigh or the trepidation in his voice, Spencer put a hand on his shoulder anyway. Aaron relaxed, and a real smile spread across his face.

"We. Will. Take. It. Slow.."

"You shouldn't have to take everything slow because of me. Maybe you should be with a guy you can take out in public, or show off to your friends, or fuck." Aaron's face heated with the admission, but he didn't look away. Spencer needed to understand what he was giving up in order to be with Aaron. He needed to know Aaron wasn't going to magically get better and be the perfect boyfriend just because they could kiss without him having a meltdown. Spencer shook his head.

"You. See. Me.. That. Is. All. I. Have. Ever. Wanted.. We. Can. Figure. Everything. Else. Out.." He placed a small chaste kiss on Aaron's lips, and Aaron felt him smile. Their fingers entwined, and Spencer held tight as he led Aaron toward the front door.

"The. South. Side. Of. The. Lake., Away. From. The. Houses., Is. Pretty. Quiet.," Spencer told Aaron as they pulled out of the Sportmart parking lot and back onto the main road. He had gotten Aaron's shoe size and disappeared into the building. Aaron had actually started to worry before he came back, red-faced, with two pairs of skates and two pairs of thick socks. From his muttering, Aaron had gathered that Spencer had to work hard to make the salesclerk understand what he wanted. Even with the hardship Spencer had to deal with, he never asked Aaron to go inside with him. Aaron could get through an afternoon of skating for Spencer. He could.

It took less than fifteen minutes to pull into Spencer's subdivision, but rather than turning on his street, they continued past it and turned on a much smaller side street, one that was barely paved. The bumps were amplified in Spencer's small car, and finally, they reached a small dirt parking area. One other car sat idling in the lot, steam rolling up from the exhaust. Once Spencer and Aaron passed, it pulled out and drove up the small road they'd just come down. They were alone.

Aaron climbed out of the car and looked around. The quiet stillness of the snow calmed his nerves. The lake was more of a large pond than an actual lake, and since the temperature had been below zero for the last week, Aaron figured it was pretty well frozen down to the bottom. Even though he'd never been to that particular lake before, he could see his mother bringing him and his brothers here as little kids, pulling them on a sled, or teaching them to skate on the ice. He could almost see himself out there, fearless, flying across the ice as his mother rushed to keep up. That invincible boy was gone, drowned in the horror and fear of monsters in the dark. He thought maybe through Dr. Thomas and Spencer, though, the boy could be a phoenix and rise from the ashes of his former life. The smallest flame of hope burned inside him, and he nurtured it as he waited for that day.

Spencer came up beside him and squeezed his hand.

"You. Okay.?" he asked as he searched Aaron's face. Aaron simply squeezed back and smiled. They walked over to a picnic table where Spencer dropped the two bags he'd been carrying. The first, Aaron recognized from the sporting goods store, and it held their skates. The second was a backpack, and the way Spencer slung it onto the table made it look pretty heavy.

"What's in the bag?" Aaron asked as Spencer looked up with Aaron's skates and socks in his hand.

"A. Bunch. Of. Muffins. And. A. Thermos. Of. Hot. Chocolate.." He dropped the skates and socks onto the bench and wrapped his arms around Aaron. "I. Like. This. Already.."

Aaron looked around as a cold breeze washed over his face.

"I like it too." He pressed his lips to Spencer's, sharing leisurely kisses like they had all the time in the world to spend next to the lake. He liked the warmth and security of Spencer's arms as they held him, his hand rubbing lightly up and down Aaron's back. It was soothing, and loving, and just… sweet. He bumped against the table, and Spencer's hardening cock pressed into his hip through their jeans. Fear rose up in Aaron's throat, and he pushed it down. They were outside in thirty-degree weather. Spencer wouldn't want to fuck in the snow. The thought persisted as the kissing grew more intimate. He put his hands on Spencer's chest and pushed back a little.

"Sorry.," Spencer said immediately and tried to discreetly adjust his erection in his jeans. Aaron watched, his own physical reactions still masked by fear and doubt. Though he'd talked about it, somewhat awkwardly, with Dr. Thomas, Aaron had no idea if he would ever be able to have a sexual relationship with Spencer. While he'd been able to jack off a couple times without completely freaking out, that was so much different than getting naked with someone, even someone he trusted, and opening himself up. Dr. Thomas said it would happen, that he'd be able to open up to someone he trusted eventually, but not to force it, and celebrate the small steps he took in his life.

“Don’t be sorry. I just wanted to ask you something.” Aaron looked over Spencer’s shoulder toward the lake, not sure how he wanted to word his question. He didn’t want it to come out sounding like an accusation, because he couldn’t blame Spencer if the answer was yes, but it hurt to think about anyway.

“Ask. Me. Anything.,” Spencer replied, and stopped putting on his skate to give Aaron his full attention. Something in Aaron’s face must have told Spencer the conversation would be important.

“Do you remember when you sent me that message over chat by accident, the sex one?” he asked and turned his gaze away from the lake and back to Spencer. A frown crossed Spencer’s face, but he nodded.

“I. Remember..”

“Do you still do that?” Aaron asked before he could lose his nerve. He didn’t know why the question was so important to him. If Spencer wanted to talk to other guys to get his rocks off because Aaron couldn’t do that for him, he should be able to. Being upset or jealous felt so fucking selfish to Aaron, and he didn’t want to be selfish. He wanted to be giving and loving like he thought a good boyfriend should be, but it hurt. It underscored all Aaron’s inadequacies.

“No.. I. Have. Not. Talked. To. Anyone. Like. That. Since. You. Kissed. Me.. It. Felt. Like. A. Betrayal. To. You. And. To. Them.. You. Are. The. One. I. Want. To. Be. With. Like. That..” Spencer reached out and touched Aaron’s face, stroking Aaron’s cold cheek with his warm fingers.

“I don’t know if I’ll ever be able to… to… give you what you want,” Aaron finished. He couldn’t even say it. If he couldn’t say it, how could he ever get up the balls to do it? Frustration filled him, and he wanted to tell Spencer he should find someone else, but he just couldn’t. He couldn’t stand the thought of not being with Spencer.

“I. Told. You. Before., Aaron., All. I. Want. Is. You..”

Aaron thought about the sign he’d looked up on the Internet. It scared him to think about sharing it with Spencer, but the feeling had been bursting inside him for a while, wanting to come out. It’s almost like if he didn’t say it, something in him would break.

"I've been looking up signs on the Internet to go along with the ones you're teaching me, and there's one I wanted to show you." Aaron took off his gloves so he could make sure the meaning came across. His face, already a little flushed from the cold, heated at the thought of what he was about to do. Spencer looked puzzled, as if he couldn't understand what Aaron would sign that would make him blush like that.

"It. Means. A. Lot. To. Me. That. You. Wanted. To. Learn.. I. Would. Love. To. See.," Spencer said.

Aaron held up his hand with his middle and ring fingers pointing toward his palm and his thumb, forefinger, and pinky stuck out. All the air seemed to leave Spencer's body in a woosh, and Aaron saw nothing but light and love, color and sound as it crossed his face.

"Oh…," he said quietly, and Aaron's smile faltered until Spencer took his hand and put it over his heart.

"I. Love. You. Too., Aaron.."

Erotic fiction is more than just moans, grunts, and physical pleasure. To J.P. BARNABY, erotic fiction consists not only of the mechanics of physical love, but the complex characters and relationships that lead to those all-encompassing feelings of need and longing. Sex without context is merely sex—but sex coupled with attraction, with explosive repercussions—that is good erotic fiction. J.P. authors all different kinds of erotic fiction including gay, straight, male, female, BDSM, sweet, romantic, and dark.

As a bisexual woman, J.P. is a proud member of the GLBT community both online and in her small town on the outskirts of Chicago. A member of Mensa, she is described as brilliant but troubled, sweet but introverted, and talented but deviant. She spends her days writing software and her nights writing erotica, which is, of course, far more interesting. The spare time that she carves out between her career and her novels is spent reading about the concept of love, which, like some of her characters, she has never quite figured out for herself.

Visit her web site: http://www.JPBarnaby.com; her blog: http://blog.jpbarnaby.com; at Twitter: http://www.twitter.com/JPBarnaby; and her Facebook Fan Page: http://www.facebook.com/#!/pages/J-P-Barnaby/361496093699. You can contact her at JPBarnaby@me.com.

LITTLE BOY LOST by J.P. BARNABY

http://www.dreamspinnerpress.com

LITTLE BOY LOST by J.P. BARNABY

http://www.dreamspinnerpress.com

Also from J.P. BARNABY

http://www.dreamspinnerpress.com

25560762R00136

Printed in Great Britain
by Amazon